MURDER IN MELLINGHAM

MURDER IN

Mellingham

SUSAN OLEKSIW

CHARLES SCRIBNER'S SONS
NEW YORK

MAXWELL MACMILLAN CANADA
TORONTO

MAXWELL MACMILLAN INTERNATIONAL
NEW YORK   OXFORD   SINGAPORE   SYDNEY

Copyright © 1993 by Susan Prince Oleksiw

Charles Scribner's Sons   Maxwell Macmillan Canada, Inc.
Macmillan Publishing Company   1200 Eglinton Avenue East
866 Third Avenue   Suite 200
New York, NY 10022   Don Mills, Ontario M3C 3N1

Macmillan Publishing Company is part of the Maxwell Communication Group of Companies.

Library of Congress Cataloging-in-Publication Data
Oleksiw, Susan.
Murder in Mellingham / Susan Oleksiw.
p.   cm.
ISBN 0-684-19528-3
I. Title.
PS3565.L42M87   1993
813'.54—dc20   92-28498
CIP

Macmillan books are available at special discounts for bulk purchases for sales promotions, premiums, fund-raising, or educational use. For details, contact:

Special Sales Director
Macmillan Publishing Company
866 Third Avenue
New York, NY 10022

10 9 8 7 6 5 4 3 2 1
Printed in the United States of America

To Susie Senecal

MURDER IN MELLINGHAM

LIST OF CHARACTERS

HOWARD O'DONNELL—*prominent businessman*
MERRILEE O'DONNELL—*his wife*
BETH O'DONNELL—*Howard's sister*
MEDGE VINTON—*Howard and Merrilee's daughter*
FRANK VINTON—*Medge's husband*
LEE HANDEL—*owner and publisher of the Marine Press*
HANNAH HANDEL—*his wife and avid gardener*
MR. STEINWELL—*a local manufacturer*
MR. AND MRS. MORRISON—*friends of Beth O'Donnell*
BOB CHAMBERS—*editor at the Marine Press*
LISA HUNT—*friend of the Handels and employee of the Marine Press*
JIM KELLOGG—*owner of the Kitchen Cast Caterers and friend of Medge Vinton*
MR. CAMPBELL—*owner of the Agawam Inn*
MRS. MILES—*the O'Donnell housekeeper*
MACK—*DPW employee assigned to the beach*

CHIEF JOE SILVA—*chief of police in Mellingham*
SERGEANT KEN DUPOULIS—*a member of the police force*

and other residents of and visitors to the town of Mellingham

1

SATURDAY NIGHT

*I*T HAD BEEN SOME TIME since Lee Handel had
ventured out willingly on a social occasion, but his wife, Hannah, had reassured him that this party would be safe. He kept
his eyes fixed on her as she walked a few feet in front of him,
her neatly pressed, dark linen slacks swinging against her legs.

The tingling smell of the ocean rose up over the nearby
cliffs, enticing him to look upward just in time to see the
O'Donnell mansion shimmering in the evening light. Built in
the early 1900s, with rambling hallways and a dozen bed-
rooms, the clapboard mansion was one of many dotting the
coast of the small town.

Mellingham had grown from a tiny fishing village,
founded in the early 1600s, to a modest trading port in the
eighteenth century, then a town of diverse cottage industries
in the nineteenth century, to a seasonal resort in the early
twentieth century, each new version of the town adding another circle of homes and streets, like rings on a tree. The
mansions along the coast represented the last and grandest
layer. Thereafter, Mellingham was compressed by its borders,
producing a nodule here, a branch there, but holding steady
in overall size and shape. When an abandoned barn collapsed
at one end of town, a homeowner sold off a gatehouse at

another end. The small town of Mellingham grew inconspicuously.

The rocky shore that had for centuries defined the nature of life for the people of the town now did so more subtly. The waves slithering on the shore enraptured children, sunsets lured painters, and rocks and boulders inspired Lee Handel to stoicism, tenacity, even hope. And so he followed his wife up to the O'Donnells' front door, the blue stone gravel crunching under his shoes. His muscles tensed as he stepped into the O'Donnells' front hall, his eyes blinking at the light thrown by the crystal chandelier sparkling overhead. He eyed it suspiciously, as though it meant to fall on him, instantly crushing him and his good intentions before he even had a chance to greet his host and hostess, Howard and Merrilee O'Donnell. As Hannah stepped forward to greet an old friend, Lee moved carefully around the edge of the hall, keeping his eye on the chandelier, then turned into the doorway on his right.

Lee Handel blinked several times at the crowd in the living room, then turned to his left, a smile ready to form on his lips. At the last moment, he realized he did not know the young couple standing closest to the door, so the smile hung half-formed on his face. He withdrew his right hand, clasped both hands in front of him, and bobbed quickly. Stepping forward, he again discovered a person he had never met. And so he made his way among the guests, gently bobbing his gray head, eagerly looking for someone at whom he could smile. Always invited to the O'Donnells' parties even after years of turning them down, Lee could not accept his wife's reassurances that the evening would be just a gathering of people from Mellingham and the surrounding area. Wherever he went now, he recognized fewer and fewer faces. He found this more confusing than disturbing, since it meant he spent a longer time at the few events he did attend searching for someone he knew and was actually willing to talk to. His body gently swaying as he crossed the room, Lee eventually found himself smiling at a large picture window opening onto a side lawn. His anticipation finally turned to delight as his eye fell on a bird feeder hanging on a crab apple tree in the garden. He leaned forward eagerly, his hands clasped even more tightly in front of him, scanning the feeder for details of its design and workmanship.

"I see you've noticed our new feeder," Howard O'Donnell said. He had come up behind Lee. "It's from the local birding club." A successful businessman since his early years, Howard O'Donnell was now in his late fifties, his softly rounded body a kind of testimony to his achievements. A short man, he stood up straight, his chin tilted upward, adding at least another two inches to his length and making him of almost average height. Long accustomed to making announcements of major import to anyone within hearing, Howard tended to deliver even the most ordinary statements with the tone reserved for a major cataclysm. "It's a new design, of special value for smaller birds." He smiled as though the information were sufficient to answer all questions, erase all doubts, though if asked he couldn't have said what those might be. Lee nodded, confusion growing on his face. After a long career as owner of the Marine Press, a small but respected book publisher, he took little at face value, including the practicality of certain designs of bird feeders.

"It's very nice," Lee finally said, "but what do you do about the squirrels?"

"Squirrels?" Howard looked again to make sure they were talking about the same thing. "We don't feed the squirrels. This is for birds." He turned toward the bird feeder hanging among the branches where two squirrels were just then swinging their way closer to the tray of sunflower seeds. Odd that he hadn't noticed them before. Never a man to overlook the expertise of another, or to pass up the benefit of unexpected opportunities, he turned to his guest and said, "What do you suggest?"

"Ahh," Lee said. "It's a very great problem." The smile vanished as he concentrated on the feeder. "I have a long tube, actually it's a new kind of piping for plumbing. That does seem to be working, for now. The squirrels haven't figured out how to get down the tube yet." The gravity that marked Lee's face as he talked about the tubing that hung in his garden might have signaled distress to another host, but not to Howard, who had known Lee long enough to recognize the sign of the scientific mind enduring the intense pleasure of profound thought. He adopted an expression he hoped would appear suitably grave to his guest.

"You hang a tube in your garden?" Howard asked. He looked at his friend and then at the garden that was rich in spring blooms. His wife had recently spent a substantial sum of money on handcrafted garden furniture, which was now arranged in various groupings throughout the yard. To Howard's mind, a yard was populated by people enjoying the fresh air and flowers. To Lee's mind—well, Howard was uncertain what population filled a yard in Lee's mind and did not inquire.

"They won't come near the house; no bushes," Lee explained.

"Who?"

"Birds, of course. Squirrels will come right up to the house if they think there's food, but not birds. They don't like the open space, too exposed. They feel too vulnerable," he said almost in a whisper. "The only time the birds have ever come close to the house was during the blizzard of '78. We couldn't get out to the feeders, so we just threw the seeds onto the back porch. The birds came right up to the house. What did you do?"

"I don't remember. Merrilee might—"

"I remember everything." The woman's voice rang loudly between the two men. Spoken in the silence of a brief pause, an incongruous remark can interrupt any nearby conversation, and so it was with Beth O'Donnell's comment. Flinging the words over her shoulder, Beth O'Donnell, a

4

younger version of her brother, swished between two people conversing in the doorway, oblivious to them, their wine glasses, and their startled confusion. The room became suddenly quiet, except for Beth, who chose a new partner for a light repartee while those around her shifted position and recovered their thoughts. The unexpectedly prolonged pause embarrassed some and distracted others, and the more nervous abruptly babbled to fill the silence.

Stalled now in his conversation with Lee, Howard wondered how to regain the flow. He opened his mouth, but nothing came out. A jovial slap on the back was the final blow and he turned to greet another guest, a business acquaintance. Howard introduced the other man to Lee, who looked the newcomer over carefully, concluded that the gentleman before him was not a bird fancier, and nodded amiably as the other man began a tale of travel woes. Still clasping his hands in front of him, Lee bobbed encouragement as he found himself relaxing with a stranger. Confidence in his wife's promise of a safe and pleasant evening seeped into his heart.

■ ■ ■

Bob Chambers curtly declined the offer of a canapé as he memorized who was talking to whom near the fireplace. He calculated he could speak later to the older man, who must be in his early forties by Bob's estimation, and still have time to enjoy himself with a few of the other guests. Still in his mid-thirties and looking even younger, Bob Chambers, editor at the Marine Press, had never accepted the premise that life was a series of accidents. On the contrary, he held himself responsible for his own life and his own success. He was a handsome, athletic-looking young man whose smile could charm, disarm, and delight an audience of one, and it was often sincere. He also believed that no opportunity should be wasted. This included social occasions, and so he found himself, not by accident, standing next to Beth O'Donnell, his host's sister. Bob was only one of many who marveled at how different brother and sister could be. Both Howard and Beth were short, tending to pudginess, with pink faces capped by increasingly white hair. But there, at the hairline, so to speak, the resemblance ceased. Whereas Howard was subdued in personality and demeanor, Beth was slightly loud; whereas Howard was methodical and meticulous in the conduct of his affairs, Beth was slightly rash and slightly impulsive. The qualification was important, for certainly Bob Chambers would never allow himself to associate with someone who was the epitome of the very qualities that repelled him. But Beth O'Donnell was only slightly all these things, and she did have one characteristic that particularly appealed to the young editor and accounted for his presence at that moment. Whereas Howard looked and sounded the same year after year, Beth was a record of any breeze wafting through the world of fashion. Her appearance at an important social function was expected, and her absence the cause of intense analysis by her friends. She was, in short, important.

Bob stepped up to her with confidence, remarking on how glad he was that they should be talking again so soon. Beaming warmly down on her, he shared his best story of the moment, an anecdote that seemed humorous but also intimate in a sophisticated sort of way, or so he had been told when he had first heard the story from a friend. He noted Beth's expected reaction, then listened politely to her response, while observing how interested the other men were in Miss Beth O'Donnell and her stories. Their wives smiled politely and looked uncomfortable. Jealous, thought Bob. The ripples of laughter spread further each time.

"I quite agree," he heard himself saying, hoping he was not agreeing to anything intolerable.

"I thought you would," Beth replied.

He glanced at her quickly, but she had turned away to the man on her left, who was less interested than Bob had been in her anecdotes.

Since graduating from a junior college in the 1950s and settling briefly into a lackluster office job in New York, Beth O'Donnell had kept a detailed record of every celebrity and important or wealthy person she had ever met. Her job had given her no leverage whatsoever, but her astute judgment of human nature had drawn her closer to her older brother, who by the mid-1950s showed all the signs of becoming a huge success in business. Beth followed him attentively as he worked his way through his first few unimportant jobs. Whether or not Howard welcomed this attention never concerned her. She meant to guide him as he approached the higher reaches of success. And guide him she did, tolerating a boring if not downright lowly job during the day and dining at the best restaurants in the evening, thanks to her brother's generosity. When she finally decided to give up her job because it interfered with her social life, she had little trouble persuading Howard that this was all to his advantage. He had listened closely to her reasoning, appearing to agree with every particular, including her assessment of his several women friends, and for years thereafter she arranged his life and her own as she wanted them. Her one failure had been Merrilee, Howard's wife. Howard hadn't even mentioned Merrilee's name until he announced he was married to her. Even today, the recollection of Howard's sudden marriage rankled deeper than any other betrayal in Beth's memory, but she had, for the most part, forgiven him.

"Now that's an old story. If you'd shown up the last time I was here, you'd have heard it fresh from the living of it." Beth winked at Frank Vinton, who stood on her left. Beth's gentle chiding of Frank, married to Howard's daughter, Medge, was accepted in good part by the man, who merely nodded, as though thinking about something else.

"Has it been two years?" he asked after a moment, raising his hand to smooth his red mustache.

"Of course it has. It's been every other year, for the last

fourteen years at least." She smiled sweetly. "And I only come to Mellingham in the spring or summer, in warm weather." She paused and looked up at him. "When I tried coming in the winter, you had an awful storm. You remember the storm, Frank? I'll never forget that visit," she said, turning to the small group around her. "How do you tolerate being snowed in every year?"

"We're not," Bob said, stepping in to quash any idea that she was surrounded by rustics. She listened with the practiced air of tolerant boredom that had turned ambitious young men into uncertain beginners on the corporate ladder, and was mildly pleased to see that her attitude had little effect on Bob. She enjoyed a challenge.

■ ■ ■

Merrilee O'Donnell had not missed her sister-in-law's appraisal of Bob Chambers; indeed, she had rarely failed to note Beth's attitude to anyone. Merrilee had learned during her first meeting with Beth not to let her guard down, even for a second. A steely caution had thereafter enwrapped Howard's wife whenever she found herself near her sister-in-law. Within a second of the dreaded telephone call announcing Beth's biennial visit, every sinew and muscle and ligament in Merrilee's body was poised for action. Fortunately, the plunge into self-defense had not yet been called for. Short and petite, and swathed in gauzy chiffon or swinging silk dresses, Merrilee gave no sign of the tense limbs beneath the soft folds of her outfits. She kept her keen eye on Beth, and expected Howard to do the same. And, in truth, she had to admit that Howard had done everything that a wife could ask of her husband, even when it came to in-laws.

From the first, Howard had warned Merrilee of Beth's determined attentions, promising her that he would see to it that Beth did not interfere in their lives. And he had kept his word. Merrilee wasn't quite sure how he had managed it, but immediately upon their marriage in the 1950s, Howard had set out to find a home calculated to repel his sister, and he had chosen well. Leaving Beth richly provided for in New York, he had moved them to Mellingham, still more fishing village than suburb as it nestled on the coast north of Boston. Beth had descended on them for her first visit only weeks after they had settled in. She decided at once not to stay. Nevertheless, she arrived on a regular basis for a brief visit, perhaps to confirm to herself that she really wasn't missing anything by having let Howard somehow slip away. She observed the natives, as she called them, sniffed suspiciously at the salt sea air, and took refuge in the company of other tourists from New York, who materialized wherever she went. She repeated to all who would listen, and some who wouldn't, how she had helped Howard get started. Every time the fateful visit was due, Merrilee hoped Howard would tire of his sister's chatter and cutting remarks and simply drive her back to the airport, but he never did, and his wife accepted this as his one act of familial duty, since his parents had been dead for many years. Beth, for her part, had been careful at first during her visits to charm as many people as she met; in more recent years, however, Merrilee had noticed an overtly malicious glint come into her sister-in-law's eye as she sized up a likely target for her mischief. That, and the steadily escalating cost of keeping Beth happy in New York, pushed Merrilee closer every year to the verge of speaking up. She wondered if this would be the year.

Merrilee shook herself mentally and reminded herself to be fair. Beth had helped Howard find his way in his early years and he was indeed grateful to her. He had been shy and self-conscious (and he still was), and Beth had introduced him to other businessmen who appreciated his intelligence and reticence. But for this Beth expected gratitude, even demanded it, and Merrilee was willing to admit that she for one resented it. She was savoring the virtue of her honesty with herself when her daughter, Medge, plucked a shrimp from the tray Merrilee was holding.

"Mother, you're paying a small fortune for someone else to serve the food so you can enjoy yourself. Give me that." Medge deftly took the tray from her mother's hands and passed it to a caterer moving through the crowd. Merrilee beamed at her only child, Medge Vinton, Executive, as she fondly thought of her, and her tense muscles relaxed. Although Medge and Frank lived in the converted gatehouse next door, Merrilee saw little of her daughter, who worked long hours in Boston in the credit card division of a major bank. Short like her mother, Medge moved with a lithe but easy grace, showing no inclination to take up the gymnastics her mother had practiced in her younger years. On the contrary, whenever Medge had free time she gravitated to the kitchen, where she experimented with recipes and made food gifts for any occasion she could think of. She had been staring wistfully at the caterers' suggested list of party foods three weeks ago when the owner of the Kitchen Cast Caterers, Jim Kellogg, noticed her look and asked her if she'd like to contribute something. Jim, an old school friend, seemed eager to have her help, and Medge promptly scheduled two vacation days to work with the caterers, although Jim had insisted he wouldn't need that much of her time.

"The food's going very well," she said to her mother with a professional air. Merrilee looked around curiously at the large living room only recently redecorated in bold flowery chintzes in salmons, pinks, and blues.

"Doesn't everything look lovely?" Merrilee said in surprise at her own home. "Actually, I'm quite enjoying myself. I was just thinking about the caterers' outfits. Do you like them?"

Medge looked at the young women in their early twenties slipping between the groups of guests. Their white peasant blouses and black or red or royal blue full cotton skirts set off the gaudy necklaces and earrings that jangled and clunked as they carried trays and smiled exuberantly at the guests. She'd had nothing to do with the serving side of Jim's business and now found it entertaining. "Well, they certainly add a festive air, but some of the guests thought they were supposed to come in costume," she said to her mother.

"Oh dear. Perhaps I should have made that clear on the invitation. Are they having a good time?"

"Yes," Medge reassured her. "It's a wonderful party. Everyone's having a great time."

"How about your father? Did he look all right?" Merrilee waffled between despair and giddiness when she thought about Howard at a party. Instead of enjoying himself, he spent the evening trying to evaluate the affair. He had once decided that the measure of a good party was how much alcohol the guests consumed, but since some guests had later not remembered much of the evening, he had doubted the value of that criterion. He had toyed with the idea of calibrating consumption of food, but their next party had included a large number of students from a nearby college, who ate with alacrity and then disappeared, leaving the party with a worn-out feeling. He had briefly accepted sound level and the number of laughs per five-minute period but had by that calculation held a dismal party for a number of earnest local writers and artists. Howard then considered the measure of time, but dismissed it almost instantly when he recalled the people who left early and the people who stayed late. He was at present considering a new criterion: how few times the weather was mentioned. Tabulating this measure posed problems, however, since he would have to question his family and the caterers and eventually they would catch on, listen carefully, and thus throw off the measure by overreporting.

If Howard had had a more discerning eye, he might have noticed the easy flow of guests in and out of groups, the quiet laughter and comfortable postures of the men and women.

Instead he wandered from room to room, noting trays of food served, glasses used, and decibel levels.

■ ■ ■

Jim Kellogg, founding genius of the Kitchen Cast Caterers, was not at that moment even thinking about his business. Holding his tray at eye level and bracing his elbow against his ribs, he leaned back against the wall and searched for a handkerchief in his back pocket with his free hand. Mopping his face, hoping the red flush would drain away, he looked across the metal tray at Beth O'Donnell's retreating back, every inch of her arching frame as smug as the look on her face a few seconds ago. She nodded and smiled to the other guests as she passed, and Jim wished he'd taken up ditch-digging. She was one prospective client he did not want to win over. Pushing a gulp of air into his lungs, he gripped the tray with both hands and scanned the crowd for a pathway back to the kitchen. He slipped between two groups, stretching his long limbs and turning toward the front hall.

"For my book?" he heard a woman's voice say. Recognizing the threatening sarcasm he had just escaped, Jim twirled around and slipped up against the wall of the dining room, looking for another way out.

"You?" he heard Beth say in the same voice that had pierced his confidence and brought the fear boiling up within him. Not for a second did he wonder who she was talking to, so stricken was he with the need to escape even the sound of her voice.

"You're not going to make me a big advance," he heard her say. Jim recognized Bob Chambers's voice in an incomprehensible reply as the caterer looked for another path, feeling in his heart that no parting of a sea could be more devoutly sought than the path he saw before him at that very moment. Lunging into the open space, he slipped away into the crowd, safe once again. The last words he heard made him wince, then marvel at what an editor would put up with to land a new author. With customers like that, Jim thought, he could well end up sprinkling his canapé trays with new concoctions like belladonna biscuits. Or digitalis toasties. So taken was he with these new names for party foods, he forgot his earlier attack of fear and gave his mind up to the playful discovery of a new theme for a menu.

■ ■ ■

"Try this," Merrilee said, slipping in behind Hannah Handel at the buffet. "Medge made it and gave it to the caterers to serve." Hannah accepted the morsel and mulled over the taste.

Now in her late fifties, Hannah had overcome the vagaries of fashion by devising a series of pants outfits and a simple blunt cut for her thick dark brown hair. After working twelve to fifteen hours a day for several years to help Lee establish the Marine Press, she had retired to her garden, where she continued to work eight to ten hours a day. She occasionally supplied bouquets of unusual blooms to the Agawam Inn or to her friends, but she refused to take the next logical step for someone with her ability and dedication and open a florist's shop or a greenhouse. Unfortunately, that had turned out to be a decision of mixed value in the past few years. The only sure thing was Hannah's willingness to work hard at whatever needed doing, a quality that had recently been called for in abundance. But she was, Merrilee noted, no longer looking haggard and no longer shadowing her husband. Merrilee was both heartened and uneasy at their appearance at the party; she had not expected them to accept, since Lee so seldom ventured out to social events. She had almost wondered if they would ever again attend her seasonal parties on a regular basis, as they had years ago.

"I think your newest plantings are lovely," Merrilee said. "I meant to get some for the cottage, but I forgot." The anger that flashed out of Hannah's eyes stunned Merrilee, and she hastily looked for something to say. Hannah stepped into the silence, perhaps unaware of what had brought her friend's conversation to a halt.

"For the cottage?" Hannah said. "I need a few days' warning. That's probably why you didn't think of it."

"Yes, I suppose so." She laughed and plucked another canapé from the tray she was holding.

"I hear from the rumor mill that your sister-in-law may write a book about all the people she knows in New York. Is that true?" Hannah asked nonchalantly. She too inspected the tray before popping another canapé whole into her mouth. Merrilee noticed the rigidity in her friend's fingers and wondered if she were now falling victim to arthritis.

"I hope not," Merrilee said. "Is that the current rumor about her?"

"It is. Surprising, isn't it?"

"Yes, it is," Merrilee agreed, relieved at the tone of the conversation, if not the topic. "Beth has never had any patience with that kind of work. She's never sought out a quiet way of life, and I don't see her taking it up at this stage. Besides," she said more thoughtfully, "what would she say about them? Just that she's met these people?"

"I don't know. That's what I was wondering." Hannah looked across the hallway into the living room where she could see the subject of their conversation waving a wineglass and nodding and smiling to a group of men encircling her. "I thought maybe that's why Bob Chambers was hanging around her this evening," Hannah continued.

"She does attract the young men," Merrilee said. "And the older ones, too. I wonder what it is about her?"

"Beats me. Whatever Bob is up to, it's probably going to be a surprise to everyone."

"Oh dear," Merrilee said, "I hope Beth doesn't get him into trouble."

"She will," Hannah said, "but he can get himself out of it. He's resourceful."

The harshness of Hannah's reply startled Merrilee and made her again forget what she was going to say. If anyone other than Hannah had made that comment, Merrilee would have been able to carry off a display of righteous indignation, but the two women had been friends for too long to hide their true feelings from each other. And yet the whole conversation was making Merrilee more and more uneasy. Perhaps to satisfy her sense of propriety as well as to relieve her own discomfort, she said as seriously as she could manage, "Hannah! How unkind of you."

"Don't worry, Merrilee, Bob is trying to get a job in New York. He may think Beth can help him."

"Oh," Merrilee said. "Does she have the right sort of contacts in New York?"

"She might, but I wouldn't know anything about that."

"I never thought of Beth as a celebrity in her own right," Merrilee said. "Just as someone who knew people." This was perhaps an overstatement. Merrilee had never given much thought at all to the names that dotted the otherwise bleak landscape of her sister-in-law's correspondence. Beth wrote to Howard alone, not to Merrilee, and his response had always been satisfactory as far as Merrilee could tell. He commented dutifully on the large number of people she knew and added to her bank account whenever the cost of living in New York seemed to be a matter of concern to her. Otherwise, Merrilee barely remembered her letters. Beth had friends in Mellingham and the surrounding area and wrote to them also, and Merrilee assumed that if anything momentous occurred, the local grapevine would eventually send a ripe green runner in her direction.

Merrilee was at that moment reminded of just how close Beth felt to her own friends when the hostess saw her sister-in-law pass by, ignoring Merrilee and Hannah as she saw the Morrisons to the door. Watching the three cross the hallway, Hannah marveled at their arch mannerisms, wondering why Merrilee invited them in the first place. Perhaps reading the other woman's mind, Beth cast a disdainful nod of recognition at Hannah, who blanched and turned away.

"I'd better say good night to my guests." Merrilee clenched her teeth and marched off to the front door.

Left alone in the doorway to the dining room, Hannah looked around for her husband. This made her appear, at least for the moment, an unattached woman, and therefore a likely audience for Mr. Steinwell, of Steinwell Fabrics, who was just then also unattached. Proud of his family business, which was known for its very fine fabrics, Mr. Steinwell was too enthusiastic about his work to be a bore but too narrow in his interest to be a pleasant conversationalist. Hannah looked around for someone to draw into the conversation but only Bob Chambers and Lisa Hunt were nearby, and they were inching their way to the door and a farewell to their hostess. Lee had only just escaped from Mr. Steinwell and was avoiding placing himself in the line of his wife's vision. Hannah understood this all too well, for during the last few years Lee had lost all interest in listening to the successes of his comrades in business. Only the persistent kindness of Howard O'Donnell had kept Lee from withdrawing completely from the society of men and women in favor of that of birds. Hannah gave up trying to attract her husband's attention and instead gave a few serious nods to Mr. Steinwell, who was now detailing computer-aided color designs for his fabrics. She was relieved to see by her watch that it was just ten-thirty, which meant that the evening was almost over and she could soon rescue her husband and take him home, if she could find him. With great relief, she realized, he seemed to have made it through the entire evening without incident.

■ ■ ■

By the end of the evening, Lee Handel had extricated himself from the few clusters of remaining guests. He noted the numbers now departing and would have followed the Morrisons out if he had been able to claim his wife before Mr. Steinwell had. He continued to back away from them and the front hall, tucking himself into corners and listening to the final chatterings of the remaining guests. He worked his way back to the window, passing a debate on the tax rate, a polemic against the fees for plowing private lanes with town trucks, and a story about a nightmarish tour to Alaska, until he finally bumped into Howard. This was a stroke of luck for Howard, who was still considering ways to get the conversation about the bird feeder back on track, since Lee had apparently enjoyed it so much.

"Perhaps you'd like to see the feeder?" Howard asked.

"Definitely, definitely," Lee answered, eager to flee the remaining guests and the story about Alaska. He followed Howard happily from the room. Frank Vinton held open the door to the garden for them, running a hand over his red hair and remarking to Howard as they passed, "Off to see the garden?"

"Uh, yes," Howard answered. He had never liked his son-in-law's man-to-man smile, his easy familiarity, though it had served him well in the brokerage business. Frank's manner generally left Howard uncomfortable, and this evening it left him embarrassed about admitting the real purpose of their trip outside to the garden at the tail end of the party. There was nothing wrong in his friend's interest, Howard reminded himself, but he still felt uncomfortable. He followed Lee across the lawn to the tree, now in full bloom and illuminated by two tall lamps standing at the edge of a stone path that ran along the side of the house, from the driveway in front to the cottage in back and the path to the beach beyond.

"Here it is," Howard said superfluously, pointing to the item in question. He explained the technical details of the discovery, purchase, and hanging of the feeder, hoping one or more of the details would interest his guest. The self-consciousness he had felt in Frank's presence a moment earlier melted away as he was caught up in Lee's scrutiny of the plastic form. Lee pointed to several design features of which he approved heartily, and Howard was gratified. He drew closer to Lee as his guest listed again the many problems he had encountered in his own backyard. It was then that Howard finally grasped Lee's love of birds. And to his surprise, Howard heard himself saying, "Why don't you take it. We have another feeder. We don't need two."

"Oh no, I couldn't," Lee said with great embarrassment, wringing his hands.

"Please do," Howard said. "I want you to."

"Really?" Lee's eyes sparkled, and he reached up to extricate the feeder from the tree branches. Grasping it carefully in his two hands, he lowered it to eye level and peered at it. He turned it over in his hands, savoring every sparkle of reflected light on its surface. In what seemed like no time at all, Howard reminded Lee of the party by offering him another drink inside. But this, Lee sensed, would be more excitement than he could endure. For the moment he was happy. And so he declined Howard's offer. Instead, Lee carried the bird feeder tenderly in his outstretched hands to the house, taking his eyes off the treasure only long enough to locate the door. Howard held the door for Lee as he passed through, and was genuinely pleased at his guest's delight, but he blushed when he saw Hannah standing in the hall talking to Frank and Mr. Steinwell and waiting for her husband. She raised an eyebrow when she saw the two men approaching and Lee's attention fully focused on the feeder. With a sigh, she steered him toward the front door; Howard quickly took refuge in the parting ritual, smiling and accepting compliments from the few remaining guests. It was just eleven o'clock, he noticed, not too early and not too late. Perhaps he had hit on another criterion for success—number of hours times number of guests times— Times what? Could he quantify the nature of an event? He missed the parting thanks from Mr. Steinwell as he pondered his new equation.

■ ■ ■

For many hosts and hostesses, the best part of the evening is just after all the guests have gone home, when the warmth of their friendliness still hangs in the air and the pleasure of their company still lingers in the heart, when the living room does not yet look starkly filthy and the quiet is calming after the sound of happy chatter. Merrilee loved this time, not the least because she did not have to concern herself with cleaning up. If the caterers had been anywhere near her age, she would have felt duty bound to help them, regardless of how much she was paying them. But they were not near her age, and so at a few minutes after eleven she found herself sliding deeper into the plush sofa, wiggling her toes in the rug, and listening contentedly to the cheerful bustle of those young enough never to be tired. She heard a screen door fall to, heard questions asked, directions given, and congratulated herself on finding such competent helpers.

She was just nodding off again when Jim Kellogg's long legs stepped over her. She opened her eyes to see a large metal tray balancing over her head. Jim moved on, collecting glasses, and Merrilee decided it was time to go to bed. It was past eleven-thirty, and Howard wouldn't settle down without her. She did not even consider for a moment passing on instructions to the housekeeper, Mrs. Miles, so complete was her faith in her staff and her daughter.

At least that was how she explained it to her friends. To herself she admitted that neither she nor anyone else told the housekeeper what to do. Mrs. Miles had come to the United States from Ireland as a girl at the end of the Great Depression and found undreamed-of opportunities. It took a while before she realized that not everyone had been so fortunate at that time, but she had never ceased to view life in her own way, and that was only one of the many ways in which she asserted herself. She had chosen the caterers as she chose every other worker who came near the house. And all on the premise that she was the one who could judge their character better than anyone else. Merrilee never argued with her, in part because she could never get a grip on the discussion. Arguing with Mrs. Miles was like chasing a greased garter snake. Merrilee sighed happily, for the evening was over and she could count it a success.

■ ■ ■

Howard stood in the bedroom doorway, looking over at his wife, who was leaning against a thicket of white pillows edged with lace. There welled up inside him the love he had always felt for her, and, as always, it surprised him. He coughed.

"Nice group of kids," Howard said as he strolled into the bedroom in his silk bathrobe. He stopped to listen to them moving around downstairs.

"They're not kids, dear. Most of them are Medge's age," she reminded him absentmindedly.

"Yes," he agreed, looking for the contradiction in this.

"Medge is going to lock up after Mrs. Miles and the caterers," she went on. Howard ahhed his approval. She patted his arm as she said this and slid further down beneath the covers. "It was a nice party, dear. Everyone had a good time." She regretted this the minute she said it.

Her husband blinked. "About the consumption of food," he began.

"People eat at parties," she said, trying to head off what she knew was coming.

"Yes, but not everyone," he went on. Merrilee settled back in the bed, wondering how long she could listen to her husband's analysis of the evening before she fell asleep. She listened to the sounds around her, leaves rustling in a light breeze outside the window, the caterers moving around below, and Howard's droning beside her.

■ ■ ■

By one o'clock in the morning, the afterglow had dissipated, leaving only good will and good humor among the caterers, who cheerily packed up their van and drove away, carrying the housekeeper with them. Loyal and hard-working, Mrs. Miles had insisted on overseeing the caterers, assisting them if necessary. And so she had. Satisfied that no one had filched the silver, broken into the safe, or pilfered the cookies, she had allowed herself to be transported home. Medge turned out the remaining lights, locked the kitchen door behind her, and walked across the narrow field to the old gatehouse, where she and her husband lived. Her way was lighted by the full moon shining on the ocean nearby. Frank had left an outside light on for her, and a light in the bedroom was on. Only then did she realize how tired she was. For a reason she preferred not to examine, she had invested much of herself in the evening. And instead of feeling envious of her husband for having been in bed asleep for the last couple of hours, she was exhilarated at her part in the success of the party. She definitely liked catering, and after apologizing profusely for the temerity of his offer, Jim Kellogg had asked her if she might consider joining him in his projects for his new client, the Agawam Inn. Medge was now satisfied she had an answer.

■ ■ ■

A single light shone from the window onto the lawn behind the large frame house. The small guest cottage behind the O'Donnell house had been designed to ensure privacy but not isolation for their guests, and Beth had appreciated that from the first. She sat now in a wing chair in front of a cold fireplace, her feet, also cold, resting on a footstool. The light of the lamp in front of the window glinted on the bud vase and sparkled on the glass bowl holding the brightly colored marble eggs, and illuminated softly the entire first room of the two-room cottage, showing to their best the antiques in a room that dealers and decorators would casually describe as tastefully appointed but Merrilee had once called overdone, like Christmas cake in July. The room was always so, intimidating some in its perfect arrangements and impressing others with its careful and expensive detail, including the leather wastebasket with the silk lining and the silver candlesticks on the mantel, the silver design of the leaves echoing the fall foliage in the painting over the mantel. Even now, with a guest occupying the cottage, everything seemed in perfect order, with not so much as a pad of notepaper out of place.

The cottage was perfectly still, the atmosphere serene. There was no breeze, no creaking door, no dripping faucet. It was simply a warm spring night, the kind that promised the luxury of a lush summer. The air was warm and fresh in the cottage. The blood that had dripped down the nape of Beth O'Donnell's neck was dry and hard now, the hand that had spastically grabbed the arm of the chair and ever so slightly frayed the fabric was limp. The sudden indrawn gasp of breath that had been punctuated by the crash of a wave on the beach below had been expelled into the soft night. There would be no other sound now in the cottage, and no sound from the road or from the beach for several hours, not until early morning. Mellingham is, after all, a small town.

2

SUNDAY MORNING

WESTERLY ROAD, a narrow old paved road, ran for a bumpy mile down a short peninsula to the rocky coast, where it ended in a tight loop. Along the way, the occasional dirt driveway wound its way up to homes whose owners had not yet felt the need to frame their wealth in macadam and gates. Most of the small mansions were hidden from view by the overgrowth along the road, some were set back in old meadows, a few sat near the road. The O'Donnell home, a large wood-frame house, once only a rambling summer estate, was set in a meadow, which previous owners long ago had broken up by planting trees to ensure privacy for their heirs if not for themselves. The pastoral sentiment had been carefully nurtured throughout the grounds, with clumps of wild roses growing thicker as they neared the cliff that fell to the beach. Other wildflowers skirted the cliff walk and the path up to the O'Donnell guest cottage, blending into an edging of white flowers ringing the side lawn. Three generations of gardeners had conscientiously watched over an array of shrubs, trees, and flowers, assiduously weeding out dandelions in favor of clover and other weeds deemed more suitable to the meadow areas of the grounds. The house and yard looked their best in high summer, but spring was also a beautiful time for the knowing visitor. At present, the only discordant note was the ambulance with its flashing red lights, the two town police cars, one state police van, and three private cars. These were parked willy-nilly on the grass. Two cars belonging to officials of the Commonwealth sat in the driveway.

The many passengers and drivers of these vehicles, with the exception of one officer detailed to send away curious passersby (of which there were none), filled the small guest cottage behind the house. Despite the number of people in that space, it was quiet, with the murmur of voices only occasionally rising to the ears of those standing outside. The officers, some in uniform and others in street clothes, moved around, behind, and in front of the well-dressed corpse in the wing chair. In death her features relaxed, giving her the appearance of a handsome, easygoing woman in middle age.

Joe Silva, chief of police in Mellingham, stood near the door with the state police officer he had called in, Captain Welch. To a discerning eye, the men stood as strangers, their different positions within the police service reflected in their appearance, but there is more to appearances than meets the eye. Captain Welch, overweight from the burdens of a desk job and his sandy hair now thinning out, had opted for the state police and its occasional political tussles; Joe Silva, tall, straightbacked, and black-haired, had chosen another path. They had begun as friends and remained so.

"Your wife taping the game?" Silva asked quietly into the air.

"Yes," Welch replied. "You got a wife yet?"

"Not yet," Silva said, grateful that circumstances prevented him from answering more fully what was only superficially a frivolous question from his old friend. He hadn't thought about Christina in years.

"Different out here, isn't it?" Welch mumbled. "Ever miss the old times?"

"This is the old times, remember?" Silva said.

"That's right," Welch said, the merest hint of a smile playing around his fleshy lips. "You always were good at homicide." Welch nodded at the irony.

"Good thing," Silva said, "since I don't seem to be able to get away from it for very long." He looked at two men unfolding a large blue plastic bag.

"My grandmother always said, 'Don't bother trying to run away. We find the same wherever we go.' She'd appreciate this," Welch said as he looked over at the corpse.

"I'll remember to hold your grandmother responsible for it." Silva glanced at Welch, but neither man smiled, though not for lack of amusement. Silva had once made the mistake of making a mild joke to ease the tensions in the station during the investigation of a particularly nasty robbery, and the victim's mother had heard the men laughing and loudly accused the police of callous disregard of her child's feelings. Welch had told him to ignore it, but Silva found in the end that he couldn't. He hadn't known it then, but that had been the crossroads. It had seemed so long ago as he thought about it now, but it wasn't, Silva knew. It wasn't long ago, and it wasn't over.

The photographer moved wordlessly, and Silva watched his own men with admiration. When he had first come to Mellingham in 1985, he had meant to leave violent crime behind him and had at first passed up training opportunities for his officers. But the younger officers had repeatedly asked for a chance to learn more and Silva, finally relenting, persuaded the residents at town meeting that there were unseen benefits from a trained force. Miss Beth O'Donnell was not what he had had in mind, but he was glad he had been persuaded. Now he looked on with relief as well, as his men worked with the officers from the state police.

"The EMT crew want to leave, sir," Sergeant Dupoulis said after conferring with two men in uniform standing just

SUSAN OLEKSIW

on the other side of the cottage door, a large blue plastic bag resting on a dolly behind them. Silva glanced at Captain Welch, who nodded, and Silva said fine, as long as Dupoulis had reports from them.

"That the officer you were telling me about?" Welch mumbled after Dupoulis had left. To the ever-increasing frustration of his men, Welch's voice became less distinct with each promotion, and some wags were taking bets on which rank would bring him to permanent silence.

"Yes. Ken Dupoulis. He's young, and very good," Silva said.

Welch nodded in agreement, allowing himself a surreptitious glance at the fellow.

"I grew up in a town like this," Welch said, looking around the room as though it represented a childhood recovered.

"Do you ever go back?" Silva asked.

"I wouldn't know how," Welch said, taking Silva's casual question metaphorically. "Must have been strange to you, after your experience," he went on in a more relaxed tone.

"Yes and no. The pace is different, but the problems are the same."

Welch glanced at him but said nothing for a moment. "No difference?" he finally said to Silva.

"Not really," Silva said, trying to sound more philosophical than he felt. "It's only a matter of degree. Or so I tell myself," he said. "But easier. A lot easier." Now in his late forties, Silva never regretted the decision that had led him to apply for the job of chief of police in Mellingham. No town could have been more different from his early years in a triple decker in a port city down the coast, but he had quickly picked up on the customs and practices of the townspeople, gently reminding them as needed of the overriding authority of the laws of the Commonwealth.

"Somehow things were easier in the city, at least for me," Welch said.

26

"That's not what it sounded like on the phone this morning," Silva said.

"I didn't say I didn't have anything to do," he replied. "Listen, we have twice the number of murders this year as last year. I hope you're not going to add this to my list," he said. "I'll be glad of any help I can get."

"So will I," Silva said. "All I have so far is a corpse."

■ ■ ■

Silva listened to the state police cars drive away before turning his attention back to the empty cottage. He had never liked the scene of violent crime, no matter how untouched the room might appear to be. But he had learned to study any discrete space objectively for information, and he looked mechanically around him as he had learned to do while a train of misgivings ran across his thoughts. He had not gotten away, as he had once believed, but belaboring this unwelcome surprise would only distract him from the job at hand. Once again the policeman, Joe Silva put his personal thoughts aside.

Silva went over each feature as it came to his eye, a skill that had saved him from the habit he had seen in others of gripping the evidence put before them. After he had looked over the room from one point of view, he went to the opposite corner and went over it again, then knelt down and looked along the floor and walls. He tried several different angles until he felt he knew the cottage well enough to know if a piece of furniture were missing or if a knickknack had been added or moved. He moved back to the front door, walked around the cottage, studying it from several angles, and returned by the front door.

The cottage was a one-story, two-room clapboard house, with a pitched roof and large windows on two sides. The wall facing the side garden of the main house and the street had no windows. Along the outside wall were planted a dozen climbing roses, which by now would have blocked any light that might have shone through a window. The other windowless side faced the neighbors. The cottage was designed for privacy, Silva mused, and certainly achieved it.

The first of the two rooms was a large sitting room with a door facing the yard behind the main house. French doors on either side of the fireplace faced the beach lying beyond a wall of low trees and shrubs. The room was plushly furnished—a comfortable sofa in a silk flowered print, antique side tables and chairs, paintings on the walls—all of it far too rich for Silva's taste. The wing chair faced the fireplace; a footstool was drawn up in front of it, and on the floor, to its right, sat a sewing bag, which had fallen open to reveal a square of linen with embroidered designs.

The second room, which could be closed off by sliding wooden doors, was a bedroom with another set of french doors facing the beach along one wall and a small bathroom and large closets on the far wall opposite the front door. Again, the decoration was plush and bright. The vanity table held an assortment of makeup tubes and bottles, hairbrush, combs, two hair dryers, and three kinds of perfume. On the bedside table were fresh cut flowers and a photograph in a silver frame of the O'Donnell family, Howard and Merrilee and Medge and Frank. Along the edge was written "Xmas 1977." The four looked much the same then as they did now, and Silva envied them for the ease with which they had aged.

The contents of the victim's purse had been dumped on the bed—leather wallet and change purse, engraved pen and pencil set, monogrammed handkerchief, and engraved lipstick and compact. The clothes hanging in the closet had designer labels sewn in by hand and nothing looked worn or old, or even well used. The clothes were spread along the rack, covering the entire space of the closet. On a table beside a reading chair was a map of the area in an embossed leather case, a car rental folder and keys, and a candy bar. The drawers in the desk and bedside table were empty.

Silva walked back through the two rooms to the front

door. From every angle a good photographer could take a perfect picture of a life of wealth, with nothing concealed beneath. There were no notes, no scraps of paper, no letters torn open and left lying about, no newspapers or cheap paperback books. Not even a dirty string of seaweed clinging to a seashell. There was no hint that life for Miss Beth O'Donnell went deeper than the right clothes, the right cosmetics, the right jewelry.

"We're ready to seal the cottage, sir," Dupoulis spoke from the doorway. He waited in silence for the chief's answer.

"Go ahead," Silva finally said. "I'll follow you out."

■ ■ ■

Howard O'Donnell stood on the stone path that led from the door of the cottage to the side of the main house, where it split, with one path leading to the side garden and the other leading to the back door to the kitchen. Dressed in slacks and a shirt with his sleeves rolled up and no tie, he stood expectantly but patiently, ready to help but unwilling to interfere. Silva recalled everything he could about the man as he offered his condolences and told him the cottage would have to remain closed.

"Certainly, certainly," Howard said, nodding his head while his eyes widened.

The surviving relatives and friends, uniformly in Silva's experience, needed time to draw back from the horror of the death and consider the implications. Their reactions, spontaneous and unguarded, could be useful, but they could also be misleading, and Silva had therefore learned to remember but remain skeptical of the comments and actions of the close relatives and friends during the hours immediately after the discovery of the victim.

"Certainly," Howard repeated a little less firmly. He stood waiting in the silence, looking around at the last of the cars driving away, back at Chief Silva. He tilted his head forward and finally said, "Did you want to ask me anything, Chief? We could go inside," he said, turning and gesturing to the house.

"I only have a couple of quick questions for the moment," Silva said. Howard nodded and pursed his lips as though he found this entirely reasonable although in truth he wondered why the police hadn't wanted to talk to everyone instantly. Howard had actually imagined himself rousting his wife and daughter and son-in-law out of bed. He was caught in the pleasure of this new sense of himself as a commanding figure of quick, decisive action when he realized that Chief Silva was watching him.

"Ah, yes," Howard said as he cleared his throat. "Why don't we sit right here?" Howard led the chief across the lawn to a group of chairs near the crab apple tree and motioned to the chief to sit down. Dupoulis stepped discreetly to the side.

"I understand you called the ambulance, Mr. O'Donnell," Silva said when they were seated.

"That's right," Howard agreed, wondering why this was the important question, or so important that Chief Silva asked it first. He was convinced that police investigations would be very different from business discussions.

"Can you tell me what happened?" Silva asked. The question was posed so casually to Howard that he first had to recite to himself what he knew to have happened this morning. And so simple did Silva's questions seem that Howard at first heard in his mind a description of how he had picked up the telephone and punched the buttons for the telephone number.

"Just what you know happened."

"Ah, well, I don't really know," Howard said. "My sister didn't come up to the house for breakfast, and it was getting late, so I thought I'd better come along to see if she wanted anything."

"What time was this?"

"Nine-thirty, I think." Howard thought about this, then repeated the time more firmly. "Yes, nine-thirty."

"What did you do then?"

This seemed to call for a mental effort, and Silva waited while Howard looked through the possible replies in his mind and selected one.

"Well, I waited a few minutes, I think," he said.

"And then?" Silva said to nudge him along.

"Then, I . . . I came down and knocked on the door, but she didn't answer." Howard stared at Chief Silva, unsure of what to say next.

"What did you do then? Did you go in?" Silva asked.

"No. I walked down and looked along the beach path. I thought she might have gone down to the beach for a walk and I didn't want to keep knocking if she'd gone out."

"Did she normally go down to the beach in the morning before breakfast?" the chief asked.

"Well, no," Howard said. "But she might have."

"Did you see anything?" Silva asked, still prompting Howard for the merest account of how he discovered the body. If every interview were like this, he thought, this could be the longest murder investigation Silva had ever conducted. The chief was not used to prompting people who were witnesses; the men and women on the sidelines were usually eager to tell their story, letting their words tumble out in such disorder that Silva had often wondered how he would ever make written sense out of them. Some were so flattered at being asked for a narrative of what they had seen that they repeated everything they could remember, punctuating every two or three sentences with, I don't know if this matters, but— Mr. O'Donnell, however, was different. A man of few words, he remained laconic and unfocused even after a shock. If it was a shock, considered Silva. "Did you see anything at all?" he prompted.

"Nothing, Chief. That's when I began to get worried. Not about the path to the beach being empty," he explained quickly. "But about how late it was. My sister always had breakfast promptly at nine o'clock. She never waited—except once when she was sick."

"So you thought she might be sick?" Silva asked, then wished he hadn't as Howard's head tilted back, his eyes rose to the top of the crab apple tree, and he pursed his lips.

"No," Howard finally said, "I never had the idea she was sick. But I was sure something was wrong so I went back to the house for the extra key." He looked directly at Chief Silva.

"So you unlocked the door." Silva made a quick mental note.

"Yes," Howard agreed.

"And?" Silva said.

"And?" Howard echoed.

"Did you go in?" Silva asked. "I have to know exactly what happened."

"Yes. I went in." Howard shuddered slightly, then took a deep breath and continued in a subdued voice. "Oh, I see. That's what you want to know. Did I find her in there? Oh yes. I saw her sitting in the chair and I started talking to her and then I realized she was wearing what she'd had on last night. I knew that wasn't right. When I got closer I saw . . ." Howard stopped speaking and the stunned look he'd had on his face when Silva first arrived returned. Silva felt sorry for him, hoping he'd be at home when the full force of the reality of his sister's death finally hit him.

"What did you do then?" Silva asked more gently.

"I went back to the house and called the ambulance. They came right away." Howard now seemed to shrink into the chair, his pudgy body molding in sorrow into the comforting embrace of the cotton-covered cushions.

"Did you speak to anyone on the way? On your way to the telephone, I mean."

"No. I went directly to the telephone." Howard blinked and looked away.

"Where did you wait for the ambulance?"

"I came back here, to the cottage, and waited outside." He looked up alert. "When I was coming back out, I told my wife that something was wrong and that I'd called the ambulance." He paused. "I told her to stay inside, that I would handle it. I hope that was all right."

"That was fine," Silva said. Even now, after almost a dozen strange cars had been up and down the quiet street on a Sunday morning no one had come by asking questions—no neighbors out walking their dogs, no children on bicycles, no young kids or teenagers drifting up the beach path, like sand dunes moving inexorably closer inch by inch to the strip of green grass and weeds above the beach. Silva looked up at the main house, but no curtains twitched at the windows, no shadows emerged and withdrew. If the neighborhood was without the usual curious passersby, the family had an equally unusual way of responding to sudden death. Instead of drawing together for comfort and consolation, they seemed to back away and steel themselves in solitude and etiquette. Howard looked stunned, but he showed no other emotion. He may simply be extremely circumspect, Silva speculated, or perhaps no one in the family had any curiosity about what was going on or felt any sorrow for the victim.

"Your sister's death wasn't accidental, Mr. O'Donnell," Silva said, hoping to push Howard to a clearer reaction.

"I know." Howard looked old and tired as he confronted the truth of the morning's events, and Silva again felt sorry for him.

"Your sister was a houseguest?"

"Yes. She came yesterday, Saturday, for a short visit." He spoke without animation, showing no relief at the change in subject. Silva was used to all sorts of reactions to sudden and violent death, but he had never before encountered such weariness, as though his sister's death relieved Howard of an enormous burden.

"She came for the party?" Silva asked. Most people in Mellingham still followed the custom of consulting the police department before every large party, which meant the police could always anticipate unusual activity. Silva found the practice useful, as did many of the local shopkeepers, who seemed to tailor their displays to the upcoming events.

"Yes, she always came in the spring or summer," Howard said.

"Are any other guests staying over in the cottage or in the house?"

"No. Beth always has the cottage to herself." Howard looked over at the outside wall covered with climbing roses not yet in bloom. He looked back at the main house, then around at the yard, finally letting his glance rest on the other chairs and sofas grouped nearby. He turned to Silva and said, in conclusion, "And we have no other guests at the moment."

"Let me ask about last night," Silva said. "I'll have to have a list of everyone who was here at the party but first I'd like to know who else stayed here after the party."

"After the party?" Howard considered the question, tilting his head back and closing his eyes, then dropping his chin down before he spoke. "Last night after the party there was just my sister in the cottage. My wife and I were alone in the house. My daughter and her husband live in the gatehouse by the road, and our housekeeper, Mrs. Miles, left with the caterers."

"We'll want to speak with everyone," Silva said. "Could you tell me now when you last saw your sister alive?"

"Ah," Howard began. "I've been thinking about that," he said and lapsed into silence again. Silva waited less patiently this time while Howard studied a distant branch of the crab apple tree. "I must have seen her during the party several times—I'm sure of that—but I don't remember exactly when she left and I don't remember seeing her after ten or a little later. I think that's right," he said as he considered his reply again. "It was very crowded most of the evening. I had to speak to everyone, of course."

"Well, keep thinking about it, sir. I'd like as exact a time as you can give me. I also need to know if Miss O'Donnell mentioned any fears or worries to you last night or any time recently," Silva said.

"No, nothing. At least, I don't think so," Howard said. He blinked rapidly as he tried to absorb the suggestion inherent in the chief's question.

Silva waited but Howard didn't add anything to his reply.

"Had she had any arguments with anyone?" Silva asked.

"I don't think so," Howard said, still blinking rapidly. Silva idly wondered if this were a sign that Howard was about to reach the saturation point in the mental stimulation he could endure. Suddenly Howard stopped blinking and said matter-of-factly, "But she didn't tell me such things, Chief. She must have had arguments and disagreements with people now and then, but she never said a word to me and I never thought to ask her about them." He sighed. "I'm afraid I knew little about her friends. I suppose that's a bad choice of words, isn't it?"

Silva smiled and stood up, arranging to talk with Mrs. O'Donnell after her husband prepared her for the interview. The two men shook hands, and not for the first time Silva noted that the nature of the place could alter the tone of a murder investigation until it had taken on the etiquette of a polite business meeting. The city was never like this, he said to himself.

■ ■ ■

Dupoulis closed the car door and said to Howard's retreating back, "That was different. It's hard to imagine someone knowing less than he does about a murder in your own home."

"Give him time," Silva said as he settled into the passenger seat of the police car to look through his notes. "Let him think about it. He'll remember little things that have been bothering him and one of them will help us."

"He doesn't even seem interested, except for getting a

grip on what happened," Dupoulis said. "Didn't seem all that upset either."

"No, he didn't, did he?" Silva agreed, looking hard at the now closed front door.

"I always thought they seemed like such a nice family," Dupoulis said.

Silva looked over at him. "A murder investigation is not the time to judge people. No one looks good at a time like this, not even the police. Make up your mind about them when it's all over. Now, what about the state team. Anything?"

"Not yet," Dupoulis said. "The state lab men didn't find much. At least it didn't look like much."

"It usually doesn't. It's the description of the evidence that makes you see what's there." Silva looked down Westerly Road, still deserted after several hours of intense police activity. Not for the first time did Silva marvel at the habits of the rich. He estimated how long it would be before the first call came in to the station for an officer to get a cat out of a tree; he would have to decide who to send with the information he was willing to release. He had a few younger officers whose tongues seemed to be glued to the inside of their mouths and Silva always worried that one or another would be the unhappy choice of a luckless resident who wanted to send information to the police discreetly, in the form of gossip. As far as Silva knew, someone might already have tried. This might be just the opportunity, he realized, to train a few of the younger ones in the tactful dispersal of noncritical information, as his first chief had called police gossip.

"Where's the rest of the family? At lunch?" Silva asked, aware of how hungry he was.

"Not yet. Not here anyway," Dupoulis said. "The daughter, Mrs. Vinton, is playing tennis and her husband, Mr. Vinton, is playing golf; both left around eight or nine this morning."

"Early birds, eh?" Silva said. "Okay. You interview the

neighbors." He looked off into the trees and beyond, to the houses that could barely be glimpsed beyond the meadows. "I doubt if anyone heard or saw anything, but you'd better check. Then take the Vintons. I'll see Mrs. O'Donnell."

■ ■ ■

Silva knew Merrilee O'Donnell by sight. She always nodded hello when they passed on the street, she sent Christmas cards to the department every year, and she was a quiet but steady supporter of the public library. He knew the O'Donnells were well off, as some liked to describe it, but Mrs. O'Donnell rarely looked any different in dress or manner from the other women in town of any level of income. And though she seemed somewhat flighty in her mannerisms, waving her hands and bouncing on her toes, she never said or did anything unusual or worthy of comment. He thought her a sensible woman, which made him all the more curious about her composure now. She was carefully pouring tea and making polite remarks while Silva settled into a chair, his eye on the tea tray precariously balanced on two stacks of books on the floor. The coffee table was covered with family photographs lying flat in cloth frames under a sheet of glass. At first he had thought it was a display for the sake of the embroidered frames, but on closer inspection he had seen the descriptions and dates on each photograph. The oldest one was of Medge at the age of five or six at a birthday party with her young friends.

"I'm sure this is a difficult time for you," she began, surprising Silva by reciting the sentiment he had meant to use to begin the interview.

"We're trained to handle these things, Mrs. O'Donnell. But it certainly must be difficult for you," he said, determined to grasp the upper hand and hold it.

"Not really," Mrs. O'Donnell replied immediately, "I didn't like Beth very much. I feel more like I've had cold water thrown on my face." She smiled awkwardly. "I didn't wish her ill, but I didn't like her either. I suppose I should be showing more regret at her death." The teapot landed hard on the tray. "Oh dear, do I sound awful?" She handed him a cup and saucer while she frowned at her own question.

In more than twenty years in uniform Silva thought he had met every reaction to violent death, but never before had he encountered people like the O'Donnells. Despite their protestations, both Mr. and Mrs. O'Donnell seemed dangerously close to the edge. Nothing else could explain their distracted conversations. Untrained in the subtleties of psychology, Silva chose by instinct to hold Mrs. O'Donnell to a mundane reality.

"I just wanted to ask a few questions about last night," Silva said, determined to keep the attention of his distracted hostess. "You had a large party last night," he said, conscious of the banality of his comment and recalling how easily the dialogue with Howard earlier had somehow slipped away from him.

"Yes." Merrilee, pleased at the change in topic, leaned forward eagerly. "We had quite a large crowd, about sixty people."

"Do you have a copy of the guest list?" he asked, confident that his interrogation could now get under way.

"Yes. Do you want to see it?" Puzzled, she looked at him expectantly.

"I think, under the circumstances . . ."

"Circumstances?" she repeated.

Silva stared at her. Either the woman was ingenuous or she really could not absorb the significance of the presence of the police officers this morning. After talking to her husband, he decided it was the latter. He decided to let her carry on in her own way.

"Yes," he said firmly. "I want to see the guest list."

Mrs. O'Donnell seemed to accept Silva's reply as a command, and rising gracefully she moved to a secretary near the front window. From the desk she took a sheet of paper containing two columns of names, neatly typed, and read it over. She added a few notes in pencil before passing it to him. He scanned it, recognizing many of the names, but not all.

"Thank you," he said. "I just want to get the time sorted out in my own mind, if you don't mind?"

"Not at all," she said, her enthusiasm once again discomfiting him.

"About what time did the party end?"

"Let me see," she said. "All the guests were gone by eleven o'clock. I think the last one was going out the door just at the stroke of eleven. I always find that so satisfying, when an event runs right to schedule, don't you?"

"Could you tell me when your sister-in-law left the party?"

"Well, it was certainly after ten-thirty."

"And was she still there after eleven o'clock?" Silva asked.

"Oh no, no, she was definitely gone by then," Merrilee said. "Try one of these rolls." She passed a plate to him, but was not put out when he declined. She left the plate on the edge of the coffee table, almost half of it extending over the edge. Silva pushed it back onto the table. "I remember now. Yes," she said with a sweet smile. "I saw her around ten-thirty or so when my guests were starting to leave. Oh dear, how thoughtless of me." She handed him a napkin and pushed the plate of rolls back to him. Silva let the plate dangle, but found his eyes drawn to it even as he asked his next question.

"Do you recall seeing your sister-in-law among the guests after ten-thirty?"

"Oh no, I couldn't. I was saying good night," she explained. "I never left the door after ten-thirty. I remember that quite well. I was talking to Hannah—you know, Mrs. Handel—and my guests started to leave, so I went to the door at ten-thirty to say good-bye. And then I just stayed there until the last one left at eleven o'clock."

"Who was that?" Silva asked, curious at an undercurrent in this recital he couldn't put his finger on.

"Mr. Steinwell and the Handels," she said. "I thought he was going to leave earlier, but he ran into Mrs. Handel, and they started talking, and well, that was that."

"So you remember seeing your sister-in-law at ten-thirty. Is that right? Did you see her at all after that?"

"I don't think so. Most of the people she knew had left by then, anyway. I assume she just went back to the cottage. She could have stayed around, but I didn't see her." Merrilee nudged a plate of cookies a few inches closer to him as she spoke. Silva let it go, recalling the luck that often went with personalities who never seemed to have both feet on the ground at once. He also worried that once Mrs. O'Donnell turned her full attention to the tea and the logistics of her ministrations, he might never get her attention again—at least not this afternoon.

"Did she mention anything earlier about any problems?" Silva asked. "Any worries she might have had?"

"Problems?" Merrilee stared at him. "Beth had no problems. She never had problems. Howard took care of everything." The sentences came in a sudden sharp staccato. Then she folded her hands in her lap and looked directly across at him, giving him the benefit of every one of her brain cells.

"Mrs. O'Donnell," Silva said gently, calming himself more than her, "your sister-in-law was murdered last night. Someone hated her enough to kill her. It's my job to find the person who did that. Did she mention anything at all that was unusual?"

"Unusual," she echoed. "No. There was nothing unusual about her. Nothing." She shook her head, her neat blond hair remaining firmly in place. Silva decided to take another tack.

"What can you tell me in general about your sister-in-law?" he asked, ready now to just let Mrs. O'Donnell speak, in the hope that something of use might fall into the monologue.

The facts came quickly and succinctly from Merrilee, who seemed relieved to be rid of them so easily. "She's a few years younger than Howard and she's always lived in New York. Always. I don't suppose she could ever have been happy anywhere else. She was so attuned to city life, so accustomed to what it had to offer. She went everywhere. At least," she paused, "we always thought she did. From what she said. Now that you ask, I don't suppose we really know much about her. We've always lived up here and she comes—came—to visit every couple of years. We're not close."

"Did she work?" Silva asked.

"No. She travels, traveled. She hasn't worked since almost right after Howard started working. He's supported her for over thirty-five years." She paused, then went on. "He thought it was the right thing to do, since he was so successful. He set up an account and added to it every now and then. And he always made sure she got her check every month. Every month."

"She must have been very grateful," Silva said; he knew what gratitude could do to a friendship, or any other relationship.

"Yes, of course," she agreed, with no sign of emotion.

"I'd like to go back to the party for a moment," Silva said. "How long were you and your family up after the guests left?"

Merrilee thought for a few minutes. "I went up to bed at eleven-thirty. We had caterers, Chief Silva." Her face brightened at the recollection. "All I had to do was say good night and go upstairs. It was wonderful," she said, then recalled the point of the conversation, letting her smile droop. "Howard was already upstairs when I went up. No doubt he was sent up by the caterers. I'm afraid, Chief, that my husband tends to study people while they're working and that can be very distressing for them. Anyway, my daughter, Medge, was helping the caterers. Her husband, Frank, left much earlier.

As I said, I don't know when Beth actually left the house for the cottage. I certainly didn't see her after ten-thirty, not to notice anyway."

"And the caterers?"

"The Kitchen Cast. They're very good, in case you're ever thinking of hiring any. Anyway, they were here until after midnight, but I don't know how late. You'd have to ask Mrs. Miles, our housekeeper. She's not here on Sunday. She'll be here tomorrow." The ability to give so many answers so easily pleased Merrilee and she eagerly smiled at the chief of police. Whatever she felt at Beth O'Donnell's death, it wasn't grief.

Silva probed a little more, but all he learned was that Beth had called on Friday to tell them the time of her flight to Boston; she had arrived at the airport late Saturday morning, rented a car, and driven, so she had said, straight to the house. It had not occurred to Mrs. O'Donnell that Beth might have stopped to visit anyone on the way to Mellingham. She had spent the afternoon unpacking, calling a few friends, and visiting with Howard and Merrilee. Nothing unusual in any of it, Merrilee had insisted, nothing at all.

3

SUNDAY
AFTERNOON

*D*UPOULIS REPLACED the telephone receiver and said, "We should have everything in a few days, but it looks pretty obvious to me." He moved a pile of papers from the second chair in the chief's office, sat down on its edge, and flipped open his notebook. In a town of fewer than three thousand people, the police were not thought to need much space, and so they had to make do with the old Victorian police station built almost a hundred years earlier as a gift to the town from a wealthy resident. The plain white building with blue trim rose stolidly from its granite foundation for a mere two stories that seemed so much more. A narrow staircase of the sort familiar to anyone who has toured the House of the Seven Gables climbed steeply to the second floor, where three old wooden desks and assorted chairs filled one half of the open floor, the other half being taken up by an elaborately wrought, cast-iron fence, with filigree work surrounding smaller grilled windows and shiny brass screws punctuating a huge black iron lock. A beautifully designed and crafted cage, the old-fashioned jail was still used occasionally, most recently by an officer on day duty who was coping with a three-week-old baby while his wife slept the sleep of the exhausted. Serious criminals were quickly transferred to larger jails in nearby cities. The station house was completely authentic, right down to the plumbing. Tourists thought it was quaint; Silva's men thought it was something else.

The cramped quarters in the station house were not the only sign that times had changed. The languid quiet of a Sunday in Mellingham had disappeared years ago when the tourists had first discovered the small coastal village and its beaches. Now Sunday meant a steady stream of cars on the main road through town and constant requests for directions to the beach, to the parking lots, to the nearest restaurant. Rarely did anyone ask anything that a good tourist center couldn't answer, but Mellingham had none and so the police officer on duty in the outer office took charge, and, as far as Silva knew, answered queries to everyone's satisfaction. For years Silva had listened on Sunday to this unrelenting buzz in the outer office (a glorious term for a large room with a high wooden desk on a platform in the center), noting the change in popularity of local restaurants and tourist sites and the consistency of the American tourist in all other matters. Today, however, he had elected to station an officer outside when the stream of questions had threatened to swamp the man on the desk. He had also hoped to have a quieter time inside so he could concentrate on his main problem: the murder of Miss Beth O'Donnell.

"I hate to make assumptions, Chief," Dupoulis said, flipping the pages of his notebook, "but it looks pretty straight-forward."

"If there are any surprises, we should be ready for them. Tell me about what you found on your end," Silva prompted his assistant. This was what Dupoulis was waiting for. Ken Dupoulis was a quiet, serious young man, and it showed in everything except his body. He walked with a zest and eagerness that would have been unbecoming for a police officer in his early thirties if he hadn't looked like a small boy still struggling to get rid of his baby fat. The wiry waves of his thick sandy hair were complemented by his surprisingly long and slender fingers, the kind normally found holding a paint-brush or a charcoal crayon. Whether or not Ken had any inclinations in that direction he never let on. He joined the police department as soon as he graduated from college and never admitted to wanting to do anything else. Much as Silva trusted the young man, he was sometimes uncomfortable with such single-minded devotion to work. Ken flipped open his notebook and began.

"Well, sir. All the windows and doors were locked from the inside." Both men laughed softly at the absurdity of this detail, and Dupoulis went on. "The front door was also locked, but it has a night latch that locks behind you, so that doesn't mean much."

Silva silently wondered at the simple trust that still flowed in Mellingham. This would probably put an end to it. Residents of small towns seemed to go from complete open-ness, with doors unlocked day and night, keys left in cars, money on kitchen counters, to rampant fear and suspicion of everyone, including old friends, whenever they perceived a threat closer to home. It was an unusual community that re-mained steady but skeptical in the face of danger.

"With the exception of the EMT men, there seems to have been little traffic in or out," Dupoulis said.

"What sort of traffic are we talking about?" Silva asked. "Can you make out anything clearly?"

"Some," the sergeant replied. "Only two people seem to have gone into the bedroom at any time since it was cleaned."

"When was that?" Silva asked.

Dupoulis turned back a page and said, "It was cleaned yesterday morning, Saturday, at ten-thirty. Mrs. O'Donnell got a call Friday evening from the victim, informing her when she was arriving for a short visit. Mrs. O'Donnell told Mrs. Miles to send someone in to clean the cottage." Dupoulis looked up when Silva made no reply.

"What does that mean? Who cleaned the cottage?" the chief finally said.

"Someone who was there getting the house ready for the party. I have the name here." He looked through his notes and read out the name of a Mellingham woman who did occasional cleaning for special events.

"Does that mean anything to you?" Silva asked.

Dupoulis considered the question for a minute. "It means that Beth O'Donnell wasn't invited along with everyone else, and she wasn't part of the plans until she called on Friday."

"That's what it sounds like to me," Silva said. "Go on. What else did you find out?"

Dupoulis again turned to his notes. "Someone, possibly a man, walked around the living room. Those carpets are pretty thick, like mud for keeping footprints sometimes."

"And is this one of those times?" Silva asked in one of his usually vain attempts to loosen up his subordinate.

"Maybe," the sergeant replied. "But there are still no clear signs of what went on. No sign of a lot of walking around, or of a struggle. Even with Mr. O'Donnell and the EMT men traipsing in and out, the place was pretty clean."

"Weapon?" Silva asked.

"That's a problem," Dupoulis said.

Silva managed to say with a straight face, "We have a very dead woman. A very real murder, and no murder weapon. That's a problem, all right."

"What I mean, sir, is we haven't found it yet." Dupoulis smiled before he went on, acknowledging Silva's parodying. "We know we're looking for some kind of blunt instrument. The pathologist should be able to give us some details."

"Let's hope so. What else did you get?" Silva asked.

"Not much. I went to the neighbors—there are three other families in the area—and no one heard or saw anything. I didn't expect much else from them because you can't see through all the trees up there and the houses are too far apart for sound to carry well."

"Okay." Silva turned around to his desk. He picked up a sheet of paper and passed it over to Dupoulis.

"This is the complete group we have to question, so far as I can tell," the chief said. "It's Mrs. O'Donnell's guest list." Dupoulis read down the list. "There aren't many there we don't know," Silva continued.

"A few of them come regularly for vacation. Some I know," Dupoulis agreed.

"Some of them we may be able to eliminate at the outset," Silva said. "Some we can leave until the end if you have questions but want to see where these people fit in. I want to go through the family first and the people who knew the victim from previous years." He made a check beside half a dozen names and then passed the list back to his assistant. "I'll take those, the ones checked off. You start on the rest."

Dupoulis read down his list, counting the names. At the total, he looked up but Silva forestalled his question

"I don't mean for you to do every one yourself. Get the other towns to help you with their people, the out-of-towners," the chief said.

"Okay," Dupoulis agreed. "Some of these people are friends of the victim, and some of them, well . . ."

"I know," Silva said. "Protocol." He sat up in his chair and turned directly to Dupoulis. "This is a murder investigation and some of these people will have to be interviewed more than once. It doesn't matter how they feel about it. I want your impressions as well as my own."

"That sounds like you feel pretty sure it was someone at the party. Do you think there's any chance of it being someone who slipped in while the party was going on or afterward?" Dupoulis asked. "An outsider?"

"Any chance of an outsider?" Silva repeated. "There's always a chance, but it's not likely. We can ask the police in New York to look into the victim's relationships down there, but it's not likely that someone would follow her up here to murder her. That would be much easier in New York. No, we have to be realistic. If the murder happened here, it's most likely because the reason is here."

He looked closely at Dupoulis. "Are you going to have a problem with that?"

"No, sir," Dupoulis replied.

"Good," Silva said even though he realized he felt a glimmer of regret that Dupoulis had not shown even a whisper of hesitation. "Let's get started." Silva paused. "Ask Mack down at the beach if he saw anyone down there last night. There's usually a couple walking the beach path and they might have seen something. I don't think an outsider is the murderer, but an outsider might have information." Dupoulis made a note.

Silva went on, "And the caterers. See if you can get them up at the Agawam Inn this afternoon. They should at least be able to tell us who was around from ten-thirty on, which is when anyone can recall last seeing the victim."

"All right," Dupoulis said. "Jim Kellogg is a friend of mine. I can start with him; he might have noticed something."

"Good," Silva said, clearing his desk. "I'll start with some of the guests. I want to know what kind of woman can so dominate a distant brother and his wife that they decorate a guest cottage to suit her and let her disrupt their private lives without so much as a passing remark."

■ ■ ■

The rumble grew louder and louder, then broke into three cracks from wood striking wood, and then silence. Jim Kellogg stretched his long arm into the shaft, grasped the rope and pulled, but nothing happened. He wiggled, tugged, and pulled again.

"It's stuck in the same place," he yelled into the shaft of the dumbwaiter.

"All right," came a muffled voice from below, and the rumble descended until Jim heard a heavy wooden box hit the platform at the bottom.

Jim leaned back against the wall; taking a handkerchief from the back pocket of his jeans, he wiped the sweat from his forehead and took a deep breath. His hand was shaking, but fortunately there was no one around to see him. Well over six feet four inches tall, Jim had sprouted up to his present height as a teenager and never filled out. He was tall and scrawny, no matter how much he ate. All through his adolescence he ate—walking to school, to work, to visit friends. He did everything with food in his mouth. He never gained weight. With his dark brown hair, brown eyes, and tanned skin, he looked like an outdoorsman and had even considered the army as a career until he had a long talk with the recruiting officer. Then one day, while eating his way through a summer afternoon, as usual, a man asked for his help loading cartons into a truck. The cartons belonged to a caterer and the workers had failed to show up. Jim got a job and a career he loved, and all the food he could eat. Surrounded by food, he reassured his mother, he was sure to gain weight. He hadn't but she stopped worrying and his career prospered, leading him to set up his own catering company, the Kitchen Cast Caterers. Now, for the first time since he had started the company, he was feeling a wave of doubt and fear swell over him, scaring him by its intensity. All he had to do was get the new client under control, he kept telling himself, and then he could relax. The Agawam Inn was going to push his business over the top and bring him the success he dreamed of—at least that's what he'd thought until last night.

Jim looked over the tables and chairs arranged on the roof deck of the inn. The small tables were set out just as he had directed, but it still didn't work. This was the third arrangement he had designed, and he was no happier with this one than he had been with the first. He groaned as he heard faint rumblings rising from below, giving voice to the volcano of dissatisfaction rising within himself.

Persuaded to cater afternoon tea on the roof deck of the

Agawam Inn, Jim was still unsure how this had come about, so convinced was he that it was a terrible idea. He remembered only asking an exorbitant fee, and being accepted. He also remembered his dismay. Mr. Campbell, the owner of the inn and a decisive man in an argument, had agreed instantly, with no attempt to haggle over the fee and no pretense of shock. The hotel owner had promised a perfect setting looking out toward the harbor, and lots of help. Now Jim was stranded in what had once been an attic storeroom, five flights up and no dumbwaiter. Hotel owners were notoriously unreliable, he repeated to himself. The man will probably stall on making his payments, Jim fantasied, pushing the Kitchen Cast to the brink of bankruptcy. Jim shuddered at the vision of what life held for him now that he had surrendered his business to the clutches of Mr. Campbell. He wondered how long he could stand it.

The rumble came again, but this time it culminated in a door opening and flinging out a huffing and puffing body. Sergeant Ken Dupoulis leaned on the door while he caught his breath.

"Gee, Ken, what're you doing here?" Jim asked, momentarily forgetting his imminent bankruptcy. "We don't start serving for another two weeks."

Dupoulis continued to breathe heavily, putting his hands on his hips and trying to look nonchalant.

"Here, sit down." Jim pushed a chair over to his friend. The policeman sat and his red face slowly turned to a bright pink. "Okay?"

"Fine," Dupoulis finally said. "How many flights was that?" He tried to speak in his normal voice but each word was punctuated by a large gasp.

"Five," Jim said matter-of-factly. "You came up the back. The guests will have an old elevator to use, if they dare." He nodded over at the newly painted black iron grill surrounding an old elevator of glass and steel.

"They actually come up here?" the sergeant asked.

"They're supposed to, but they haven't yet," Jim said. Looking at his friend, he studied his rosy face and the dark patches of sweat on his shirt. "Rough climb, was it?" Jim asked, his eyes suddenly twinkling with malicious delight.

"Next time I'll take the elevator," Dupoulis promised.

"Next time wear street clothes." Jim looked at the uniform.

"I'm here as a police officer, Jim." Ken pulled out his notebook.

"I knew it," Jim said. "Campbell forgot the permit and you're going to shut us down." Jim's eyes shone and he gleefully clapped his hands together. "I just knew it."

Dupoulis stared at him. "This has nothing to do with Mr. Campbell, as far as I know." Deciding it was better to move ahead calmly rather than tackle his friend's strange behavior openly, Dupoulis took out his pencil and began. "I have some questions for you, Jim. Last night Miss Beth O'Donnell was murdered."

Dupoulis waited for Jim's reaction, but when it came it wasn't what he had expected, although after the last few minutes with Jim he wasn't sure what to expect.

"Wow," Jim said, slumping down in a chair, more thoughtful and relaxed than Ken had seen him in some time. "Really?" he asked. "We did a party there last night."

"I know. That's why I'm here."

"What happened?"

"We're not sure yet," Ken said, unwilling to give away any information. "We're interviewing everyone who was there last night. You might have seen something that could help us."

"Whatever you want, Ken. Whatever I can do. Shoot." Jim paused. "Or was that a poor choice of words?" He folded his long legs over another chair, his back to the deck and the view beyond.

"What?" Dupoulis asked, looking up from his notebook.

"Was she shot?" Jim asked.

"No. Where'd you get that idea?"

"I didn't get any idea—"

"You just said—"

"I was kidding. Bad taste. Start over," he said in exasperation.

"All right," Dupoulis said, glaring at his friend and holding his pencil poised over his notebook. "Did you know Beth O'Donnell?"

"No," Jim said firmly, determined not to derail the questioning with ambiguity. "Not personally, that is. I knew who she was. She comes up here to visit the O'Donnells every now and then."

"Do you remember seeing her at the party last night?" Dupoulis asked.

"Sure. She was there."

"What was she doing? Do you remember anything? Anything stand out?"

"Not much, Ken. It was really rushed. We didn't have a free moment until everyone started to leave."

"What time was that?" Dupoulis asked.

"Between ten and eleven. There was a rush at ten-thirty, and then a few were still leaving at eleven."

"Do you remember seeing Miss O'Donnell leave?"

"No, I don't think so." Jim considered the question a bit longer. "I thought she was staying there."

"She was," Dupoulis agreed, "but at the cottage, so she would have had to go out some time. Did you see her during the evening?"

"Sure. Let's see. She was talking to that Chambers guy for a while and Frank Vinton and that new guy who lives over near the lake. And some others I didn't know. And the Morrisons. They're staying here at the inn."

"Bob Chambers?" Dupoulis repeated as he wrote down the names.

"Right. The editor. He works for Lee Handel at Marine Press. Know him?"

"I know who he is," Dupoulis said.

"He was with her a lot. At least I remember seeing him talking to her."

"Did you happen to hear what they were saying?"

"Come on, Ken, get serious," Jim said.

"Listen, Jim, this is a murder investigation. I have to ask these questions, you know that."

"Yeah, yeah, I know. I'm sorry," he said, pulling out his handkerchief and wiping the sweat from his forehead. "What did you want to know?"

"Did you overhear her say anything to anyone that might help? Did you hear what she said to Bob Chambers, for instance?"

"They were talking about a book," Jim said as he drew himself up straight in his chair and crossed his legs. "I think she's writing a book that's supposed to be a hot property. Or something like that."

"Can you remember anything else about it? Anything specific?"

"Hey, we were working. I had other things on my mind last night. I just got an impression of what they were talking about; that's all. I'm lucky I heard even that much."

"Maybe someone else in your crew heard something," Dupoulis said.

"I'll ask around."

"I also need to know if anyone in your group saw anyone outside on the near side of the house, anyone walking around to the back to the cottage."

"You mean instead of going around by the side garden along the path?" Jim asked. "I doubt it. We would have noticed that. The whole house was lit up last night. People parked along the road and then walked up along the path across the field. We kept an eye on that too, but there wasn't any trouble. There never is at this kind of party."

"Does that mean for the time after everyone left, say, after ten-thirty or eleven?" Dupoulis asked.

"Oh, sure. We're real good about that, Ken. We keep our

eyes open," Jim said, "not that we could do anything if we saw anyone making any trouble. I mean, I'm not brave. That's your job."

"Thanks, I'll remember that," Dupoulis said. "What about Mr. O'Donnell? Did you by any chance see him around after eleven o'clock?"

"See him around?" Jim repeated, his voice rising. "Man, I wish that's all it'd been. That man may mean well, and—don't get me wrong—he really pays well, but, man, he was there every second."

"What was he doing?"

"Counting glasses," Jim said.

"You guys have some kind of problem with losses?"

"Hell, no. He was counting dirty glasses; he wouldn't let us wash them until he counted them, some idea about popularity and dirty glasses. Or was it noise and dirty glasses." Jim frowned at the floor as he tried to recall the conversation from the night before. "I think it had something to do with dirty glasses being noisy."

"Are you sure about this?"

"Don't look at me, man. I finally told the guy to go to bed and leave it to us. I promised not to make any noise at all."

"What time was that?"

"It must have been about eleven-thirty. Maybe a little later."

"Okay. Thanks. What about the Morrisons?" Dupoulis continued.

"Tourists. I don't know anything about them except they're not really summer people; they stay here once in a while. They're here now. They wanted to know when the hotel serves tea." Jim winced slightly.

"I'll go down and talk to them while I'm here." Dupoulis closed his notebook. "By the way, I'll need a list of everyone who was working for you last night."

"No problem, Ken." Jim jumped up with alacrity as his friend rose to go.

"Thanks, Jim," Dupoulis said, eyeing him suspiciously. "Not at all, Ken, not at all. I'll even go down with you now. We can take the elevator." And with those words, Jim jumped to open the elevator door.

■　■　■

"Mr. and Mrs. Morrison?" Dupoulis said to the young waitress leaning against the wall near the door to the kitchen. Her mouth slightly open as though undecided about a yawn, she clenched her jaw deftly and cracked her gum, then nodded toward a couple in their fifties eating dessert at a table by a large picture window. Appropriately dressed for an afternoon lawn party, they were the only diners still in the dining room, which had been cleared and reset for dinner, with the exception of their table. Dupoulis calculated that if they spun out their lunch a few minutes longer, they could roll over into teatime without an odd minute uncovered by a meal.

In some hotels this devotion to a meal would have seemed reasonable, but the Agawam Inn was not known for its cuisine, which tended to be whatever the cook was also having at home later in the evening; or for its rooms, which tended toward the simple, even the ascetic, on the grounds that guests who could afford the Agawam could go elsewhere for luxury and here could get a safely controlled dose of the simple life, at least as far as it extended to hotel rooms; or for its decor, which had not been changed since the late 1920s, when the owner returned from Europe and in a flurry introduced an early version of Art Deco, which was kept dusted, scrubbed, polished, and unchanged; but for its view, the only feature of the inn that startled everyone with its beauty and brought people back year after year. It was perhaps an uncanny wisdom that kept successive owners from changing the inn, which would have transferred attention from the perfect beauty supplied by nature to the imperfect beauty created by man. None of this had ever been articulated by Ken Dupoulis or other residents of Mellingham, but they felt the same proprietary right over the inn as they did over the appearance of their own homes. When Ken went in search of the Morrisons in the dining room, he did so without any feeling that he was wandering through private property.

Dupoulis introduced himself to the couple and the Morrisons managed a wary nod. He reported Miss O'Donnell's death in long slow sentences so he could watch their reactions and was gratified to see their reserve fall away and their mouths fall open.

"What happened? Do you know?" they both asked at once as soon as they had contained their sadness.

Like many other couples who had been married for more than twenty years, even thirty years, the Morrisons looked like each other, the softness of one hardening to meet the softening in the hardness of the other. Straight hair took on a suggestion of a curl and curly hair fell a little straighter. Both wore navy—he had on a navy blazer and white shirt with a tie and she had on a navy sweater set with a white skirt. Both looked nautical, sturdy, robust, though Ken doubted if they got more exercise than moving from dining table to terrace to restaurant. He didn't really like the idea of questioning them together, but he had no reason to separate them, so he answered the questions flowing from their surprise and shock before turning to those that he considered important. Dupoulis had to repeat himself before he finally brought them to focus on their actions during the previous evening.

"Well, we left around ten-thirty, Officer," Mrs. Morrison said, an indignant tone rising in her voice now that Dupoulis had satisfied her curiosity and was no longer necessary to them. "Wouldn't you say so, dear?" She turned to her husband, who nodded.

"Then we walked back here," she went on. "Dear me, when Beth walked us to the door and we said good-bye, who would have thought—" She sniffed and looked away, determined to stifle a genuine feeling.

"Yes, ma'am," Dupoulis said. He wondered why he kept thinking of a soap opera he had been forced to watch years ago when he was home from school with the flu. "You walked all the way back?"

"It was a lovely evening. And we do so enjoy a walk." She gave him a warm, gracious smile that moved Dupoulis to wonder if murder was a catalyst for insanity in otherwise ordinary people. They had recovered their poise so quickly and noticeably that he couldn't help doubting their sincerity. He decided to keep these two in mind—for what he wasn't sure.

"That's quite a long way. Did you know you were going to be walking back?"

"I should think so, Sergeant, since we walked out there," Mrs. Morrison said. "We walk as much as possible. Good for the figure, don't you know." Her lashes fluttered toward Dupoulis's torso. "And I dress accordingly. Flats." She waved her foot, shod in a low-heeled blue shoe, toward the edge of the table. Dupoulis made a note, his first suspicions deflated before he even got a chance to try them out on the chief.

"About what time did you arrive here, at the hotel?"

"Just about eleven o'clock," Mr. Morrison broke in with his first contribution to the questioning. He had listened closely to his wife and the sergeant and at the last question seemed to come to a decision. Until then the two were virtually indistinguishable to the sergeant. Mr. Morrison, however, pushed himself up in his chair, stretched his neck and straightened the lapels of his blue blazer, and thrust his chin out at Dupoulis. "We walked back at a steady pace," he said. "A lot of people passed us along the way. A lot of people."

"Did you meet anyone else out walking?" Dupoulis asked politely, intrigued by the man's change of demeanor.

"No one. The only people we saw were others from the party, driving."

The sergeant carefully wrote all this down, wondering if

the Morrisons appreciated how easy it would be to check on their statements. He was equally careful to keep his tone of voice consistent and let the Morrisons play out their own perception of the interview. He was beginning to enjoy the process and tried to think of ways to string it out. "How well did you know Miss O'Donnell?" he asked.

"Not well," Mr. Morrison said to his wife's apparent surprise. She stared at him, then snapped her mouth shut. Dupoulis made a note to suggest to Silva that he reinterview husband and wife separately.

"Did you know Miss O'Donnell would be there last night?" Dupoulis asked.

"It seemed a reasonable assumption," Mr. Morrison said, disdain creeping into his voice.

"Miss O'Donnell lives in New York. Is that right?" Dupoulis asked.

"I believe so," Mr. Morrison said, apparently growing bored.

"Then how could you assume she would be here this weekend?" the sergeant asked.

"Isn't this her regular visit?" Mr. Morrison said casually, cutting off his wife again, who slid back down in her chair.

Dupoulis underlined the word "separately" in his notes. "Is it?" Dupoulis asked.

"If you need any specific information, Officer, I hope you'll call on us," Mr. Morrison said, abruptly ending the interview.

■ ■ ■

Hannah Handel stood quite still with her hand resting on the wall telephone in the kitchen, and wondered about Bob Chambers. Like everyone else in Mellingham, she had thought him a likable fellow when he had first arrived to work for her husband, but lately he had made little effort to conceal from her his annoyance with his work and frustration at the limitations of his job. She had first wondered idly why he had taken the position at the press, and now wished she had paid closer attention to her suspicions. Hannah was the kind of woman others described as "no nonsense," and they would have been surprised to learn that she based her sensible, rational decisions on her gut reactions, her deepest, most inchoate feelings, which she could dress up any way she wanted to logically. And she had a gut feeling about Bob Chambers that she didn't like at all. She heard her husband's step, reminding her why she hadn't told anyone about her feelings.

"Who was that on the phone?" Lee asked as he came trotting into the kitchen.

"No one." She turned at once to pick up a packet of seeds on the counter.

Her husband looked at her intently. "It must have been about Bob. If it were anyone else you'd tell me. And it can't have been Bob in person because he would never call here. So it must have been someone else calling about Bob. You really don't like him anymore, do you?"

"No, I don't," she said with a shrug. "Are my feelings so obvious?"

"Only to me. What was it about?"

"Nothing important." She opened a drawer beneath the counter and poked through a collection of odds and ends. "Have you seen my new gloves?"

"If it's not important, then you can tell me, Hannah," he insisted. "Who was on the phone?"

"You're very placid today," she said as much to herself as to him. Then she mentioned the name of an acquaintance in answer to his question. "Bob's been trying, discreetly, of course, to find out about Beth's contacts in New York," she explained. "That's all it was about. Nancy just thought I should know."

Lee shook his head. "I told Bob that Beth was all talk. He should have figured that out for himself last night." He turned away. Hannah watched him with open curiosity.

"He did spend a lot of time with her," Hannah said. "I

didn't think anyone could put up with her for that long."
When he nodded his agreement with no other sign of emotion,
Hannah blinked away tears of relief and added a few other
comments. She felt the muscles in her arms relax, unaware
until then of how tense she had been, and was suddenly
warmed by the beauty of the deepening afternoon light. Leaning against the counter, her whole body relaxed, she was
caught in the intimacy of a moment she had once thought
would never come again. Remembering her resolve to recover
the husband she had first married, she felt settle in her heart
an acceptance of all she had done. She closed the drawer and
turned to a basket sitting on the floor near the back door.

"Bob is willing to do almost anything to get ahead," Lee
said.

"He seemed so nice at first."

"He was nice at first," Lee agreed. "But people change."

Hannah glanced at him. "I hate to see you go through all
that turnover again."

"It doesn't matter. Lisa and I will manage." Lee smiled
so reassuringly that Hannah was caught off-guard. She smiled
and hummed while she rifled through another basket. When
she had found what she was looking for, she returned to watching her husband, who was then absorbed in attaching a thick
wire to a chain, from which hung a bird feeder in the shape
of a miniature wooden house.

"Do you think there is a manuscript?" she asked after
several minutes of silence.

"I don't know," Lee said as he tightened a screw holding
the bottom of the feeder in place. "I don't care either. That
woman would only write gossip." He kept on with his work,
not looking up even as he answered Hannah.

"Suppose there is one," she said softly. She waited.

He finally stopped what he was doing and looked at her.
"It would only be gossip, and that's all." He turned back to
the bird feeder, but before he could continue working on it,

his attention was taken by the sound of a car stopping on the street in front of the house.

"I'll go," he said as he glanced through the kitchen window. Still more nimble than most younger men, he was out the door and along the stone walk before Hannah could say anything.

■ ■ ■

Chief Silva watched Lee Handel coming to meet him, Lee studying Silva just as Silva was studying him. The chief knew Lee only slightly, and when he had seen his name on the guest list, he was surprised. It was no secret that during the last few years the Handels had withdrawn almost entirely from the social life of the town, confining most of their contact with the outside world to telephone calls and an occasional holiday card. The gossip about this change in their affairs had been divided. A few thought the Handel marriage was failing, a few that one or the other Handel was dying of an exotic or even mundane disease. And still others thought they'd had an argument with someone or had taken offense at a minor (or even major) slight. More recently, when Lee and Hannah had reappeared in public—at town picnics, at the local diner, at town meeting—people had taken to speculating on whether or not Handel would retire soon, since he was evidently losing interest in his business, or at least that was how they explained his recent irritability. Few had wanted to talk about his earlier financial troubles, and these had remained vague, dropping from the list of topics approved for general gossip after he had apparently overcome his business difficulties. The few times he had snapped at people during those years were dismissed as aberrations, hardly worth recalling or passing along. But Silva wondered, nevertheless. Lee often had a steely look in his eye that reminded Silva of some of the men who worked the docks near where he grew up. It was not the sort of look he expected to see in the eye of a publisher in a picturesque hamlet like Mellingham. Mrs. Handel, on the other hand, was an enigma. People rarely had anything to say about Hannah. Her demeanor never changed from her well-known composure, not even during the couple's recent rough patch, leading her acquaintances, though certainly not her friends, to comment on her calm or her callousness, her stoicism or disregard, but nothing more.

"Yes? Yes?" Lee asked as he approached the chief.

"Good afternoon, Mr. Handel," Silva said. "Something unfortunate has happened at the O'Donnells. Beth O'Donnell died last night," Silva said, watching for Handel's reaction. To Silva's surprise, Lee seemed perplexed for a moment, and then a hardness passed over his face.

"Why are you coming to tell me?" he asked. "Couldn't you have telephoned? I'm busy."

"We think she was murdered." Silva thought he saw a flicker of a wild smile at the mention of murder, but no more. "We're interviewing everyone who knew Miss O'Donnell or who was at the party last night. You were there. Is that correct?"

"Yes. We were there, but we don't personally know Howard's sister." He turned away, saying, "I'm busy. I have to hang this up." He indicated the bird feeder he was holding and walked with short, quick steps to the backyard. Silva let him go, following easily behind, and watched him climb into a tree from a stepladder. The older man worked his way out on a limb, punctuating his progress with grunts and long looks at the ground below. At the end of the branch, he hung the feeder, his gift from Howard O'Donnell the night before. From his back pocket he then took a plastic jar, opened it as he lay precariously on the branch, and smeared the contents of the jar along the chain from which the feeder hung. He closed the jar, put it back in his pocket, cleaned his hands with a rag, which he pulled from another pocket, and worked his way back along the branch. He offered no word of commentary during this exercise.

"Squirrels," Lee announced to Silva when he stood on solid ground again. "They climb down onto the feeder and eat everything." He shook his head as he recalled his most recent skirmishes with the rodents. "They drive off the birds and leave them nothing." Lee was disgusted.

The two men talked about bird feeders and squirrels for several minutes, reminding Silva of the time his father had taken up history when the fishing was so bad he had feared losing his boat. At four-thirty in the morning, six days a week, he threw a water-logged volume of Churchill's epic history of World War II into his lunch pail. He'd read all four volumes seven times before business got better. Silva appreciated Handel's love of birds.

"I'd like to ask you about last night, Mr. Handel," Silva finally said.

"All right, all right. I suppose you have a job to do. What do you want to know about last night?" Lee now turned his full and intense attention on the chief.

"Did you see Miss O'Donnell at the party last night?"

"Yes, she was there," Lee said, nodding several times.

"Did you talk to her at all?"

"No. I barely know her. And I have no reason to talk to her." Once again, a mask of cold disinterest fell down on Lee's face, shutting in whatever his deeper feelings might have been.

"I see," Silva said. "What time did you leave the party?"

"About eleven. Almost everyone else was gone. Mr. O'Donnell and I had been talking just up to eleven." His voice softened as he spoke the name of his host.

"And is that the last time you saw any of the O'Donnells?"

"No, Chief." Lee smiled. "That's the last time I saw Howard and Merrilee. I hadn't seen Beth since much earlier in the evening."

Silva acknowledged the correction with a nod. "Did you ever hear of anyone who strongly disliked Miss O'Donnell?"

"I strongly disliked her, Chief Silva. I suppose that's

obvious. But I certainly didn't kill her if that's what you want to know." Lee succeeded in checking his anger but not the belligerence in his voice.

"There's a lot I'll have to know before this is settled," Silva said.

"Before what's settled?" Hannah asked.

Silva swung around at the sound of Hannah Handel's voice; he hadn't heard her come up behind him and he was startled. He was also embarrassed at having slipped up on something so basic as to let himself be caught up in a conversation to the exclusion of attending to what was going on around him.

"Beth O'Donnell died last night; she was murdered," Lee explained.

Hannah glanced at her husband and then at Silva. "What happened to her?" she asked with controlled surprise.

"We don't know for certain yet," Silva said. "That's partly why I'm here. We're interviewing everyone who was at the party last night. I was just asking your husband a few questions about the evening. Can you recall what time you left?"

"Yes, I can. We left around eleven o'clock," Hannah answered.

"And then?"

"We came straight home," she said. "It was late."

"What time did you arrive here?" Silva tried to decide if her tone suggested only impatience or something more.

"We arrived about quarter after eleven. It's less than a mile from here to the O'Donnells, after all."

"Did you talk to Beth O'Donnell during the party?" the chief asked.

"No," Hannah said. "Not one word." Lee Handel was obviously taken aback by his wife's swift and sharp reply; he opened his mouth to speak, but his wife cut him off. "Howard and Beth are very different people, Chief Silva," Hannah said, in an attempt to smooth over her bluntness. "Lee and Howard are friends, but Howard doesn't expect his friends to also be friends of his sister."

Silva was impressed with how reasonable she could make her hostility sound. If there was any connection between the two women, just the same, he would find it soon enough.

"Did you like his sister, Mrs. Handel?"

"I only met her a few times. I knew her to say hello to, but that's all."

"Mrs. O'Donnell didn't include you in any groups when Miss O'Donnell was visiting?" he asked.

"No. Why should she?" Hannah replied.

"Seems natural to me," the chief said.

"Well, it doesn't to me." Hannah's face still gave away nothing of her true feelings.

"Did you know she would be visiting this weekend?" Silva asked both husband and wife.

"No," Lee said.

"I understand she arrived on short notice," Silva said.

"Really?" Hannah commented.

"Mrs. Handel," Silva said, trying the direct approach, "did Mrs. O'Donnell ever indicate to you any problems in her relationship with her sister-in-law?"

"No, none. She never said a word against her, Chief," Hannah replied.

"I see." Silva noted that Mrs. Handel had politely avoided answering his question. "I understand Miss O'Donnell had friends in this area."

"Yes. She saw them when she stayed with Merrilee and Howard," Hannah replied.

"Do you know them?" he asked. She recited several names Silva had seen on the guest list, but refused to comment on the nature of the friendships, whether they were of recent vintage or of long standing. Most of the people she knew only by sight, she explained, and some only by name. When asked directly about the previous evening, she answered in the modulated voice he always associated with her.

"It was all quite normal," Hannah said. "Just the usual people one meets at parties around here. No one special. Nothing out of the ordinary." And this was delivered, to Silva's mind, with complete honesty.

Nothing out of the ordinary, Silva repeated to himself as he drove away, except that someone was dead soon afterward and no one seems unhappy about it. Certainly not Mr. and Mrs. Handel.

■ ■ ■

Dupoulis drove into the beach parking lot and parked the police cruiser beside a battered pickup. Everyone in town knew Mack's rust-red truck, and everyone expected to see it first at the beach. Few could blame Mack and many envied him. He had chosen his life's work when one summer morning before he was ten years old he had stood on the narrow wooden walkway that deposited beach-goers onto the white sand. At the end of a narrow, bumpy, crooked road, the beach stretched out its white arms to the gray rocks on both sides and embraced the blue-green water of the Atlantic Ocean. The beach was long, even, smooth, tapering sharply at the ends into slowly rising rock cliffs. The ocean rose and fell along the smooth sand, a single line of breakers on a singularly beautiful beach; there were no sandbars at low tide, no tidal pools from end to end, no fingers of land turning inward to create a cozy cove, protected from squall or hurricane. The beach was open to the sea and the sky and the sun, with a direct view of Spain.

Mack was not the only one who loved the beach. Throughout the year, people of all ages walked the beach from early morning until late at night. As soon as it was warm enough, the younger ones arrived with beach towels and suntan lotion. Even in May in Massachusetts, a few were determined to begin the summer season with a swim and a tan, even if the temperature had barely reached seventy degrees in the sun. Dupoulis never thought twice about where to find Mack. He walked across the sand to a body lying still on an old army blanket, and stood in front of him for a matter of seconds.

"You're blocking the sun." The well-tanned former athlete's body remained still on the blanket. Mack had taken off his shirt but was wearing khaki shorts instead of a bathing suit. His light blond hair was already showing signs of being bleached by the sun.

"Don't you ever go home?" Dupoulis said, giving Mack's foot a friendly kick.

"Ken?" Mack sat up and looked him up and down. "What's the matter? Someone die?"

"Yes," Ken said.

"Oh yeah?" Mack jumped up and looked around him, as though expecting to see the corpse on the beach. "Who?"

"No one you know. Relax." Dupoulis sat down on the edge of the blanket. "You've got the life, Mack." He looked up and down the beach, the sand sparkling in the sun.

"I thought you were working today," Mack said.

"I am. I came down to see you," he said, leaning back.

"Oh yeah?" Mack was inordinately pleased with the attention.

"Yeah. I wanted to ask you about last night. Were you working?"

"Sure. Every night. All year round. You know that. Listen, if you really want to talk, let's move up to the bathhouse. I'm thirsty." Mack picked up his sunglasses and blanket, and the two men walked toward the bathhouse. Mack disappeared briefly inside and reemerged with two cold cans of soda, and the two sat down on a bench overlooking the beach.

"Last night a guest at the O'Donnells' house was murdered," Dupoulis said.

"So that's what all that ruckus was this morning. I slept on the beach last night," Mack said.

"You could get arrested for that."

Mack dismissed his friend's comment with a side glance. "I could tell there was a lot of action up there this morning so I went up to take a look. I saw the ambulance leave a few hours ago."

"We didn't see you," Dupoulis said.

"So?"

"So about last night," Dupoulis said. "Miss O'Donnell was murdered in the cottage there, we think."

"Is that where you found the body?" Mack asked with the excitement of a child.

"Yeah, this morning," Ken said. "What I want to know from you is whether or not you saw anything last night that might help us. Was anyone out on the beach path last night? Any couples? Anybody out walking their dog?"

Mack threw his arms over the back of the bench. His body slackened as he surveyed the beach he patrolled day and night, usually for pay. He and Ken had gone to school together, played sports together, and now guarded the beach together, but Mack didn't like the idea of crime spilling over into his territory.

"Last night," Mack said, trying to concentrate. "About what time?"

"Don't know yet for sure, but probably after ten or eleven," Ken answered. "Aren't there usually a few couples out walking?"

"Usually, but not last night after ten." He paused. "There were a couple of kids chasing their dog along the path sometime after nine, but I don't think they were here much later than that."

"Tell me about them." Ken took out his notebook.

"I was just heading for the north end of the beach when I saw them—just two kids chasing a dog. The dog thought it was a game and they must have chased the mutt for a mile already. Anyway, the dog raced off down the path and the kids went after it. I never saw them coming back."

"Do you know who they were?" Ken asked, eager to have something concrete to pursue.

"No."

"What about the dog?"

"The dog I've seen before." Mack stared intently at the ground as he tried to conjure up the image of the animal. "White, short hair, stocky."

Ken wrote down the description. "I've seen it around too," he said. "The owners may live near the O'Donnells. That may be why the kids didn't come back this way. They just kept going until they got to their parents' house further down." Ken made a few more notes before he said, "The kids. Do you remember them?"

"Nope. Just kids. Two boys about ten or twelve years old. That's all. Nice dog, though."

4

SUNDAY EVENING

*I*T IS A TRUISM that some people seem destined for fame from an early age. Lisa Hunt firmly believed this about herself, but being a modest and patient young woman, she was willing to wait for it to happen. In her early thirties and for several years employed by Lee Handel at the Marine Press in whatever capacity the day's work called for, Lisa was known for her prodigious energy, quick intelligence, and general lack of ambition, sometimes even of curiosity. She would have gone far, had she wanted to go anywhere. Instead she marveled at her own perfect and beautiful body, considered its anatomical design, the way an engineer considers the design of the newest automobile, and idly wondered what she'd look like if she'd grown up eating yams among the Dobu or whale blubber among the Eskimos.

Lisa read a lot but it never seemed to motivate her to a higher anything. At the most, she brought her vast knowledge to bear on any decision, large or small, that presented itself. She could discuss at length the history of painting the hands in various cultures, and had done so during her last visit to the drugstore, where she had purchased the small bottle she was holding in her left hand while she waved the applicator brush in her right. She examined the sparkle of the late afternoon sunlight on her Purple Passion toenail polish, pleased with the color against the slate of the terrace. She would have to get a pair of steel gray sandals for the summer, with high heels to accent her long slender legs.

Lisa's concerns with her toenails did not mask a shallow woman, despite her best efforts, in Hannah Handel's view, to create just that impression in other people's minds. For several minutes now, alternating with her concerns for her wardrobe, Lisa had been considering the twists and turns of the path of destiny, and there were many. Her mother had just stepped out of the house to tell her about Beth O'Donnell's death, strange news for a Sunday afternoon. Among all the experiences she had prepared herself for, sudden violent death was not included. True, Beth O'Donnell was a woman whose personality might stimulate such thoughts, but Lisa had not known her well—and certainly had not cared for her. Perhaps if Medge Vinton had spoken of her fondly, Lisa might feel differently. Medge and Lisa had been friends for many years, but Lisa had never heard Medge speak affectionately of her aunt. Lisa admitted to feeling sad at the news of Beth's death, but little more. She hoped Medge wasn't taking it hard. Perhaps a rose dress against the purple nails, she considered.

Lisa's ultimate lack of interest contrasted with her mother's feelings, leaving the older woman noticeably frustrated. Indeed, sometimes Mrs. Hunt wondered if Lisa could truly be her own child so different did her nature seem, but Mrs. Hunt's curly white hair atop her long-legged and still-slender body underscored the limited extent of their differences. No one need wonder what Lisa would look like in her later years or what Mrs. Hunt had looked like in her earlier years, but their views had never exhibited a comparable similarity. The older woman wondered what was wrong with her daughter that even a murder in town didn't get her fired up. Mrs. Hunt was still struggling with her own conflict between curiosity and revulsion when she went back into the house.

"Didn't you notice anything?" she had asked her only child, who was just then reviewing Beth's outfit and behavior of the previous evening.

"There wasn't anything to notice, Mother." And in the image Lisa had in mind at the moment, this was true.

"Did you meet the dead woman?" her mother asked, standing over her reclining daughter.

"Not this time. I met her last time she was here," Lisa said, tossing back a curl of her honey-blond hair.

"What was she like?"

"Not like Mr. O'Donnell," her daughter said.

"That, Lisa, is not an answer," Mrs. Hunt had finally said to her sunbathing daughter, returning to the house to try her luck on the telephone.

Alone again on the terrace, Lisa reviewed her mother's questions. There was nothing unusual about Beth O'Donnell last night as far as Lisa could recall, other than her death. The older woman had a habit of offending everyone she talked to for anything longer than five minutes. That was no secret. And it was no secret that such people are regularly explained away as unhappy. But Lisa wondered. Beth showed intent, planning, determination in her sallies, so much so in fact that Lisa had to admit that Beth's mind must be as skilled and as controlled as that of a chess player. This image of Beth hung before Lisa's eyes before dissolving into a hazy image of another, and that, Lisa acknowledged, was the real question. Who was that hazy figure? Who got angry enough to fight back? Who murdered Beth O'Donnell? Without any hesitation and following the pragmatic side of her nature, Lisa recited the names of the guests, considering each one as a prospective murderer. This exercise forever altered her view of some and brought interesting clarity to the image of others. Most of the guests were impossible in the role of murderer, but not all. Not all, thought Lisa as she drew together in her mind's eye a cluster of well-dressed men and women.

So intent was Lisa's concentration on the group that she had isolated in her mind that she did not immediately notice the policeman her mother ushered through the back door. Lisa had little trouble redirecting her thoughts at the sight of Chief Silva. She and the chief had progressed at one time to the stage of first names but more as a result of what seemed to be expected of them than as the reflection of a genuine desire to know each other better. After a few months they had drifted back to a comfortable formality. At one time speculating on Silva's future had been one of Lisa's entertainments during idle moments, but after it became clear that he preferred talking about her future rather than his, Lisa's fertile imagination moved on to other topics. She still occasionally wondered why he hadn't settled down with one of the more attractive single women in town, but only because she didn't look closely at the relationships he did have. If she had, she might have noticed a striking pattern: each woman he became involved with underwent an unexpected change soon after she started seeing Joe regularly. Joe Silva had the knack of hearing in others the dream too deep for words. And once heard, the dream came alive. If Lisa had wondered about the abrupt changes in the lives of the women Chief Silva dated, she never connected them to the nature of Silva the man. Now that he was standing in front of her asking questions, however, she began to think again. Perhaps she might introduce him to a few of her friends.

"I'm sorry," she said, "what was the question?"

"You were at the party last night. Is that correct?" Silva asked after he had settled himself in a lawn chair facing her.

"Yes, I was. A lovely party." Lisa could think of no reason why Joe Silva should be sitting in her backyard asking her questions, but if an inane comment would move the conversation along, she was willing to make one. "Such a tragic ending to such a lovely evening." She was also willing to say the right thing, but wondered if anyone cared at times like this.

At moments of great sadness and stress, Lisa was shockingly practical.

"Did you know Miss O'Donnell?" Silva asked.

"I knew the family."

"Did you know Miss O'Donnell?" Silva repeated. Lisa Hunt was, to Chief Silva, one of the enigmas of Mellingham. Perhaps fifteen years younger than he was, she was pretty, intelligent, good-natured, single, and had no ambitions that he could see. He pegged her as a woman who would start late (what he wasn't sure) and be unstoppable once she got going. In this she reminded him of Christina, the woman he had felt sure he would marry when they were both in their twenties. In truth, he was seeing in Lisa what he had seen in Christina and in every other woman he had known well—potential. Joe responded to the woman as she might be, and the results were inevitable.

Silva asked his question a third time while she put away her nail polish.

"I'm just collecting my thoughts," she said. "No, I didn't know Beth O'Donnell personally," she said in answer to his question. "I only met her once or twice before. She was just Medge Vinton's aunt."

"Did you see her or talk to her last night?" he asked.

"Yes, I saw her. But we didn't talk."

"Do you remember when you last saw her?"

"No. It must have been halfway through the evening. I wasn't noticing her much."

"What time did you leave the party?" Silva asked, wondering how many guests would block all recollection of Beth O'Donnell from their memory once they learned how she had died.

"About ten-thirty."

"Did you leave alone?" he asked.

"No. I went with Bob Chambers and left with him," she said.

"And where did you go after the party?"

"Home, of course." Lisa was irritated by the question, and Silva knew enough about her to know that this would probably be her answer.

"What time did you get home, then?"

"Eleven o'clock. The clock was chiming when I came into the house," she replied with a satisfied grin. "So how's that for knowing the time?"

"Pretty good. It took you almost half an hour to drive less than two miles," he pointed out.

"Oh," she said, caught by his observation. She thought for a moment before she said, "I forgot. Bob had to go back for something just after we drove out. He walked back up the driveway and I waited in the car."

"For how long?" Silva asked, curious that such an incident could be so easily forgotten.

"Just a few minutes."

"What did he go back for?" Silva asked.

"He didn't say. Nothing important." She looked directly at him as she spoke, apparently unaware of any suspiciousness inherent in her escort's behavior.

"Did you see anyone else leave while you were waiting for him?" Silva asked, wondering what she had been thinking of during that time.

"I saw a few cars drive out, but almost everyone had gone already. People started to leave after ten o'clock," she explained.

"Tell me about the party," he suggested, hoping another approach would reveal more.

"It was just a party. The O'Donnells have two or three every spring and summer—big ones. You know that."

"I'd rather you didn't assume what I know, Lisa. Just tell me about the evening from your perspective."

"All right. Well, there were about fifty or sixty people there. It was just a nice party," she said after describing the

SUSAN OLEKSIW

food, the guests, the O'Donnell home, and the general run of the evening.

"Who did you talk to?" She sat quietly for a few seconds before reciting several names Silva recognized from the guest list. "You didn't talk to Miss O'Donnell even to say hello?"

"No. I had no reason to," she replied, and Silva thought he heard an undercurrent of hostility.

"I thought maybe you might have found yourselves in the same group over drinks or something like that," Silva said, probing her reactions. "Did you see her around?"

"Around," Lisa said. "She was here and there."

"Here and there?" he repeated. "What does that mean?"

"Nothing. She was just near the door as we were leaving but not there when we actually went out."

"Where'd she go? Did you notice?"

"The living room, I think," she said, moving around in her chair.

"You didn't try to catch her while you were going out, just to say hello?" he asked and was rewarded with a flash of anger in her eyes.

"No. I saw no need to make a point of speaking to her."

"Even though she's the aunt of a good friend?"

"They're not close." Lisa sat up straighter and pulled her legs over to the side of the chaise longue. "Beth just calls the day before she wants to come and then arrives. The O'Donnells always pretend that she's been invited, but she never has been." She repeated this in a sharper tone than she had used so far, then added in a softer voice, "I think Medge was getting tired of it."

"Did she tell you that?"

"Not in so many words." She frowned. "She doesn't seem relaxed about it anymore. Her aunt's visits seem to make everyone tense now. Especially Medge."

"How long has this been going on?" he asked, wondering if Beth O'Donnell's death had roots reaching down before 1985, the year he first came to Mellingham.

76

"Forever. Well, at least for as long as Medge can remember, anyway."

"How often has Medge mentioned this to you?" As soon as he asked this, he regretted it. Lisa pulled herself up in her chair and said coldly, "She hasn't complained to me. She just mentioned it once or twice."

"No one complains about the uninvited guest?" Silva asked, trying to lighten the interview and get her relaxed attention again, but he could see in her expression his efforts had failed.

"She's family and the O'Donnells don't complain about anything," Lisa said with exaggerated politeness.

"I see," said Silva. "Was there any reason you didn't talk to Beth O'Donnell at the party?"

"No. I was having too much fun talking to some friends I hadn't seen in a long time." She was trying hard not to sound peckish, but not doing very well. She finally looked up at him and asked, "Do you have any other questions?"

"Yes, but they can wait." He promised to return again, for there was one question he sorely wanted answered. Either Bob Chambers had so charmed Lisa that she didn't mind sitting alone in a car on a dark road for almost twenty minutes, or she had something else on her mind last night.

■ ■ ■

Mrs. Miles refilled Silva's cup with coffee as she sat across from him at the table in her small, neat, all-white kitchen at the back of her small, neat white house. Mrs. Miles had worked for the O'Donnell family long enough to feel a certain right to know and be consulted about what happened in the home or to the family anywhere. She had felt this way since her second week of employment, when she had decided she would stay with the family indefinitely. She had remained in firm control of the household ever since, but she had a gentle hand with the reins. A stout woman who looked as though she were solid muscle, Mrs. Miles moved through the town like a swan on a pond, a not unlikely comparison to anyone used to seeing her walking the two miles to the O'Donnell house in her white nylon uniform and white shoes every morning at seven-thirty. On rare occasions when she was sidetracked, she dispensed the same exhausting interest she usually reserved for the O'Donnell household to the person who had drawn her attention, watched it percolate through the person's being, and turned again to work. Youngsters under the age of ten eagerly waved to her; teenagers were more circumspect: they knew the cost of idle conversation with Mrs. Miles. When Chief Silva put her on his list of interviewees he knew the price would be several minutes on the receiving end of her questions, not all of them suitable for a chief of police conducting a murder investigation.

Resigned, he accepted her offer of coffee and waited for the first question. During the several minutes Mrs. Miles had spent brewing the drink, she had probed into his pastimes and checked up on his cleaning lady, a woman she had once worked with years ago. By the time she had placed the coffeepot on the table, she had satisfied herself about his personal life. By the time she sat down to pour, she had chided him for not coming to see her directly after discovering the body. She advised him on who to listen to during the investigation and who to ignore, when to expect the grapevine to choose the first suspect and what that would tell him about the other suspects. Finally, she warned him not to overlook the value of a good gossip. She had, after all, known about the death of her employer's sister for several hours. As she put it to the chief, what else were people going to talk about on a quiet Sunday afternoon?

"It's too bad this had to happen to the O'Donnells," Silva began.

"Well, it had to happen to someone," she said. "And the guests didn't know about it, so I don't see how it much matters as far as the party goes, do you?" She sighed. "One of life's little ups and downs."

Silva decided to be more direct while he still had control of the interview; he could explore her philosophy of murder at another time. Slipping into the tone of voice he had been using for most of the day, he said, "I understand you stayed to help the caterers. Is that correct?"

"In a manner of speaking." She nodded.

He sighed for opportunities lost. "And what manner might that be?"

"Well, they're in and out so fast that I might lose track of what's going on if I didn't watch closely. But good they are. I'll say that for them. The Kitchen Cast. And what a show they put on." She laughed heartily at the recollection of last night's sample.

Silva knew some of the young people, and appreciated their unorthodox methods. They rarely, if ever, came dressed in the uniform of black pants or skirt and white top adopted by other caterers; they preferred to come in costumes suitable to the party of the hosts, though sometimes unfortunately for the hosts, the caterers decided unilaterally what was suitable dress. More than one hostess in Mellingham had been nonplussed to see the caterers' perception of the type of party and guests they would be serving. The costumes were the result of the youngest member of the company and the early decision by Jim Kellogg, the founder, to assign each person a task and trust everyone implicitly. He never argued about costumes. Luckily, so far, no one had been offended, for the members of the Kitchen Cast adored their business and their customers.

"Did you stay in the kitchen the whole time?" Silva asked.

"I did not," she said indignantly. "I went round the guests, making sure things were running smoothly."

"And were they?" Silva asked this automatically, feeling sure that no one—guest or employee—would dare overstep the bounds of good taste as long as Mrs. Miles was standing in the background.

"That they were."

"Tell me about the end of the evening. What time did people leave?"

"Most left by ten-thirty or so. And everyone was gone by about eleven." She sat with her hands in her lap, letting him run through the mundane questions of his business.

"And then you were cleaning up?"

"Well, I was watching them, wasn't I? They did some washing up, and they cleaned up the front rooms. Very careful they are. They even vacuumed out there. Most unusual, but it's one of their services. Had everything cleaned up and done by one o'clock." Mrs. Miles assuredly approved of the caterers.

"So they were gone by one o'clock," Silva repeated meditatively.

"Didn't I say so?"

Silva sighed and went on. "When did you leave?"

"I left with them. They drove me home." This had evidently pleased her, and she smiled happily.

"With sixty guests and caterers in the house, there must have been people milling about everywhere," Silva said, hoping Mrs. Miles would just start talking.

"Not really. Whenever we have a party, Mrs. O'Donnell and I work it all out beforehand. We know how much space we need and how we're going to keep the guests in it. We used the living room, the dining room, the halls in front and at the side, and the terrace and garden off the living room." She ticked off the areas on her fingers. "The rest of the house is tactfully not open. And no one wanders off, as you might say."

"Women don't go upstairs?" Silva asked, amused by a decorousness he had not known he had a few years ago.

"They do not. There's a powder room down off the side hall."

"But people could still go out into the garden and wander around if they wanted," Silva insisted.

"I suppose so."

"Even out to the cottage, if they wanted?"

"Ah, the cottage." She nodded as she thought over his question. "I suppose they could."

"The sliding glass doors in the kitchen face it. Is that right?" Silva asked. Mrs. Miles nodded. "Were they in use last night?"

"Only when the caterers came and when they left," she said. "They brought everything in when they first arrived, and then took everything out at the end. During the evening they just worked in the kitchen. They had no need to be going in and out, and they didn't."

"If there had been any guests walking out back, would you have noticed them?" Silva asked.

"Might have," she allowed.

"Did you notice anyone?" Silva prodded.

"No, not a soul, but then I was busy."

"Could someone have come around the other side of the house and gone into the cottage without your seeing them?"

She clenched her teeth and glared at him, then finally said, "No."

"No," Silva repeated. "No one could have come around the other side of the house without your noticing them. You're sure of that?"

"Isn't the house lit up like an altar on Saint's Day? Didn't we have a dozen young ones running around looking here and there for anything they could light their eye on?"

"Did you?" Silva asked.

"Yes, and doesn't it break my heart to say so."

"You understand this is a murder investigation, Mrs. Miles," Silva said.

"Oh, don't I? At first I thought of just telling you I had my eye on the food and the caterers, not on the cottage or the garden." She paused for a moment to look him over, and Silva could see the struggle in her eyes between pride in how well she did her job and a desire to protect her friends and employers. "Whenever we have a party," she went on, "I'm supposed to keep an eye out to make sure no one comes up from the beach or around the other side, but no one ever does."

"So no one came from that direction last night?"

"No one as far as I know." She frowned, thinking. "I thought maybe there was someone out back for a bit but I looked for several minutes and it was perfectly still out there."

"When was this?"

"About when the guests were leaving. Either side of ten-thirty. Hard to say. If there was something, it could have been just kids." She dismissed the possibility of a serious intrusion.

But Silva was less willing to let the possibility dissolve so easily. He asked, "Could it have been guests in the garden?"

"Maybe," she admitted. "There were some as went out there, not too many. Mostly people didn't go out unless the family wanted to show them something. Let me see now," she said as she peered into her coffee cup. "There was Mr. O'Donnell and Mr. Handel and Mr. Vinton and Mr. Steinwell, and the new owner of the health food store, and the architect who converted the cottage. He comes every year to look at his work, though you can't see much in the dark," she explained. "That's all I remember."

"That's very helpful. Do you remember seeing Miss O'Donnell out there, perhaps on her way to bed after the party?"

"You do want a lot, don't you, Joe?" she said.

"Yes, I do, Mrs. Miles, especially today," he said with a wink.

"Well, I think she went out about the same time most of the guests were leaving."

"You saw her go?"

"I saw her going out," she said, qualifying her earlier statement.

"Through which door?"

"The side door, into the garden. She wouldn't come through the kitchen, not that one."

"Did you see her again after that anywhere?" Silva asked.

"No. I just saw her going out the side door." Mrs. Miles was definite on this point.

"And the party was almost over by then?" he asked.

Mrs. Miles was not so sure of her memory this time. "Well, not empty, no. Others went out into the garden after her, but it was so near the end of the party that it made no matter," she concluded.

"What do you mean?"

"Well, you know how at a party, all of a sudden everybody seems to decide all at once that it's time to go and the place suddenly clears out. That's how it was. There were still some close friends about, I guess, at eleven o'clock, and then they went too. But that was after Miss O'Donnell had left. I guess she left when the people she knew had gone."

"Who did she know in particular?" Silva asked.

"The Morrisons and some others," she said. "Especially the Morrisons."

"It sounds like you really don't like them."

"Does it now? Well, makes no matter what I think now."

"It does to me," Silva said. "What about the Morrisons?"

"What about them, indeed. They had no business being there in the first place."

"They were guests, weren't they?" Silva said, remembering the list of names Mrs. O'Donnell had given him just a few hours earlier.

"Were they now?" she said. "And whose I'd like to know?"

"They're on the list Mrs. O'Donnell gave me," Silva said, watching the housekeeper closely and recalling the only two names written in pencil.

"Is that so?" Mrs. Miles ruminated on this bit of news.

"When were they added, Mrs. Miles?"

"Added, is it?" she said. "Well, they weren't. They simply arrived and Miss O'Donnell greeted them at the door. Fair turned me blue, it did," she said. "Miss O'Donnell must have invited them. They weren't on the list this year. For the first time in years they weren't invited, but they were there. Invitations make no matter to that sort."

"And no one said anything?" Silva asked, noting the ease with which good manners can give the upper hand to the bully.

"Well, what were we going to say? I ask you? Old friends they've been. We all made like it was an oversight. No more than that," she said. "But a lot more it was," she said darkly.

"Were the Morrisons there for the entire evening?" Silva asked.

"The whole thing," Mrs. Miles replied in disgust.

"So Miss O'Donnell left when they left," he said.

"That's right. Had to have her friends around her, and when they left, she left. Went off to bed, I guess."

"That would have made it closer to ten-thirty," Silva recalled.

"I suppose so," she said. "We were very busy so I didn't really notice what time it was until it was almost over."

"Is eleven o'clock the usual time for the O'Donnells' parties to end?"

"Yes. Sometimes the late summer parties go until midnight, but not much later."

"So Miss O'Donnell knew exactly what kind of party to expect?" Silva asked.

"To be sure, Chief. The same every time she came. That's probably why she expected the Morrisons and called them to make sure they were coming."

"She came every few years; at least that's what I've been told," Silva said.

"Every two years," she corrected him.

"How long has she been doing that?"

"Years. Let me see," she said, touching her fingers. "Ten, twelve, fourteen years, I think. At least as long as I've been working there full time."

"Did she ever come more often? In earlier years?"

"Not that I ever heard."

"You're very certain of that." Silva commented from mild curiosity.

"Bad enough every two years, it was," she said with feeling. "Takes two years just to get over it all."

"Over what?"

"The trouble, of course." She looked at him with disdain for his ignorance.

"What trouble, exactly?" he asked.

"Mr. O'Donnell looks just as confused after his sister's visits," Mrs. Miles said, "but this time I think he finally got it." She sighed.

"Got what?" Silva asked, hoping he would not end up as disengaged from reality as Howard always seemed to be, because of the influence of Mrs. Miles.

"Why his sister comes to visit," she said.

"Why, Mrs. Miles, did his sister come to visit him?" he asked as clearly and as unemotionally as he could.

"Money, Chief Silva."

"I see." The mention of money at least promised to put him back on a track he could recognize. "I understand he gave her money every month. Mrs. O'Donnell said they supported her and had done so for years."

Mrs. Miles poured out two more cups of coffee, remembering how much milk he took, and placed it in front of him. "Dear me," she sighed, "you and Mr. Howard do think alike."

"Now is the time to help me overcome that, Mrs. Miles," he urged with good humor.

"Money, Chief. She wanted money. Not monthly checks. Now do you see?"

"Keep going," was all he dared say.

"Mr. O'Donnell sent her a check from an account he set up a long time ago, so if anything happened to him, there would still be money for her. That was fine, until Medge got married. Then Miss O'Donnell realized that Medge might have children and the Mister might care more about helping them than supporting her in her old age."

"So she asked him to transfer the account to her. Is that it?"

"Not exactly," she went on.

"How exactly, Mrs. Miles?"

"She probably didn't want a flat no for an answer, so she kept hinting. Only thing was that the Mister didn't get the hint until this time." She shook her head over the denseness of the male mind.

"Are you sure of that?" Silva asked.

"I'm sure all right. I heard them, the Mister and the Missus, talking about it before the party."

"Do you remember exactly what they said? Did they say Miss O'Donnell would get her money?"

"No. Mister didn't see the point of that," she explained. "The only thing they finally understood was that she wanted control over the money."

"She didn't say why?" he asked.

"I don't think so. It didn't sound like it, anyway. Besides, Miss O'Donnell couldn't come right out and tell him she didn't like having him run her money, now could she?"

"And you think this was the purpose of all of her visits?"

"I know it was. She came up here regularly and hinted. And she didn't get anywhere," Mrs. Miles said with satisfaction.

■ ■ ■

The Agawam Inn was a rambling Victorian hotel built on the side of a hill as it rose to the rocky coast beyond. From the roof deck and the front veranda, as well as from the rooms on the floors between, guests could look out at the picture-perfect view of the harbor filled with pleasure crafts of all sorts and a few commercial fishing boats. On the far shore were the large red barns of the marinas. Since the coastal area on the other side of the road running in front of the inn was all salt marsh, no developer had or would ever inconsiderately and tastelessly block the view of the visitors to the inn. This was fortunate, for over the decades the successive owners of the Agawam Inn had sold off most of the other assets: the land on which guests had enjoyed a few holes of golf, the private dock and private boats tied thereto, the pond tucked away in the woods, and the lawns on which men and women had played croquet and badminton. Now the Agawam was no more than a gracious old painted lady with an enviable view.

And yet, for most of Sunday evening, Mr. and Mrs. Morrison had found no pleasure in the view of the quaint New England village and placid harbor spread before their window. Indeed, for the last hour, Mrs. Morrison had kept her back to it while she folded and packed her clothes. Since she was alone in the two-room suite, there was no one to count the number of silk blouses with misaligned buttons and buttonholes carelessly packed into the first suitcase, which was now sitting near the door. Her actions were so hurried that an observer might think nothing could halt her activity and would have been surprised to see her hands still and her head rise at the sound of footsteps stopping outside the door.

"Oh, it's you," she said to her husband when he opened the door and stepped into the room. She returned to her packing.

"Who were you expecting?" he asked as he watched her. When she failed to answer, he asked, "My dear, what are you doing? Surely you're not packing?" he said, ignoring the obvious condition of the room.

Mrs. Morrison stopped to look at her husband. "Of course, I'm packing. What does it look like?" His expression was no different from that of any other husband whose wife argues about an obvious point, and Mrs. Morrison's was that of a wife who wonders why her husband can't see what is plain in front of him.

"Why," he said, "why are you packing?"

She closed a bureau drawer and turned to him. "Surely you can't mean for us to stay."

"Of course, I do," he said. "I've been having a chat here and there downstairs." He swept his wife's nightclothes from a chair and sat down.

"With whom?"

"Oh, just the odd sort who wanders in from the village."

"You've been talking with anyone who might know something about Beth."

"Quite."

"Well?" she asked.

"Well, first of all, I see no reason for us to be packing. Quite the opposite," he said, raising an eyebrow.

To this Mrs. Morrison made no reply except a long hard stare. Finally, she said, "I don't know, darling, I really do think I'd be more comfortable if we vacationed elsewhere. This sort of thing is so, so," she cast around in her mind for a suitable adjective and said, "distasteful. It really is."

"I agree, my dear," he said with exaggerated graciousness. "But I also think it would be, how shall I put it, not the expected thing." He paused, and then added, "To cut and run, I mean."

Disdain and anger mingled in Mrs. Morrison's face. "That's not how I see it."

"I know it isn't, my dear, but others might. And I just think that we should stay on. It won't be for long, I assure you," he said. "I hardly want to stay here any more than you do, but I think we should."

His wife considered his suggestion, then sat down on the bed, defeated perhaps, but not persuaded. "You think it might not look right, and I think it won't look right either way, whether we stay or go. Poor Beth," she said in a rare moment of honesty.

"We should stay to offer to help out any way we can," he said.

"Oh, I agree," she said, his suggestion capturing her

imagination. "I quite agree. The family must be simply, utterly devastated. And we simply couldn't just leave without offering some comfort. And certainly we too are utterly destroyed at this awful event," she said with great deep breaths. "Perhaps a card," she said turning to him with a dramatic dip of her shoulders.

"Do whatever you think is best, my dear," he said with a nod of approval.

■ ■ ■

For almost his entire working life Joe Silva had lived in apartments that had been little more than places to hang his uniform and shine his shoes, a place usually located to enable him to move fast on public transportation or by car. And then he had come to Mellingham and found himself spending longer and longer at the breakfast table in an apartment he rented when he first arrived. When he caught himself driving the long way to work just so he could smell the salt marshes and the fishing boats, he dismissed it as a sign of the weakness that he called middle age. But he knew that wasn't it. First of all, he was barely forty. Second, he used to do the same thing when he was a boy. Then one day, after he had been in Mellingham for a year, his landlord told him about a small condominium in an old colonial house tucked into a crook in the arm of the harbor and Joe went to see. He and the owner passed papers three weeks later and Joe moved in the following week. It was a dimension of his life he rarely looked at too closely, so different did it seem from the image he had of himself as a man. This was his home in a way no other place had ever been.

To the outside world the black-shingled colonial presented a plain, even austere facade. Joe pulled into the driveway, careful to park within the wavy white lines painted with more enthusiasm than correctness by the grandson of Mrs. Alesander, the elderly woman who owned the house originally and now lived in the upstairs condo. He liked the wavy lines for the rare variety they introduced into a life used to straight lines and strict rules. Joe walked around to the back of the house to a porch that opened from a large glass door with colonial sash windows on either side. The front door gave access to both condos, but Joe preferred his back door, which opened into a cozy sitting room cut from the center of a large keeping room that at one time ran the entire length of the house. To his right was now a small study, and to the left a small kitchen and bathroom. The two front rooms of the house were a living room, on the left, and a bedroom, on the right. The sitting room faced a narrow strip of back lawn, which opened into a marsh and the harbor beyond, open to the smells caught by the grasses and trees. In the winter Joe awoke to the sounds of mallards and the thin ice on the marsh crashing under the heft of a dog after prey.

For the six years he had lived there Joe had never come to think his home ordinary; instead he found in it an almost unnatural ability to gather his thoughts, write out his ideas about his cases, and shine the lens of his policeman's eyes. He knew when he had received the call earlier that day that he would return in the evening to sort through the suspects and discern the early shadowy outline of the case. And he knew he would come back to the one question he could not answer: had his luck as chief of police finally run out? For in his entire time here he had faced nothing as serious as murder and had found it easy to work with the townspeople on the issues they cared about. But murder was different, and there were no exceptions for the fourth-generation family, the prominent local businessman, or the favorite soprano in the church choir. Silva leaned back into the cushions of the wide sofa and pulled a pad of paper onto his lap, knowing it might well be the last uncomplicated evening he had for a long time.

The list of suspects stepped down the lines of the yellow paper, falling onto the sheet without hesitation: Merrilee and Howard O'Donnell, Hannah and Lee Handel, Medge and Frank Vinton, Mrs. Miles, Jim Kellogg and the caterers, Mr.

Steinwell, Lisa Hunt and Bob Chambers, Mr. and Mrs. Morrison, and a list of names that surprised him by its completeness. Since few of these knew the victim personally, Joe was ready to remove them, provisionally at least, from his working list. Tucked away in the back of his mind was the ready awareness that no one could be ruled out at this stage, and sometimes the quietest, least likely suspects proved to have the strongest, most passionate motives and the most unexpected capabilities when it came to carrying out a murder. He glanced back up to the beginning of the list, and heard a voice reciting what he knew would be the first and most persistent refrain of outrage at the suspicion that would settle over the main figures just because of the police interest in them. But the family was always the first suspect, and the housekeeper and caterers were there last and had the easiest opportunity.

Silva looked again at the list of names and jotted beside each one his personal reactions and questions, writing freely after pausing to gaze out through the large glass door to the marshland and harbor beyond. When he was finished he looked back through his comments, once or twice startled at his feelings about one or another of the people. Lee Handel had always been a kind if eccentric local businessman, but his eccentricity now seemed less than innocuous. Merrilee also took on a new dimension as he recalled the gossip he had heard about her early athletic endeavors. She was certainly strong enough, if the gossipers were correct, to smash a woman's skull. The same could be said, he realized uneasily, of several other women who were guests last night. Lisa Hunt, for all her apparent flakiness, was capable of bursting into astounding energy, and he was not at all satisfied with his preliminary interview with her. Silva sighed, added a few more notes, and threw the pad of paper onto the coffee table. One more night, he thought, one more night to enjoy the illusion that he was just an ordinary chief of police in an ordinary New England town. Tomorrow the work would begin in earnest.

5

MONDAY MORNING

*S*ILVA DREW the window shade against the glare of the morning sun and listened to Dupoulis in the next room dictating his notes into the tape recorder. He could see his assistant's foot in the doorway of the other tiny office, now serving three men with two desks. Frankel was seated at the tall desk in the center of the large main room, looking for all the world like an intruder into a miniature set as he sat hunched over the mundane tasks that kept life running smoothly. Silva moved one name on the duty roster for the week, and initialed it. Only one problem remained and he was toying with the idea of giving the task to Maxwell, who for all his bulk had shown an unexpected delicacy in negotiating the social and political byways of small-town life.

The problem was Elm Street, a long, narrow road with a straightaway that successfully tempted youngsters to test their take-off skills in their new cars. Neighbors complained as the noise increased in the spring and Silva had over the years regularly stationed an officer in a cruiser at a strategic point along the road. The strategic value of the point in question was derived in part from its location on the straightaway and in part from its position in front of a particular house, one of the rare few that had an uncut lawn, unpainted clapboards, patchy roof, and torn screen door. Here the police could park for up to an hour at a time to clock and stop speeders without a complaint from the homeowner. Unfortunately for the police, however, the house had been sold during the winter and over the last two months the new owners had quickly dispelled the fog of neglect. It would be impolitic, Silva knew, to station a police cruiser in front of the home now. For the moment, therefore, Silva had no method for dissuading the younger generation from testing the laws of physics at odd evening hours, and he would have to find one soon, judging by the weather and the number of calls coming in from Elm Street. He scribbled a note and left it tucked into the corner of his blotter.

"How did you get on, Ken?" Silva asked his sergeant as he stepped into the doorway of the other office. He wondered now which would come first: an arrest or a complaint about the hours.

Dupoulis pulled out the list of names and his other papers and said, "So far, things are going okay." He cleared his throat and began his report. "This is what I have so far. Almost everyone arrived around seven o'clock and left by ten-thirty. Some left earlier, but none left later than eleven." He leaned back in his chair and looked up at the chief standing in the door. "And none of them was a fan of the dead woman. They really didn't like her, Chief."

Silva smiled and sat down. "Did you expect something else, Ken?"

"No, sir, I guess I was just surprised at how much some of these people hated her."

"Yes," Silva agreed. "Hate can run deep and quiet for a long time. How well did these people know the victim?"

"Most barely knew her, despite how strongly they felt about her, and the few who did know her only knew her slightly, from meeting her at the O'Donnell house. The Morrisons and Mr. Steinwell seemed to be the exceptions."

"What do you know about them?"

"Mr. Steinwell seemed to be someone who knew her well because he was talking to her a lot, but after you talk to Mr. Steinwell, you realize that that doesn't mean anything. He didn't know very much about the victim at all, even though he talked to her for almost half an hour and then later in the evening for a few minutes more."

"What did he have to say about her?" Silva asked.

"He said she was a good listener, very interested in new manufacturing techniques," the sergeant said. "I tell you, Chief, that man can talk. But he doesn't seem to have done anything more than talk to everyone at the party, anyone who would listen. He doesn't seem to have known the victim personally; she was just another guest at the party."

"Okay," Silva said. "What about the Morrisons?"

"Out-of-towners. They come for a few days or a few weeks at a time," the sergeant said, checking his notes. "They always stay at the Agawam."

"When did they arrive?"

"Friday. And they planned on staying until next Friday. They used to live around here, so they come out to see old friends," Dupoulis explained.

"How close were they to the victim?"

"Closer than they want to admit now."

"That's what you surmise, is it?" Silva asked.

"Yes, sir. If I may, sir?" Ken said deferentially.

"Sure," Silva said. He was always on good terms with his force, but he never made the mistake of getting chummy and his men understood this.

"I'd like to suggest that you take a second interview with them and talk to them separately," Dupoulis said.

"Did one of them seem to be keeping a blanket over everything?" Silva asked, having heard if not felt a few dozen kicks exchanged between husbands and wives during previous investigations.

"Yes, sir. Mr. Morrison didn't want his wife to say anything, and cut short the interview. I thought I'd just pretend to go along with it and then one of us could go back and hit them from a different angle, each one alone."

"Good idea," Silva agreed. "What did they actually admit to? Anything?"

"Just that they knew her. They left the party around tenthirty, and they walked straight back to the inn."

"How far is it to the Agawam?"

"About a mile." Dupoulis checked his notes and read out the exact figure. "I checked it in the cruiser."

"Not far in a small town," Silva mused. "But it still means they were walking a mile on a quiet village road with no streetlights late at night."

"That's what they said," Dupoulis agreed.

"How old are they?"

"Fifties," Dupoulis estimated. "And Mrs. Morrison made a point of telling me that she dressed for it. She wore flat shoes so she could walk out and back." Dupoulis omitted the sly look she gave his midriff, and left Silva wondering at the resentment in his sergeant's voice.

"What did she have on when you talked to her? Did you notice?" Silva asked.

"Sort of loafers. Flat shoes, anyway."

Silva mulled this over, then asked, "Healthy?"

Ken nodded. "I'd say so."

"Anyone say they saw them?"

"A couple of guests mentioned seeing them walk down the driveway and two others saw them crossing the street further down. I'll check the neighbors to see if anyone spotted them along the way to the inn. I checked with the desk and the clerk said they got in around ten forty-five or eleven, so that fits okay."

"Keep checking," Silva said. "Let's make sure they didn't go out again. Anything else?"

"Yes, sir," Dupoulis said. "I talked to Jim Kellogg from the Kitchen Cast and he's pretty sure no one went around the near side of the house while they were there."

"So is Mrs. Miles," Silva said, repeating his conversation with the housekeeper. "If they're both right, then that means the murder had to take place between ten-thirty, after the victim was last seen at the front door, before she must have left for the cottage, and eleven o'clock, when the last guest left and just the family and caterers were around."

"That sort of narrows it down."

"It sure does," Silva agreed. "What else did Jim have to say?"

"He overheard the victim talking to Bob Chambers. Apparently she was writing a book. Jim heard Bob and the victim talking about it. At least that's how he interpreted the snatches of conversation he heard."

"Does he remember precisely what they said?"

"No, he doesn't. He's vague about it, seems like he doesn't want us to put too much emphasis on it," Dupoulis explained.

Silva considered this, then said, "Did anyone else mention she was writing a book?"

"No one. But I never even heard she was a writer until Jim came out with this," Dupoulis said. "I'll do some more checking with the caterers about what they overheard. Maybe we should ask Mr. Handel about her."

"I already did," Silva said, recalling his earlier interview.

"What did he say?"

"That he barely knew her, he didn't like her, and he didn't speak to her last night."

"He really gets to the point, doesn't he?" the sergeant said. "I didn't realize they even knew each other. Did he say why he didn't like her?"

"No, he didn't. But he doesn't mind admitting it," Silva said.

Ken frowned as he listened to his chief before saying, "I

never thought of him seriously, Chief. I guess I was still looking at someone who was more of an outsider. But Mr. Handel—" He broke off in midsentence.

"He's an early surprise and there'll be more," Silva said.
"So keep your ears open."

"Do you think he's told others how he feels about Miss
O'Donnell?"

"I don't know, but I'd like to. He didn't seem at all
reluctant to tell me how he felt about her, even after he knew
she was dead." Silva thought for a moment. "He's either very
shrewd or very honest."

■ ■ ■

Dupoulis closed his notebook and stood up. "I guess the real
disappointment," he said, "was Mack."

The chief swiveled around in his chair to look directly at
his subordinate. Mack lived as he did partly because Chief
Silva let him, tolerating his prideful possession of the beach
and his caretaking chores with an understanding and kindness
that surprised more than a few old-timers. No one could recall
any other chief of police tolerating the quirks, passions, or
idiosyncracies of youngsters who flocked to the beach throughout the year, and many in town wondered at the magic Silva
wrought by his trust in Mack. Only a few intuited the psychology behind the chief's stance: Mack cared for the beach as
though it were his own home—no interlopers, no beach bums,
no litter. Ever.

"You mean a night actually passed when Mack wasn't on
the beach?" Silva asked in mock surprise.

"No, he was there all right," Dupoulis said, "but the only
people who headed down the beach path after nine or so were
two kids chasing a dog." He tucked his notebook into his
pocket. "And Mack said he never saw them again. They never
came back. He thinks he's seen the dog before down past the
O'Donnells' place."

Silva stepped over to the large street map covering one

wall of the office. There were half a dozen houses beyond the O'Donnells on Westerly Road.

"What kind of dog was it?" Silva asked.

Dupoulis repeated Mack's description.

"I think he's right," Silva said after meditating in front of the map. "Send Frankel out on that. Should be easy. Two kids and a dog. He can tidy that one up without any trouble."

■ ■ ■

Medge stood in the doorway of the living room watching her mother rearranging knickknacks on a table and listening to her humming quietly to herself. Learning about Aunt Beth's death had been a shock but not so serious as to keep Medge from work. Nevertheless, she had decided to use her aunt's death as an excuse to take some time off and do some thinking, at least that's what she told herself now. Mostly she felt in limbo from life—her job didn't draw her or repel her. Developing new credit card services never became more than a sales job for her, and life at the bank moved at a dulling pace, making her long for the rhythm of rush and rest in her earlier years. Listless after the party, she had drifted into the day, not getting up and dressed until midmorning. She had avoided thinking about the Kitchen Cast, feeling a twinge of embarrassment at being so excited about her future at a time like this. With no ambition to do anything and no clear purpose, she had wandered across the field to her parents' house, meandering noiselessly through the kitchen and into the hallway when she heard a series of odd clicking and clashing sounds like china hitting glass. When she got to the doorway she saw her mother rearranging knickknacks on a side table. Medge stood silent and watched. When her mother did not sense her presence, Medge wondered if her being were now as light on the earth as her will, which was apparently not heavy enough to fill the air and warn her mother that another person was near.

Merrilee O'Donnell's lightheartedness was almost fey; all morning she had been cleaning and sprucing up the house.

This alone bothered Medge because her mother had not cleaned her own home for as long as her daughter remembered. Mrs. O'Donnell helped the household employees, she could even be prodded to supervise for major affairs like Thanksgiving, but she never turned eye or hand to dust or grime. Medge had grown up accustomed to a home that reflected the personality of the housekeeper of the moment as much as that of her mother. Now, seeing her mother dusting and arranging and plumping and tidying left the younger woman perplexed, even uneasy.

"Hello, Mother," she called out as though she had only just walked in.

"Hello, dear," the older woman answered automatically. When she turned, her smile was radiant and relaxed. "I was just putting a few things in order."

"It looks wonderful," her daughter said sincerely. "I came over to see how you were holding up, but you seem fine. Maybe you should rest before you wear yourself out."

"Nonsense. I don't feel the least bit tired," her mother said. "I really feel quite energetic, in fact. When I got up this morning, I felt so peppy so I thought I'd put it to good use. So I've been doing the housework—all those little details that so easily get overlooked." As if to prove her words, she went from window to window, straightening the draperies and arranging the folds.

"Do you know," she turned suddenly to Medge, "that your aunt has been coming here for the past several years with only one purpose. And we never even knew." She turned back to the draperies. Medge waited for her mother to elaborate, but when she did not, Medge prompted her.

"What purpose, Mother? What are you talking about?"

"Your father told me Saturday night, only he hadn't noticed either," she said by way of explanation.

"Noticed what?" Medge was now following her mother from window to window.

"Her real reason for coming every two years."

"Mother, stop. Stand still." Medge grabbed her by the shoulders and held onto her. "Tell me from the beginning. Why did Aunt Beth come every two years?"

"You know your father supported her?" Merrilee asked.

"Yes, I know that. He's always done that."

"Well, she wanted to take over her account and handle it herself. She's been hinting at it for years and years and I never even realized it until something your father said Saturday."

"What did he say?" Medge asked.

"It wasn't any particular thing," her mother said, her eye drifting back to the draperies.

Medge sighed. "How did you decide that Aunt Beth was asking for control of her money?"

"The fulcrum," Merrilee replied.

"The what? Mother, you're not making any sense. What fulcrum?"

"Oh dear. I'm sorry I'm so confused." As she spoke her hands fluttered up to her hair, her fingers lightly touched her head, and then her hands fell to her shoulders, where her fingers hovered lightly on the padded shoulders of her silk blouse. "Saturday Beth called your father the fulcrum. Two years ago she called him an anchor holding fast a catamaran." Merrilee smiled, pleased with her memory.

"An anchor?" Medge echoed.

"Yes. And before that he was a foundation for a house trailer," said Merrilee frowning, "although I may have got that one wrong. But you get the idea."

"No, I don't, Mother. What are you talking about?"

"All right, I'll spell it out for you. Money," she said. "Money. For years Beth has been hinting about how her money—actually it's your father's money—is handled. We thought she was complimenting him on his generosity, although I'll admit that the reference to the house trailer did confuse your father."

Medge groaned and her mother quickly returned to the point. "But all this time she was saying just the opposite. She was saying that she wanted to control her own money, without your father's help." She sat down on the sofa, and smiled up at her daughter. The two women pondered this matter for several moments.

"You say that as though, as though . . ." Medge stopped. "I don't understand this." She finally capitulated.

"Darling, all this time," Merrilee said, "I thought she was after more money. But she wasn't."

"You mean she just wanted to control her fund rather than ask Dad for money all the time?"

"That's it," Merrilee agreed.

"Why didn't she say so?"

"Well, I don't think I know," Merrilee said.

"Oh well, it hardly matters now," Medge said.

"No, I don't suppose it does," her mother agreed.

■ ■ ■

Medge poured her mother another cup of tea and finished her story about the tennis match on Sunday. Over the last half hour she had managed to hold her mother's attention, but Medge was still worried. She was only beginning to realize what a strain her aunt's visits had been over the last several years.

"I think I'll ask the police if I can clean out the cottage in the next day or so," Merrilee finally said, "and start redecorating."

"They may ask you to wait," Medge said. "Unless, of course . . ."

Mrs. O'Donnell didn't hear her daughter and instead went on with her own thoughts. "At least I can get started thinking about it."

"What did you have in mind?" Medge decided she might as well humor her mother.

"Something sporty. Right now it looks like a New York penthouse."

Medge said nothing.

"Perhaps a seashore motif," she said, looking to her daughter for agreement.

"Maybe I should finish the needlepoint Aunt Beth started," Medge offered.

"Don't bother, dear. She never started that. She bought it like that. She just brought it up here for show. She told me once that she thought the design matched the decor of the cottage." She put her teacup down on the tray. "I'll just throw it out." Merrilee looked at her daughter closely, forgetting her own concerns for the moment. "I didn't realize you were so fond of Beth," she said with suspicion.

"I wasn't. I just find the whole thing upsetting."

"Yes, of course you do. You didn't hate her. It must be hard for you. And Frank too. How is Frank? Not upset too, is he?" Merrilee asked in her disconcertingly bright tone.

"No. Mother, you don't mean that you really hated her."

"Yes, I do. She was an appalling, evil woman and I hated every inch of her. I have no intention of telling your father that, but it's true. If he asks, however, I may just let it out."

"How is Dad?"

"Fine." Merrilee was suddenly shocked at the callousness of her reply, but merely shrugged and said, "He wasn't close to her, dear. He's sad, of course, but not terribly upset."

"He must be upset about how it happened," Medge said, aware of the lunch meetings she had canceled and the people she knew she would avoid over the next few weeks.

"Yes, that does bother him. He likes to think he has his eye on everything. He doesn't, but there's no point in telling him that."

"Where is he now?"

"Just sitting in the garden, staring at the crab apple tree."

Medge laughed. "That has nothing to do with Aunt Beth. He gave the bird feeder away, to Lee Handel. Remember?"

"Is that why he's out there? I wondered about that." She nodded to herself, and said, "He misses it. I'll get him another one."

"What came over him? I never saw him do anything like that before," Medge said.

"I guess he was so glad the Handels came that he wanted to show them how glad he was to see them."

"They used to come to all your parties. Why should this one be any different?" Medge asked.

"Well, with Beth here and all." She eyed her daughter suspiciously.

"They've met Beth before," Medge said, growing curious at her mother's short replies.

"So they have, dear," Merrilee said. "I think I'll just go and see how your father is doing."

"What were you getting at, Mother?"

"Nothing, dear. Beth and the Handels aren't alike, that's all. I suppose if they'd known she was coming, they might have thought it was a different kind of party and not come."

"They probably did know," Medge said.

"How?" Merrilee asked, her eyes widening to stare at her daughter.

"The Morrisons. They're staying at the Agawam and Mrs. Handel sends over a special bouquet for them whenever they come. And Beth always comes when they're here, every two years. So the Handels could have easily figured out that Aunt Beth would show up. She was due."

"But they—" Merrilee broke off. "Well, isn't that nice?" she said. "And they came along and had a good time." Merrilee looked genuinely pleased.

"Why shouldn't they come and have a good time?" Medge persisted, but her mother quickly rose and escaped to the garden.

■　■　■

Silva leaned against the police car in the Vinton driveway. Just down the road from the O'Donnell house and separated by a small field, the gatehouse was hidden from view on three sides by tall poplars and firs. A path cut across the field and through the trees between the two homes. Neighbors used the path to get to the beach, and the area children could be seen skulking through the tall grass, ambushing enemies, hunting wild animals, or spying on police officers. Not having known the pleasures of an open field at that age, Silva took the opportunity to watch them, studying the layout of the O'Donnell house from the perspective of a person approaching from the outside. The house had privacy, but this had not yet advanced to the extreme form that is isolation. Silva guessed that a stranger could work through the neighborhood by moving among the trees, but would soon be noticed. A far safer route for the outsider would be to step boldly into the light of day, acting as though he belonged there. Such people went unnoticed until the damage was done, and then it was too late.

The Vinton housekeeper had said, as she was leaving for the morning, that Mrs. Vinton was just on her way back from the other house. When Silva saw movement at the front door, though obscured in part by the trees, he assumed it was Medge Vinton. He waited by the police car until he could see her coming through the trees and the field, noting that she moved in the open areas even though a less visible path ran parallel to the road.

"Have you been waiting long?" she asked politely when she was only a few feet away.

"I saw you when you came out of the house, so not very long." Silva noted the determined look of the successful young woman, but also a reserve that might hold her back. She was less a social animal than her mother, from what he had heard. He had never had the opportunity to speak to her at length before, though he had come to know her through her habits. She took the 7:37 into Boston every day, along with several other young women and men in their cookie-cutter suits, and returned most evenings on the 6:57. She had halfheartedly worked on the Garden Club with Mrs. Handel, occasionally spoke in the high school on career day, but otherwise kept a low profile in the town. There were others like her, and Silva, like other chiefs before him, had learned early on to expect the day they woke up to an issue and turned serious.

"First, I'm sorry about your aunt," Silva said after the formalities. To his surprise, she relaxed considerably.

"Thank you. In all the talk about how it happened, we seem to have forgotten that someone has actually died. Thank you." She turned toward the house. "Shall we talk inside?" She led the way into the living room. Silva wished he had time to look over the room and glean what he could about its owner; he felt at a disadvantage simply by not having a better sense of the woman he was interviewing. All he noticed quickly was a room comfortable and subdued. He was acutely aware of how little help could come from superficial information like a commuting schedule or job description. Knowing that Mrs. Vinton worked in the credit card division of a Boston bank and Mr. Vinton was a sales rep for his father-in-law's brokerage house did not tell him what he really wanted to know, which was what kind of people they were.

Mrs. Vinton motioned him to a chair and sat opposite him as though she expected a fistful of questions to be thrown at her without introduction. This was all that he needed to remind him of the true weight of his life now. He began to speculate on the hidden depths in Mrs. Vinton as he explained what he wanted.

"We're interviewing everyone who was at the party Saturday, and anyone who might help us with your aunt's death," he said as soon as they were comfortably settled. She was completely different from her mother, not offering him anything to drink but making sure he could take notes where he sat. His last hope of finding her a willing narrator of her story evaporated as he looked into her placid face. "What time did you leave the party?" he began.

"Close to one o'clock. I was helping to clean up."

"Can you be more precise about the time?"

"Not really. But I'll try to remember and let you know," she said, dismissing his question.

"Was your aunt still up when you left?" he asked, trying to explore her reactions.

"No. I think she left when most of the guests did." Again, she delivered her answer in quiet, unemotional tones.

"Do you remember when you last saw her?"

"I think she was saying good night to the Morrisons."

"What time would that have been?" He tried to make his questions conversational and noticed a wary look come into her eye.

"Maybe ten-thirty. It's hard to say with so many people leaving at once."

"And that's the last time you saw her?" he asked.

"Yes. No, wait." She stopped to think. "Bob Chambers came in looking for her, I think. I don't know if he found her or not. I was out in the kitchen, but I heard him ask someone if she was still there."

"You didn't go out to help look for her?"

"No."

"Do you know when he left?" he asked.

"Yes."

"When was that?" he asked, his curiosity heightened by her reserve.

"Maybe ten or fifteen minutes after he came in."

"So he could have found her, spoken to her, then left," Silva suggested.

"He could have, but as I said, I didn't see her," she repeated. "Or hear her, either."

"Did he give any indication that he had spoken to her?"

"No. I didn't speak to him. I just saw him marching out."

"Marching? Is that how he looked?" Silva was intrigued at her choice of words.

She reconsidered what she had said, then replied, "Well,

he looked angry, frustrated. But that doesn't mean anything. Everyone gets angry dealing with Aunt Beth. She specialized in getting people upset."

"Including you?" he asked. His thrust hit home, for there was no mistaking the anger in her eyes. She laughed quickly to cover her feelings and said, "Absolutely. I'm human too."

Silva gave her credit for a good comeback and a delicate cover. "Did she upset anyone in particular last night?"

"I suppose I have to answer all these questions?" Her tone was light but Silva noticed her foot pressed hard on the floor and her back stiff against the sofa.

"Did she upset anyone especially?" he repeated.

"No more than she usually does when she comes here," she said slowly. "Those who knew her well enough to know what to expect avoided her. Those who met her for the first time last night probably wish they had, too."

"Does that include Bob Chambers?"

"It could," she replied.

"Who else was meeting her for the first time?" Silva asked.

"Lots of people, Chief Silva," she said, not trying to conceal her irritation. "It was a pretty big party."

He took a copy of the guest list from his pocket and handed it to her. "Would you just check off those people you think hadn't met her before last night."

"Wouldn't it make more sense for you to ask my parents this?"

"I want your opinion." He pushed the list across the low table between them.

She hesitated, then pulled the sheet of paper closer to her. She read down through the list, marking a few names. She handed the paper back to him, and he glanced at it quickly. One name stood out.

"Your husband had never met your aunt before last night?"

"That's right."

"How long have you been married, Mrs. Vinton?"

"Fourteen years this June."

"And in all those years he's never had the chance to meet her?" He wondered how his relatives would react to a new member of the family remaining unmet and unknown for so long.

"That's right," she repeated.

"How did he fail to meet Miss O'Donnell during those years?"

"He just wasn't here for her earlier visits," she said. "That's not hard to understand. He travels a lot."

"But he met her last night?" Silva asked just to be sure.

"Yes. And they got along just fine."

"I'm glad to hear it," he said. "If I could just go back a bit, Mrs. Vinton. You said you left close to one o'clock. Did you and your husband leave at the same time?" he asked, turning a page in his notebook.

"No. He left first. I stayed to help with the cleaning-up." She delivered the second statement with the first feel of warmth he had heard in her voice.

"Was there a lot to do?"

"Not a lot," she said, stretching her arm across the back of the sofa, "but I wanted to make sure everything went well."

"And then you went home?"

"Yes, and I went straight to bed," she said coldly. "Frank was already asleep."

"Did you walk home along the path?"

"Yes. I always walk that way at night."

Silva had hoped to have her relaxed by the time he came to these questions, but Mrs. Vinton was a surprise in a lot of ways. "Did you see anything while you were on your way home? Anyone moving around outside the house?"

"No one."

"Were you the last one to leave the house?"

"Yes."

"When you left, the house was closed, locked for the night?"

"Yes."

"No lights on?" he probed again.

She hesitated for the first time, her eyes drifting up to the ceiling as some image came to mind. She had seen something, Silva was now certain, but she might not be willing or able to pass it on to him.

"Were there lights on?" he asked.

"Not in the house, of that I'm sure. But I do remember . . . somewhere," she said.

"How about the cottage?"

"I don't remember," she said. "I may have thought I saw a light, but I don't remember for sure noticing one way or the other." Her eyes were again on the chief, her composure intact.

"Well, we think the light must have been on, but we don't know if anyone came into the cottage after one o'clock or so."

"I can't help you with that one way or the other," she said.

"How about later," he said. "Did you hear anything during the night?"

"Not a thing. Slept like a log," she said unhelpfully.

"And your husband?"

She paused. "Well, I was asleep. He was too. But you'll have to ask him, won't you?"

"I intend to. Just a few more questions if you don't mind," Silva said.

"Go ahead."

"How often is the guest cottage used?"

She considered before answering. "Maybe three or four times a year for long visits. Possibly five or six times a year for short overnight stays."

"So you're accustomed to looking out your window and seeing the cottage lit up as well as the house?"

Medge glared at him, but instead of throwing the question back at him, she puzzled over it and finally answered.

SUSAN OLEKSIW

"We can see there are lights on in that direction, but the trees block most of the view of the house and the cottage."

"But you can tell if the lights are on in the cottage?"

"Yes," she agreed.

"Can you see if someone is moving around blocking the light or going in or out of the door?" he asked.

"Sometimes," Medge reluctantly agreed. "But I didn't Saturday night."

■　■　■

Chief Silva looked across the coffee table at the eager, smiling face of Mrs. Howard O'Donnell, who readily dismissed his apology for dropping in to ask a few questions after speaking with her daughter. She seemed to want to talk, and Silva felt an odd pressure to produce a long litany of queries. Instead, he turned to the page in his small notebook where he had noted his questions.

"There are just a few minor points," he said. "If I have a clear idea of where you were from, say, ten-thirty on, then I'll have a better idea of how to place other people."

"Oh, fine," Merrilee said, sitting forward on the sofa. "At ten-thirty, let me think." She looked down at the floor, thought hard for a few moments, and said, "I was at the door saying good night to my guests at ten-thirty."

"Good, thank you," Silva said. "Then, where did you go?"

"Well, I just stayed at the door saying good night and chatting with people as they left."

"Can you recall where your sister-in-law was then?"

"Well, the Morrisons went out and Beth said good night to them, and then I think she left," Merrilee said, snapping out the last few words.

"You weren't fond of her, were you?"

"No," Merrilee agreed. "I hated her. But you needn't wonder, Chief. It didn't matter how I felt about her. I didn't

110

have to deal with her more than once every two years. Anyway, after she said good night to the Morrisons, she was smart enough not to stand by the door as though she were the hostess, at least not while I was there. And I did not leave the front door until all the guests were gone, at eleven."

"Well, that's very helpful," Silva said, her replies opening up unimagined possibilities.

"Who left during that time?" he asked, and Merrilee recited a number of names. "Who was the last to leave?"

"Mr. Steinwell and the Handels," she replied. "Hannah and Mr. Steinwell were talking to each other for most of the time I was at the door."

"Most of the time?" Silva echoed.

"Well, I think Hannah went off for a moment or so and Mr. Steinwell went off to talk to someone else. But they went out almost on each other's heels."

"When did Lisa Hunt leave?" Silva asked, probing around in Merrilee's memory.

"Oh dear, do I have to remember everyone? Oh dear. Well, I must say, let me think. Oh, I do know. She left with that handsome young man, Bob Chambers. I think they left at about ten-thirty."

"Did you see Bob Chambers come back?"

"Oh yes, now that you say that, I did. That was confusing."

"Tell me what happened," Silva said.

"Well, I turned my back and then turned around again and saw him standing in the front hall talking to one of the caterers. I thought he had left and so I was a bit confused. Then he looked around and I started to say good night to someone else and when I looked again he was gone."

"Did he go by you on his way out?"

"Well, he must have, but I didn't notice him," she said.

"How long after that did the last guests leave?"

"Well, that would have been the Handels," she said.

"You shook hands with the Handels at eleven," Silva said as he looked at his notes.

"That would have been a bit difficult," she said, taking his comment literally. "Lee had his hands full. My husband gave him a rather large bird feeder and he was carrying it with both hands," she said, shaking her head at the strange behavior of men.

"What did you do after the guests left?"

"Nothing! Isn't it too wonderful? The caterers, Chief Silva," she said when she realized he was lost for a meaning. "I just stretched out in the living room and sank down in the joy of having others clean up for me. Then I went to bed," she said matter-of-factly.

"About what time was that?"

"I think eleven-thirty. Howard had already gone upstairs, and we were both tired so we went straight to bed."

"So the only people in the house were the Vintons, Mrs. Miles, and the caterers," Silva said.

"Not Frank," Merrilee said. "He left at eleven, right after the Handels. He walked home through the field. I saw him go out and across the field. It was a lovely night," she said, leaning back into the sofa and smiling at him. "Well, except for Beth, of course."

6
MONDAY AFTERNOON

*T*HE POLICE STATION on Mondays had its own quiet hum of activity, and on this Monday the hum was a little louder, or maybe it only seemed a little louder to Silva as he tried to find something solid to lean on in all the notes he had taken in the investigation so far. Unable to shake the feeling of vague dissatisfaction that had descended on him after the interview with Merrilee O'Donnell, Silva went over it a third time in an effort to glean a few grains to feed his growing hunger for a solid clue to the murder and the relationships of the people involved.

Beth O'Donnell was dead. No one liked her but no one hid their feelings about her either, so he couldn't rely on narrowing down his list of suspects by identifying who hated her. No one saw her after she left the Morrisons at the door—around ten-thirty—but a dozen or more people were still milling around and making their way to the front door. Even at eleven o'clock, there were still seven people in the front of the house, plus the staff and caterers moving between the kitchen and the front rooms.

Again, no one admitted to going out to the cottage at any time, not even at the request of the victim for a chat, but Miss O'Donnell was found dead still dressed in her evening clothes.

Someone had slipped away and caught her relaxing after the party, before she had had the time or the inclination to get ready for bed. She could have stopped somewhere in the garden or at the side of the house to talk to someone for a while, but no one had come forward to say so. More likely, she went straight back to her cottage and settled down for a few moments before getting ready for bed and the murderer joined her then, making the time of her death between, say, just after ten-thirty and eleven o'clock. It was also possible, Silva knew, for the victim to have fallen asleep in her chair for an hour or more, and for one of the guests or someone else to have come back long after the party was over, find her there, and murder her. But that was a mere possibility, not a probability. Mrs. Miles and the caterers had been pretty definite that no one came around the other side of the house while they were there. Anyone who approached the cottage before eleven o'clock had to do so by the side garden and the path. The idea of the victim falling asleep only to be murdered where she sat by a late night intruder was more than implausible. To Silva's mind, the victim was not the type to fall asleep in a chair in an expensive dress.

Far more likely was his first idea, that she was murdered some time between ten-thirty and eleven, while the party was winding down and guests were wandering around as they said good-bye to friends and got ready to leave. And those who were both still on the scene and tied in some way, however tenuously, to the victim were always first on the list. Not unexpectedly, in this case pride of place went to the victim's relatives. The family was followed, in Silva's mind, by Lee and Hannah Handel, and Lisa Hunt, Bob Chambers, and Mr. Steinwell, all of whom were in the house or near it after ten-thirty and up until eleven o'clock. These were the people who interested Silva, the ones who had opportunity and who left him unsettled after his initial interview with them.

Merrilee O'Donnell and her husband, Howard, and

Medge and Frank Vinton did not look like murderers, but looks had nothing to do with it, Silva repeated to himself. Even Mrs. Miles and anyone among the caterers had plenty of opportunity to slip away after the last guests had left. And the last guests—the Handels—had the same opportunity. The Handels were there until eleven o'clock and Lee Handel made no secret about how he felt. Neither had Hannah. Either one of them could have gone out to the cottage. The same was true, at least for opportunity, for Mr. Steinwell, who was one of the last to leave. If the victim went straight back to her cottage, even Bob Chambers could have slipped outside to the garden and gone along the side of the house and killed her when he came back the second time to look for her. And that, Silva mused as he looked at the next name on his list, meant a closer look at Lisa. Was she in the car waiting for Chambers when he came back? Would she have had enough time to make her way around the house to the cottage and kill Beth?

Silva reexamined the list of names. Except for Lisa Hunt, Bob Chambers, and Mr. Steinwell, every major suspect belonged to a pair; he had three sets of spouses, which meant he had six people who had someone to cover for them or someone they could cover if guilt came too close. He drew a line under the group of names, and mentally called it his short list. These were the people he was the most interested in.

He considered the other names. The Morrisons left at ten-thirty and walked to the inn. Could one or both of them have slipped around back to the cottage? Then or later? He posed the same question about the other guests who had left after the Morrisons; none of them provoked anything worthwhile in his reasoning.

But the real question was why, thought Silva. What was going on around this woman, Beth O'Donnell, that left so few people willing to say a good word about her? He mulled over a few of the expressions dropped by guests, idle gossip, they had said apologetically, before eagerly passing on every rumor of the last few years. And none of it added up to anything at all, as far as Silva could tell. For all the people he had found with opportunity, he didn't have a single motive to share among them. Right now, he admitted to himself, all he could do was follow up every lead, every hint, and narrow down as much as possible the range of the unknown. Though he was ready for the inevitable accusations from the victim's family that the police were taking too long, neglecting the tragedy of the situation, and on and on, Silva wondered if the O'Donnells might not run on a different track. So far there had been no complaints, no curious phone calls, and no suggestions to speed up the investigation. Silva would be grateful if they remained so understanding and so remote while he gathered information that might ultimately lead him back to one of them or someone close to them.

■ ■ ■

Silva looked through his office door at the two youngsters sitting on a bench in the outer office—two more details to cover—and wondered how long it would be before he had regular meals again. Homicide had always been bad for his digestion.

"They were chasing their dog," Frankel said in a lowered voice. Frankel had gone off to follow up on Mack's story of two boys and a dog, and in less than an hour had called in his report. Apparently, Frankel knew the town's dog population almost personally. He had arranged for the two boys to come into the police station on Monday afternoon. They were now sitting in the front room, staring up at the main desk and craning their necks to look around corners without forgetting the manners instilled in them by their parents, and doing their best to look nonchalant throughout an experience that could easily become the most thrilling one of their summer. Frankel passed on his initial report to the chief, his bulk filling the office door and his voice rumbling softly below the hum of the office. "It seems the dog runs off every evening, down to the beach, along the beach cliff, and back through a field to their house," Frankel explained.

"Does the dog ever take an adult along?" Silva asked.

"Yes, sir," Frankel said with a smile. "The boy's father usually takes it for a walk when the boys are away at school. They decided to do it on their vacation." He looked over his shoulder at the two boys sitting on the bench in the outer office.

"So they were on the beach path—when?" Silva asked.

"When the guests were leaving the party," Frankel replied.

"Fine," Silva said, hoping this wouldn't take most of the afternoon. Interviewing children was always a challenge. "Why don't you bring them in?"

■ ■ ■

The two boys, aged ten and twelve, home for the summer from boarding school, were wearing shorts and cotton shirts. Poised and polite, they followed Frankel into Silva's office, pretended to be too sophisticated to gape at the insides of a police station, and addressed everyone in sight as sir, including a very surprised teenager being reprimanded for speeding in his father's pickup. Silva marveled at how wealthy children could be so worldly, so confident, and so naive. He gave them thirty seconds more before their excitement broke through their upbringing.

"Officer Frankel reports that you were along the beach path Saturday night," Silva said conversationally after telling the two boys about the investigation.

"Yes, sir." The boys spoke in unison, jostling each other in Silva's small office. They declined an offer to sit on stools, and their furtive glances around the room threatened to derail the conversation at every question.

"There was a murder, wasn't there?" The ten-year-old could contain himself no longer.

"That's right," Silva said in measured tones, determined

to keep the boys in line. "And the police are looking for anyone who can help us." The two boys stared back at the chief of police, their mouths open, but too young to catch the cue he had thrown them.

"Can you help us?" Silva asked. "Can you tell me about your walk along the path?"

"Sure," said the older one, determined now to take the lead. "We were following Crabs—"

"That's our dog," the younger one interrupted. "He used to chase crabs along the beach when he was a puppy—"

"He doesn't do that anymore," the older one said, reclaiming his position as spokesman. "Anyway, he ran down the path."

"He ran up to the O'Donnells' house," the younger one broke in again.

"Let's go one at a time," Silva finally suggested. "Who went up the path first, after the dog?"

"I did," the older one said.

"How far up the path did you go?" Silva asked. "Did you go far enough to see anything?"

"I could see the back of the house. And the cottage," the older one said.

"Me too. They were having a party," the younger one said.

"That's right," Silva said. "We knew about the party. Did you see any of the guests?" Silva asked.

The boys looked perplexed and Silva silently cursed himself for his clumsiness. He tried again. "Did you see any people out back?"

"Oh sure. A woman," the older one said.

"Yeah, me too," the younger one said, not to be outdone by his older brother.

"And what did she do?" Silva prodded.

"Nothing," the older one said, looking blankly at the chief.

"Yeah, nothing," came the echo.

"You mean she just stood there?" Frankel said, who had a knack for conversing with children on their own terms.

"No. She just came down the walk and went into the cottage," the older one said.

"Yeah, nothing," the younger one said, "just like her husband."

"Her husband?" Silva asked calmly.

"Yeah. He came down the walk and went in, too," the younger one said.

"Yeah, nothing," the older one nodded in confirmation. Both looked expectantly at the chief, waiting eagerly for the big question they were sure would come. They weren't sure what it would be, but they were sure it would come.

"What was he like? Her husband," Silva asked.

"Dunno. Couldn't really see through the bushes," the older one said, still hoping for a block-busting question. "It was dark."

"Yeah, it was dark," came the echo.

"Yeah, all we could see were the guy's legs through the bushes," the older one said.

Silva thought hard for a few seconds. If Beth O'Donnell was murdered as soon as she went back to the cottage, that meant the murder took place around ten forty-five or so, while most of the guests were leaving, at the moment of peak confusion, just as he had earlier speculated. Silva looked up at the two boys, who had been studying his expression closely for a clue to the import of what they had told him. True to their age, they read his thoughts.

The younger one suddenly gasped, "Hey! Was that the murderer? Wow!"

"Wicked good," both boys said and started babbling together. Silva calmed them down and tried to put them off the idea of their having seen the murderer. He posed a few more questions, but it was clear they had nothing more to tell him.

They had caught their dog after chasing him up and down the beach for a while, and hurried home before they got into trouble for sneaking around the neighbors' backyards. When Frankel had informed their father about the investigation, their father had sent them down to speak to the police as an exercise in civic responsibility, with no thought of their producing anything of significance. Both father and mother would have to be informed now of what their children had seen and its importance for the investigation. Silva wondered how the boys' parents would feel about their children being prosecution witnesses.

■ ■ ■

"I think I settled it with their father," Frankel said when he had returned from driving the boys home. "He'll humor the boys, and let them think they're just playing it up."

"Good," Silva said, relieved. He did not want two young kids running around town telling their friends that they had seen the murderer.

"Just in time, too," Frankel said.

"How do you mean?" Silva asked.

Frankel looked into the main room, then said in a lowered voice, "That guy from the *Traveler*. Someone must have called them."

Silva frowned. Newspaper reporters were rarely a problem in a small town, no matter what the crime and no matter who the suspect. But that seemed no longer an absolute truth. Some of the new reporters were so young and from so far away that they had none of the grounding in small-town life in this area that ensured tact and reports that conveyed only information no one would get upset about. Some of the new reporters wanted to win an award for dramatic writing with their first news job. Silva shuddered when he thought of what was riding on newspapers these days.

"Okay," Silva said, "give him just what we have and I'll talk to him later if he wants something more."

■ ■ ■

The reporter from the *Traveler* was still chatting with Frankel when Silva went out, and the chief didn't stop to talk. He walked swiftly and quietly out the side door, grateful for Frankel's measured, not to say sometimes painfully slow, speech. As the chief unlocked his cruiser, however, the young man appeared beside him. Mickey Concini, as he introduced himself with an outstretched hand, was young and eager, and very new to the business, which left Silva with the comforting thought that the young man's editor hadn't yet decided that this was an important story. In his jeans, shirt, and neatly pressed jacket, Mickey looked his age, physical and emotional. Not yet cynical and not yet too sophisticated to smile at the chief of police, Mickey displayed the easy friendliness of the recent college graduate. He smiled openly and looked directly at the chief. Silva had heard him laughing at one of Frankel's jokes and tagged him as a neophyte. Now the young man wanted to question him on every detail Frankel had given him, and Silva let him, considering it his contribution to his education. As ever, Silva answered with patience and courtesy. Satisfied that he had at least a small story to report to his editor, Concini finally put his notebook away.

"You know, Chief, there are a lot of rumors about the dead woman," the young man said.

"Are you looking into any of them?" Silva asked, still wary of the young man simply as a reporter.

"No, I'm just keeping my eyes open," he said with a wide innocent smile. "Someone said she was supposed to be really important in New York," he said, "but no one has tried to reach us from down there. My boss even made a couple of calls earlier today to some people he knew, but they didn't seem to think she was anything big." He paused to let Silva reply, but the chief said nothing. The reporter finally added, "So he put me on it."

Silva said nothing, unable to tell if the young man was

pulling his leg or not. It would be just like his editor, Silva thought, to send him a ringer. "You don't usually do the police desk, do you?"

"No," Concini agreed, "but if I'm going to stay in this area I'll probably have to get used to it."

"What do you mean, stay in this area? Do you want to stay or are you here for a few years of training?" Silva had long ago given up hope that the police departments in the area would have the same reporter for more than six months. The turnover rate among reporters-in-training at the local and regional papers irritated him when he found himself explaining the basics to young kids more than twice a year.

"I hope to stay, Chief," the reporter explained. "I grew up near here. I figure it's all in how well you write, and I can do that right here."

"Well, good luck," Silva said to him. As he got into his cruiser grumbling about how young the new reporters were and how ill-prepared they were to interpret and protect the First Amendment, he turned his mind from the soft whisper that what was really bothering him was that he now noticed how young they were. That was not a good sign, he felt, and he shook off his annoyance with himself for caring about it one way or the other.

■　■　■

The evidence of the two boys had opened up possibilities Silva had not imagined. He had never considered, for instance, the possibility that Beth O'Donnell had had a close male friend in the area when she visited. If a man had followed closely behind her to her cottage, which is what the boys insisted they had seen, she must have known him well, or at least well enough to feel comfortable bringing him along to the cottage late in the evening. It was also possible, Silva considered, for her to be simply delivering to him a note or a gift she had carried up from a friend in New York, but so far nothing like that had come out in any of the statements taken by the police. And that left him with a man who went with the victim back to her cottage and murdered her. Whoever he was, he had to be someone she knew well, felt comfortable with, and wanted to spend a little time with alone. So far nothing had pointed to any particular person. Flushing this bit of information out from under the thick shrubbery of gossip and rumor was not going to be easy.

Silva dropped the tempting morsel of the victim perhaps having had a secret male friend onto the ground in front of Mrs. Miles, remarking casually that he had never considered the idea, even the few times he had seen the victim alive during her earlier visits. From the look on Mrs. Miles's face as she polished the O'Donnell silver, listening politely if impatiently to the chief, she wasn't about to consider the idea now either, no matter what the chief of police might suggest.

"She never went out alone with a man, if that's what you're asking, Chief Silva. Not here in Mellingham in the sense you mean." Mrs. Miles finished a spoon and laid it on the kitchen table, then started on another one. When Silva had called to speak to Mrs. Miles, she had settled him at the kitchen table, where she obviously felt at home and in control, and continued with her work. "Miss O'Donnell," the housekeeper said, "went out with couples she knew or with a woman friend. But no gentleman friend."

"You make it sound almost impossible," Silva said.

Mrs. Miles looked across the table at him. "It is to my mind. She didn't come to see her friends. They were just extra."

"Well, her family, then," Silva prodded.

"Listen, Joe," she said, letting her hands fall into her lap. "She didn't come here out of any love for us or anyone else. Leastways, no one felt any love for her when she left. No one was sorry to see her go and no one wanted her coming back too soon."

"Then there's more to her visits than asking for money," Silva said.

The housekeeper studied him in silence. "I'll say," Mrs. Miles finally agreed. "Much more."

"Such as?"

Mrs. Miles finished another spoon and placed it neatly on the table. She was that odd mix of reticence, discretion, and gossip which translated into a woman who had a lot to say about most people but was careful about whom she spoke to and could as easily withhold as give away information. Silva waited, hoping she would see her way clear to speaking freely with him. After she had meticulously selected another spoon to receive her attentions, she said as though speaking to the spoon, "Nothing you could put your finger on, but Beth never liked not getting her own way."

"Why don't you tell me exactly what you mean, Mrs. Miles," the chief said, and settled back to listen. Mrs. Miles seemed relieved to get the story out of her system, and to one as sympathetic as Silva.

"She came up here every two years, fiddle faddled around trying to get the Mister to let go of his money, but he never understood that. Then she just got fed up and spent the rest of the time upsetting people. She didn't like coming up here and she didn't like not getting her own way. By the end of every visit, she had usually stirred up some trouble. It might take two months just to get people to settle down again. Sometimes even longer. She doesn't have a man friend because no man could stick with her for very long."

"Exactly what trouble," Silva asked.

She again studied him silently, listening to the quiet house. A door shut, footsteps came down the carpeted front stairs and crossed the hall, and a door closed. A car started and moved down the gravel drive. The house was still again.

"Missus has an engagement. Funeral home." So saying, Mrs. Miles again settled into her chair. "This is all gossip, Joe. You understand that?"

"I need to know what's going on, Mrs. Miles, even if it does seem like nothing to you."

This way of looking at the matter seemed to satisfy her, and she said, "Well, all right, then. Miss Beth didn't like not getting what she wanted," she began, "so she took it out on others. Usually it was just something small—a nasty little insult just when you're meeting someone new at a party—or something embarrassing like a wild goose chase. But a few years ago, she must have been mighty angry because her mischief got serious, you might say."

"What do you mean by serious?"

"At a party the O'Donnells had a few years ago when Miss O'Donnell was here, Mr. Handel was talking about finding his business easygoing and wondering what he should do next," Mrs. Miles began.

"Easygoing?" Silva repeated. "How do you mean?"

"He had a good steady income from his business—nothing grand, but steady—and he had a good reputation, but the challenge was gone," she said. "Well, don't you know Miss Beth stepped right in and started talking about how he could teach the young ones a thing or two about ambition and drive. And the next thing you know, he's talking a mile a minute about expanding and maybe getting others to come in with him. Grand plans, he had."

"That doesn't seem like anything," Silva said.

"Nor is it," she said, her voice rising in anger. "But then she goes back to New York and she gives Mr. Handel's name to an investor down there. And he was a shrewd sort. In no time, he and Mr. Handel were just great friends, seeing eye to eye on everything. Think they'd known each other all their lives."

"What happened?" Silva asked, knowing the answer already.

"He offered to loan Mr. Handel all the money he needed, and Mr. Handel took him up on it. He borrowed the money, spent it on the business, I guess," she said. "That wasn't so bad, I don't suppose, but it didn't stop there. One day, out of the blue it was, the investor called for his money, not six months after he'd loaned it. That was real bad, it was. What was the poor man to do, I ask you? Mr. Handel had to mort-gage everything he had and even then he had to borrow from friends to pay it all back. My God," she said, shaking her head. The mere thought of all that debt seemed to terrify Mrs. Miles.

"What did that mean to him financially?" Silva asked, wondering how much of her story was truth and how much the embellishment of a loyal friend. If this business loan proved to be relevant, Silva was going to have to get someone to interpret it for him. He could understand panic from the need to scram-ble for a large amount of money fast, but the bitterness in Mrs. Miles's recital suggested a more complex threat. Then again, the housekeeper might be taking on the grievance out of loyalty, unconsciously exaggerating the injury until it matched her feelings for the family. "How bad was it for him?"

"Almost broke him, it did. Spent it, he had, just as he was supposed to, and that man wanting it all back at once."

"He didn't consider it a loan come due? He must have known what could happen," Silva suggested, wondering just how much Mrs. Miles knew about it.

"It wasn't a loan coming due, Chief," she said.

"What do you mean?"

"It wasn't due. Only five months into the loan. Recalled for emergency something or other. Some special clause. I heard Mister and Missus talking about it and Mister said he'd never heard of that clause being used." She sat back in her chair, triumphant with her final evidence. "Never heard of it, he said."

■ ■ ■

Silva stirred his tea, thinking over what the housekeeper had told him. The problem with this kind of information was the spotlight it put on the speaker as well as the subject, but she had given him his first inkling of a motive and he wanted to explore it as rationally as was possible with Mrs. Miles. He had therefore asked her for a cup of tea, hoping the familiar domestic activity would calm her down, and it had.

"Did Mr. Handel ever talk to the O'Donnells about the loan and its recall?" Silva asked.

"No," she said with a deep sigh. She stirred her tea, clicking the spoon against the side of the teacup at each twirl through the creamy liquid. "Mr. Handel never told the O'Donnells, so Mister couldn't do anything openly. But he must have known. We all thought he must have had a hand in helping get things worked out."

"Do you think Mr. Handel blamed Miss O'Donnell?"

"Well, wouldn't you?" she said indignantly, not answering his question. "Of course he did. And so did I."

That, thought Silva, was obvious. Aloud, he asked, "What about the O'Donnells? Did they blame her? Did you ever hear them say anything to her?"

"Well, no, not exactly. I never heard them say anything to her over the phone, but the Mister was never the same to her afterward. Mister never wanted to talk about it. Not to anyone, not even the Missus. And don't go asking me how I know that," she said to him. "I know how it was. All that anyone would own up to was that there was a private problem. It was just Mr. Handel, a good friend, in unexpected money trouble."

"You're suggesting, Mrs. Miles, that Beth O'Donnell, because her brother wouldn't hand over control of a substantial sum of money, deliberately set out to bankrupt a friend of her brother," he said carefully.

"Not suggesting, Joe. Not suggesting. I'm telling you that's exactly what she did."

"You're also saying that the investor agreed to help her do this."

"No. No, I'm not saying that." She pondered this. "Not that. I'm saying that Miss O'Donnell was one of those people who know how to set people on the path to trouble even if she doesn't walk every step with them. That's what I'm saying."

"What about the last time she was here, two years ago?

SUSAN OLEKSIW

Who did she upset then?" Silva asked, trying to probe from a different angle.

Mrs. Miles became quiet. "You think I'm fanciful about this," she said to him. "I know you do, but I'm not. You learn to be alert with that one around. You can believe me or not, Joe Silva. It's all the same to me. I'll not change my mind. That one was trouble," she said. "I never relaxed while she was here, nor did she; not her and not me." She sighed. "All right. Two years ago you want to know about? Two years ago she took a new interest in Medge, not a kind interest either."

Silva shook his head and added this to his notebook. "What form did this interest take?"

The housekeeper stopped tapping her toe. "Kept asking Medge about what sort of things she and Frank liked doing."

"That doesn't seem so bad," Silva commented.

"They don't do these things together," she said. Silva didn't glance up, but he was surprised nonetheless.

"Do you think Miss O'Donnell knew that?" he asked.

"She knew that all right. They've been taking separate vacations for a few years now. Beth was just rubbing it in, making Medge feel bad." Mrs. Miles's distress at what she imagined to be Medge's distress was palpable.

"That still doesn't seem so bad," he repeated.

"Maybe not to you," she said. "But the two, Frank and Medge, were at one of those sort of delicate times, you might say. Anyway, Lisa Hunt kept it from getting any worse."

"Lisa? What did she do?" Silva had not envisioned Lisa in the role of protector.

"Beth dropped in on a luncheon Medge was having for some friends and started to comment about Medge's marriage as though she didn't mean to let the secret about their troubles slip out of the bag, but Lisa put a stop to it." Mrs. Miles smiled at the memory. "Turned to her and said bold as you please, 'Why don't you wait for everyone so we can all hear what you have to say?' So then everyone looked at Miss Beth and what

128

could she say?" Mrs. Miles chuckled. "Then Lisa just smiled at her."

"And Miss O'Donnell?"

"Well, she started to say something, but Lisa stopped her again by telling everyone to pay close attention to what Miss O'Donnell said next." Mrs. Miles chuckled at the recollection.

"What did she say?"

"Nothing. After that, what could she say? She had to leave," the housekeeper explained. "Lisa made sure everyone kept staring at her."

Silva permitted himself a smile as he made a note.

"That Lisa," she said warmly, "always was a nice girl."

"And that was the end of that?" Silva asked, enjoying Mrs. Miles's definition of a nice girl.

"Beth was careful with Medge after that," she said. "Kept her distance, she did." The recollection of Beth finally having been confounded obviously pleased Mrs. Miles, and she continued to chuckle softly to herself some moments longer.

"How long would it take her to set her sights on a likely target," Silva asked, his picture of the victim growing clearer minute by minute.

"Not long," Mrs. Miles said. "That one got riled up so easy, she did. Couldn't handle not getting her own way. Went right to the Mister soon as she got here."

"This visit?" Silva asked quickly. "Did she go after him on Saturday, as soon as she arrived?"

"That she did. Fair ruined his day, she did, not that she'd care, not that one. Never cared about anyone but herself."

"Mrs. Miles," Silva said, "did she actually ask him for control of her money before the party?"

"That she did. Didn't I tell you I heard the Mister and the Missus talking about it?"

Silva considered quickly what that might mean in terms of suspects, and then changed directions. "There's been some talk that she was going to write a book. Did you hear anything about this?"

"A book?" Mrs. Miles was outraged. "That one? What sort of book?"

"I don't know. I thought you could tell me," Silva said, intrigued at her reaction.

"Gossip it would be," she said indignantly. "Every malicious story she'd ever heard. Probably get sued. Spend the rest of her life fighting libel suits. Serve her right." Mrs. Miles contemplated this delightful prospect until she recalled with disappointment that Beth could no longer be expected to live out this promising scenario. Her smile faded.

"It must have been just a rumor," Silva said.

"Some people will say anything," Mrs. Miles agreed. "If she were alive, she'd probably say it herself. Brag about her journals and all the people she's known."

"She kept journals?" Silva said calmly, almost stunned.

"She kept records of everything, or so she said." She cast a stern eye at Silva. "Not a good thing to brood over the day gone by. You wouldn't be doing that, would you?" So saying she cast an accusatory eye on his notebook, and Silva, unconsciously, drew it closer to him.

"Just notes of things I have to do or to remember to check. That's all." He smiled lamely.

"Well, I suppose that's all right," she allowed with a skeptical look.

"How do you know she kept a journal?" Silva asked, hoping he had indeed heard her correctly and that she had meant what she said. "There wasn't one in the cottage."

"What? What do you mean no journal out there?" She rose heavily as if she meant to go check that very moment. Silva persuaded her to sit down again, assuring her that they had thoroughly searched the cottage but had found no journal. But Mrs. Miles was adamant, describing at great length the small clothbound books that had appeared regularly on the dressing table during every biennial visit, sitting right next to the bottles of expensive perfume that were, in the housekeeper's opinion, wasted on a woman like Beth O'Donnell.

7

TUESDAY AFTERNOON

SILVA ROLLED UP the white deli paper from his sandwich and tossed it into the wastebasket by his desk. The late spring afternoon worked its magic on the town and the police department as well, softening worries and emergencies to milder matters and leaving the police department quieter than it usually was in the middle of the week. Silva was grateful for the time and quiet to go over what he knew now about the murder with Sergeant Dupoulis, who was using every opportunity to learn more. "And that's it," Silva said. "It doesn't sound like much, but it is."

Dupoulis nodded while he assimilated the information. "I see what you mean by the murder taking shape even though we don't know what the shape is yet."

"The woman's journals should tell us something when they get here," Silva continued, "but I think she must have followed her usual pattern this year. If she had her first go-round with Mr. O'Donnell right after she arrived, and if she'd already failed, then she'd have been angry by the time of the party."

"And she probably looked around for a likely victim," Dupoulis said, following the chief's train of thought, "and found one." He paused. "That means, Chief, that any one of the guests could have been a victim."

"Not quite," Silva said. "If Mrs. Miles is right, Miss O'Donnell had a different victim every visit. But from the sounds of it she wasn't arbitrary or scattered in her attentions," he said wryly. "This is speculation, but she sounds like she had a pattern, and she would have been following it by the time of the party. She would have picked out someone in a conversation and taken a few preliminary shots, just to test her victim's resistance or vulnerability," he said. "And she was subtle. She didn't go in with a sledgehammer. She picked at her victim, a little at a time."

"Except that this time," Dupoulis said, "she grossly miscalculated how her victim would feel about it."

"That's right. This time she picked a target and the target fought back," Silva said. "She could not have known how serious the situation was and she probably didn't pick up any warning signals either. She may even have reached that point where she was no longer aware that her behavior was way out of line." He added, "Once something gets to be a habit, we stop wondering if it's right or wrong."

"So the murderer has to be someone she spent more than a few seconds with, someone she could have talked to long enough to scare," Dupoulis said thoughtfully. "Someone who was at the party long enough for her to bump into more than once, without making it look obvious."

"That's going to be a short list: Howard O'Donnell, Bob Chambers, Mr. Morrison, Frank Vinton," Silva said.

"Mr. Steinwell," Dupoulis added.

"And Lee Handel," Silva said, "if we include the possibility of an earlier victim being the murderer, someone still bitter who decides to fight back."

"They're all men," Dupoulis pointed out.

"Do you think I'm being sexist?" Silva asked good-naturedly.

"Yes, sir," his sergeant responded in kind. "You're thinking of what the kids said, about seeing the man coming right behind Miss O'Donnell."

"That's right," Silva agreed. "They saw a man coming right after, someone they took to be her husband."

"But they only saw a pair of legs wearing pants," Dupoulis pointed out.

Silva kicked himself for not catching it first, but congratulated his sergeant for picking up on it and correcting him. He nodded as the younger man went on.

"Several of the women guests were probably wearing slacks, particularly Mrs. Handel. She probably hasn't worn a dress in years," Dupoulis said.

"You're right, Sergeant, you're right," Silva said, "and that works both ways. It seems to leave out all the other women at the party, including Lisa Hunt. And Mrs. Handel could have the same motive as her husband—revenge for what Beth did to her and his business."

"According to what we've got so far, Mrs. Handel didn't speak to Miss O'Donnell," Dupoulis said, "but Miss O'Donnell is supposedly to blame for how bad things got for the Handels. It may not be reasonable, but if the Handels went to the party, saw the victim, the woman who almost ruined them, saw her going after someone else, or even thought she was going after one of them again, well, it could have triggered something."

"That's definitely a possibility," Silva said. "Add her to the list, and her husband. Anyone else?"

"Yes, sir," Dupoulis said. "Jim Kellogg."

Silva raised an eyebrow. "From the caterers?" Silva was skeptical, but only said, "Go on."

"He's very jumpy, sir. Doesn't like talking about anything connected with any of it. I asked him about anything he could recall about the party, any scraps of conversation, anything odd. For him it should have been just a report of a job, but when I was talking to him up at the Agawam, I got the feeling something else was going on."

"Something to do with the murder?" Silva asked.

"I can't tell, sir," Dupoulis replied. "But it made me uncomfortable, and I didn't think I should overlook it."

"Okay. Follow it up. It's probably something unconnected with the murder," the chief said more hopefully than he felt.

■ ■ ■

"One tongue, a dozen hearts, and how many fingers?"

"Four dozen should do it," Jim Kellogg said, sitting languorously on the porch of the Agawam Inn and surveying the rich pink blooms of the wall of rhododendrons on the edge of the lawn.

"Okay, I'll do the fingers," Medge said, and copied down a recipe for finger sandwiches. They were sitting at one end of the veranda at a table strewn with small recipe cards, pages torn from *Gourmet* magazine, and pictures of rooms in English hotels set for savory or sweet teas. The breeze was soft and slow, enough to ruffle the leaves of a nearby bush but not enough to flip a card from the table. The sun was pink behind the clouds, and the warmth was enough to slow down the determined pace of the young.

"Sorry about your aunt," Jim said into the silence.

"Thank you," Medge said without looking up. She went on copying, her sandaled feet crossed at the ankles beneath the table.

"I think I've talked Mr. Campbell into laying out the weekend tea on the side lawn. Not too much sun. Nice breeze. Nice gardens. Fragrant." Jim delivered this news in a cheerful voice as he looked around him.

"No view of the ocean," Medge said without lifting her pen from her notes.

"Listen, Medge," Jim said. "People come for the food, not the view. If they want views, they can go up in an airplane or a balloon." With a scowl spreading across his face, he wiped out the hotel's one remaining asset.

Medge watched him politely through this tirade before saying, "Did you have a run-in with someone?"

"What?" he asked in confusion.

"Did you have an argument with someone?" she repeated, looking directly at him for some sign.

"No," he said, nonplussed. "Why do you ask?"

"I just thought you seemed a little jumpy."

"Me? Jumpy?"

"Yes, you."

"Really?" he said. "Well, I'm not. I'm not jumpy. Never have been. I run a nice, smooth business, and I've been doing it long enough to know what I'm doing."

"Jim, what're you talking about?" she asked. "All I said was that you seemed on edge about something, that's all."

"Listen, Medge, business is a risk, that's all. I want this new sideline to go well. So just work with me, not against me. Okay? Okay?"

"Sure, Jim, sure." Medge smiled, and nodded at him and Jim slouched back into his chair, turning to the list of foods for the tea and arrangements for the coming weekend.

"I think ten tables of four seats each should be enough," he said. "Then people won't feel crowded and conversations will seem intimate." He looked over at the side garden, which had become so lush that the neighbors could no longer see through the bushes.

"I still don't understand what was wrong with the roof," Medge said as she followed Jim's eye to the garden. "The view is gorgeous. And the dumbwaiter works now."

"Unreliable. Entirely too unreliable."

"But—"

"Look," he said, cutting her off. "We have to get these details straightened out. Could we stop talking about the roof?" He sat up in his chair and hunched over his notes. "You're just like your aunt."

Stunned, Medge stared at him with her mouth open until he turned to her when she failed to answer a casual question about sandwiches. His self-defense of a moment earlier dissolved as soon as he saw her look of shock and hurt.

"Oh, Medge, gee, I'm sorry, I only meant—" he said. "I

meant . . ." He stumbled around for an explanation while Medge pulled herself and her notes together.

"It's all right, Jim," she said as she put her pen in her purse.

"No, please, don't go," he said in a rush. "I didn't mean that."

"What did you mean?" she snapped back.

"Nothing, nothing," he said, looking around wildly for an answer to his dilemma. "I only meant that your aunt liked the roof deck, too, that's all, and she said she might have a party for her friends at the Agawam while she was here."

"Aunt Beth wanted to have a party here at the Agawam?" Medge asked in surprise.

"Yes, that's what she said, and she asked me at the party the other night if I'd be interested in catering it. Just a small thing, she said. So I said yes. I thought it would be a good deal for the business."

"Yes, it would have been," Medge agreed.

"Then she said she'd heard about the new roof deck," he said, finally running out of breath. "Oh God, I thought I'd die," he said softly to himself.

"Why?" Medge asked. "I don't understand why you think it's such a terrible spot."

"It just is," he insisted.

"Is that what you told her? That it wasn't a good spot?"

"Yeah. How did you know? I didn't see you around. Were you nearby?"

"No," Medge said. "But I can see why you'd be edgy after talking to Aunt Beth about it. I can just imagine it. She never liked anyone telling her she couldn't have something. If you tried to get her to accept something else, like a party in the garden, she probably wanted the roof deck all the more. Telling her something she wanted wasn't a good idea was like a red flag to her." Medge shook her head. "No wonder you don't want to hear about the roof deck right now."

"Yeah." Jim laughed with relief as he settled back in his chair.

"I'll admit you had me worried, Jim."

He watched her while she reopened her purse, pulled out her pen, and again spread her notes out on the table. "Where was I?" she said. "Oh yes. The pâté. I don't think a pâté in the shape of a heart is appropriate."

"Okay. You know best about something like that. You pick something else," he said, standing up. "I want to check on the cutlery and the china." He dropped the notebook on his chair and went off in the direction of the dining room, wiping the sweat from his forehead and leaving Medge satisfied by her insight into the transformation of the lanky and amiable Jim Kellogg.

■ ■ ■

The offices of the Marine Press were located in the wing of the Handels' home. The main house, a colonial with gray painted clapboards, sat at the edge of the brick sidewalk. The wing, perpendicular to the main building, formed with it a small courtyard, which also faced the street. The only indication that the house contained a business was a small sign of black letters on a white board nailed to the side of the wing facing the street. Since the door to the business was at the far end, both home and business had a feeling of privacy if not independence. The old iron anchor that had been used as decoration in the courtyard was now overrun with vines of ivy and blocked from various angles by clusters of columbine in the summer. Only in the dead of winter could anyone get a good look at it, and then only if there was no snow. The courtyard was part of Mrs. Handel's overall scheme of gardens, and so far none of the old-timers had objected to the loss of the anchor from their view.

Although Silva knew the site of the press well, he had never had reason to go inside and he was curious to see where

Lee Handel worked and the business that had appealed to Lisa Hunt, enticing her back to Mellingham from a better-paying job in Boston. He opened the screen door and stepped into an office, where Lisa sat behind a desk reading a recent issue of a high-fashion magazine. Her desk was bare except for a blotter, a telephone, and a pile of four neatly typed letters with envelopes attached. On a low table behind her sat a small bud vase with three pansies in it and a photograph whose subject Silva couldn't make out. She held in her hands, according to Silva's quick glance around the small office, the only magazine in the room. The wall behind her, which was to his right, and the wall directly opposite him were lined with bookshelves, which held the many titles on business history and cartography the press had published over the years. There was an occasional bright paper dust jacket, but most of the volumes had the serious look that came from dark cloth or leather bindings with minimal stamping on the spine. Although it had been many years since the Marine Press had been a publisher exclusively of marine books, the office probably looked much the same as it always had. The old back room of the wing was painted off-white, the oak desk was small and old but serviceable, and the few prints hanging on the walls depicted ships of various periods. In a few years they would probably have a value unimaginable to their original purchasers. Silva turned to greet Lisa, who had been watching him with a smile on her face.

"You've never been here before, have you?" she asked him.

"No," he admitted. "But now that I see what you have, I wish I'd come sooner." He indicated the shelves of books.

"Those are the old ones," she said. "Our most recent titles are over there." She nodded to a new bookshelf installed by the front door, and Silva turned for a moment to look over half a dozen shelves of books with brightly colored dust jackets. When he turned back to the desk, he looked directly at her magazine and then up at her. She followed his eyes until they reached hers and said, "I'm maintaining my balance today. Most of the week we're all improving our minds. Every now and then I take a break to improve my sense of humor. After summer fashion I expect to move on to a book about absurd place names." She smiled up at him and waited for a reply. Silva didn't dare. He asked for Bob Chambers's office and followed Lisa's directions, leaving her leaning back in her chair with the magazine sitting in her lap, propped up against the desk.

Bob Chambers's office was up a narrow flight of stairs, typical of a colonial house, and a few steps down the hall. Since the door was open, Silva stepped into the room quietly, listening to Chambers talking on the telephone. Having swung his chair around so that he faced the small colonial windows that looked onto the courtyard and the street, the young editor was going head to head with someone over the cost of shipping boxes. Although he could hear only one side of the conversation, Silva sensed that, for Chambers at least, this was more than a simple business call.

"That wasn't our agreement," Chambers said to the voice on the other end of the line. "There may well be a clause for that, but we'd still have to come to some sort of understanding about whether or not this is an emergency for you. We'd have to have some sort of evidence—" Chambers broke off in midsentence and then continued. "Editor," he said. "I'm sure Mr. Handel is glad to know you predate him," Chambers continued, "and we're glad you've worked with the press for so long, but that doesn't really have anything to do with this problem, does it?" The insinuation of superiority in his voice must have irritated the other person, because Chambers finally replied firmly with more than a trace of pleasure, "A contract is a contract, and we expect you to honor it." He swiveled back to face his desk and dropped the receiver onto its cradle without a final salutation. Silva thought he could hear a voice from the receiver as the phone hit the cradle. Only then did Chambers notice that Silva was in the room.

"Hello, Chief," Chambers said in surprise. If it was anything more than that Silva couldn't tell. The younger man recovered himself quickly, stretched out his hand for a brief handshake, and motioned Silva to a chair. The room was painted white and had the wide plank flooring of colonial houses. The windows, six panes over eight panes, were set low in the walls and the ceiling was barely seven feet, Silva estimated, glad he was not wearing his hat. The chairs and the desk were modern office furniture. Against one wall was a wooden unit of large square cubby holes, most of them containing a manuscript in one of the various stages of production. There was a calendar on the wall opposite the wooden unit. This was the only decoration in the room and Silva guessed it was there for practical rather than aesthetic reasons. To the bare bones of the office Bob Chambers had not added a picture, a statue, a photograph, a book, a coat rack—not a thing that revealed his taste or interests or connections in life. Silva settled back in his canvas chair and noted that it was the regulation three inches or so lower than the one Chambers was using. Glad of his height, Silva was still better than eye level with Chambers, who did not fail to notice this.

Chambers's answers to Silva's preliminary questions did not lead Silva to change his mind about him: a reserved and ambitious young man who knew where he wanted to go if not exactly how he was going to get there. More to the point, however, the young man was answering the questions so easily that Silva was afraid he'd slide right by something important.

"Had you ever met Miss O'Donnell before the party?" Silva asked.

"No," Chambers said, the failure of the seating arrangements still rankling in him.

"Had you heard about her?"

"Not much," he said, sitting up as straight as possible.

"Just her reputation for entertaining and being seen with all the right people."

"Who introduced you to her?" the chief asked.

"I don't recall," the editor said shortly. He caught himself and explained, "I may have introduced myself. There were so many people moving around. It was all very informal."

"But you got to speak to her anyway."

"It was a party, Chief. I spoke to lots of people," Chambers said, backing off from any involvement.

"What time did you leave?"

"It must have been about ten-thirty," Chambers said.

"And where did you go?" the chief asked, making a note.

"I took Lisa Hunt home," he said.

"Arriving when?"

"I'm not really sure. I drove her straight home. We didn't go anywhere else." Chambers's manner was becoming more abrupt as Silva's became laxer.

"Did you arrive just after ten-thirty? Maybe ten-forty?" Silva asked.

"Probably."

"Not closer to eleven?" Silva suggested.

Chambers stopped swiveling back and forth in his chair and looked hard at the chief. "Is that what Lisa told you?"

"It's what I'm asking you, Mr. Chambers," the chief said, no longer smiling.

Chambers looked steadily back at him. "Then, yes. It must have been closer to eleven," he said without emotion.

"Does that mean you left closer to eleven than to ten-thirty?"

Chambers glared at Silva but finally said, "No. You've spoken to Lisa, I suppose." He waited. "Well, if you have, then you probably know that I went back to talk to Beth O'Donnell one last time," Chambers said with more than a hint of resentment in his voice.

"Go on," was all Silva said.

"I thought if I could speak to her alone we could settle a business matter."

"And did you speak to her?" Silva persisted, reminding himself that it was at such moments that a good officer was scrupulously fair regardless of his opinion of a suspect. "Did you?" he repeated more strongly.

"No," the younger man said. "She was gone. I saw her earlier saying good night to people at the door, but I didn't see her when I went back. I waited around for a few minutes, but I never saw her. And by that time almost everyone else was leaving and I felt a little foolish standing there as though I wanted to say good-bye a second time, so I left—again." Bob Chambers was never going to be one who found honesty a rewarding experience; he was growing testier with each of Silva's questions.

"Did you speak to anyone when you went back in?"

"I asked one of the caterers if Beth was around, but he said he hadn't seen her," Chambers answered.

"That's all?"

"Yes. No, actually. I saw some of the last guests getting ready to leave but I didn't want to ask them if they had seen Beth, so I just left."

"Who was left?"

"Just the caterers and the family and a few of their close friends."

"Where was Lisa all this time?"

"I asked her to wait in the car," he said. "This was business, Mr. Silva. And Lisa is nice, but . . ."

"She didn't mind being left alone in the car all that time?" Silva asked.

"No, at least she didn't say anything to me about it," Chambers said, dismissing his companion's feelings.

"Tell me about your business with Miss O'Donnell," Silva said, noting that the sudden change in topic threw Chambers momentarily off balance, but he recovered instantly.

"Certainly," he said smoothly. He smiled, and settled back in his chair. "I thought she might have a book in her. She seems to know a lot of people in New York and has for a long time. I thought we might work something up."

"What did she say to that?"

"I think there was interest," he said with satisfaction.

"That's all?" Silva asked.

"That's all," Chambers repeated. "We never had a chance to get down to specifics."

"How far did you get?"

Chambers was stymied by this question, his ego pushing him to challenge every question Silva raised but his sense of caution telling him to answer only the minimum and answer carefully. This question wasn't as easy to deflect, and he glared at the chief.

"We just talked about it," Chambers said, caution winning out over ego, "in a general sort of way."

"Too bad you didn't get any further," Silva said, standing up. "It might have led to something."

■ ■ ■

The warm spring breeze on the veranda of the Agawam Inn was known to turn into a stultifying summer air that drove guests into the bar for a cool drink. Most of those arriving for tea, elderly women who had outlived at least one husband, had not yet found the veranda at all unpleasant, and were contentedly spread along its breadth to enjoy the sights and smells of Mellingham, at least to the extent they could still make them out at their age and their distance from any other inhabitants of the village—all except one. Mr. Morrison, who had chosen to find the light breeze oppressive, had removed himself to the lounge, where he was at that moment sitting at the bar, slowly sipping a gin and tonic and desultorily chatting with the bartender, a young man in his twenties who had only recently graduated from college and then taken a course in mixing drinks, much to the horror of his middle-class and still-aspiring parents. The young man, for his part, was just following his curiosity. At this moment, Mr. Morrison might have hoped he would show some curiosity in another area.

"Actually, there was something else my wife heard," Mr. Morrison said, but the young man merely nodded while flipping through a bartender's guide. "Something about an outsider," he said vaguely, but still the young man showed no sign of interest. Chief Silva could not fail to notice this as he stepped to the end of the bar and asked for a soft drink. He had come here looking specifically for Mr. Morrison on the premise that those who were unwilling to give information would be the most likely ones to be out looking for it. For Mr. Morrison that meant discreet eavesdropping or insinuating himself into local groups gossiping about the murder. And the most likely place for that in the afternoon was the Agawam Inn. Unfortunately, Mr. Morrison hadn't counted on the bartender's ignorance or lack of interest. All of which meant there was no conversation for Silva to interrupt and no polite way for Mr. Morrison to demur when the chief invited him to sit down with him for a few minutes at a table by the window.

Chief Silva was not averse to the beauty of the old inn and was willing to show the proper appreciation for Mr. Morrison's comments about the attractiveness of the inn, the quaintness of the village, and the obvious pull of sentiment for a former home.

"Makes it an ideal spot," Silva finally said. By now Mr. Morrison was thoroughly relaxed and readily agreed.

"Indeed, indeed," he said. "And it never changes," he added. "Never. Always the same. One of Mellingham's chief attractions to my wife's mind. Hasn't been worried, don't you know, by all these modern fellas putting up houses everywhere they can knock down two trees for space."

Silva nodded, and Mr. Morrison went on. "Can't even think how many years it's been that we've been coming back here," he mused. "Actually, probably more than twenty or twenty-five, I would say," he calculated as he turned a smug face to Silva. "Before that we lived here, you know."

Silva allowed as how he had known this, and said, "You lived here for some time, didn't you?"

"Indeed, indeed," Mr. Morrison said heartily. "Grew up here. Both of us. Knew everyone back then. Everyone. I even remember when this hotel still had its pond, don't you know."

Silva admitted that he hadn't known that, and hadn't really known anything about the inn in its halcyon days.

"Really?" thundered Mr. Morrison, though he thundered only in a decorous manner. This, in Mr. Morrison's view, was a great lapse, on whose part he didn't say, and he proceeded to educate Chief Silva on the fascinating and intricate history of the Agawam Inn. Silva listened to the tales of famous guests who had taken tea on the veranda during a visit with friends who owned estates nearby and a catalogue of dinner parties and small, exclusive dances held in the 1950s. Silently working out Mr. Morrison's age, Silva realized that the older man was not being careful to distinguish between debutante parties he attended as a college man and those he must have heard about from his parents. Everything was being run together into a single glorious memory.

"The parties today must be pale by comparison," Silva said.

"Nothing like the old days," Mr. Morrison agreed.

"I suppose the O'Donnells' parties have changed over the years, too," Silva said, looking over at his companion.

"Indeed, indeed," he said automatically.

"Certainly fewer people, I guess," Silva said.

"Indeed, indeed," Mr. Morrison said. "I recall they had parties of well over a hundred guests when they first moved here. That would have been the end of the 1950s or thereabouts. Wonderful affairs," he concluded. "Everything just so."

"I once heard they had a big party with over twenty-five people just to serve," Silva said.

"That's what's called doing it right," Mr. Morrison said superciliously. "Linen cloths, tables and chairs with outside lighting, flowers on all the tables."

"Dance floor set outside," Silva suggested, and the other man nodded in agreement.

"At least a ten-piece band," Mr. Morrison said.

"Tents over the dance floor and seating."

"Attendants to park cars," Mr. Morrison said.

"Engraved invitations," Silva said. Mr. Morrison nodded and the chief continued, saying, "Quite different from today and what Mrs. O'Donnell sent out this time."

"Quite," said Mr. Morrison abruptly, raising his glass to catch the attention of the bartender, who was still closely reading his manual.

"What color was the paper now?" Silva said into the air. "Not plain white like most invitations. What was it?" he said turning to Mr. Morrison.

"I don't recall," the older man said, on the verge of getting up when the bartender disappeared through a door into another part of the inn. "Do you take a holiday?" Mr. Morrison suddenly asked Silva.

"I'm sometimes persuaded to accept an invitation from friends," Silva said.

"I see," said Mr. Morrison with a sigh. He relaxed again in his chair and said, "Ah well, man to man, you know how it is?" He tried a hearty laugh, but what came out sounded like a strangled frog. "These women have their own ideas and one just has to go along with them." He tried another laugh, this time with some success. "Well, as my wife said, they've been friends for such a long time. We can overlook a little confusion."

"Old friends, yes," Silva said noncommittally. "So you and Mrs. Morrison learned about the party on Saturday, when Miss O'Donnell arrived."

"Oh no, no, no," Mr. Morrison said indignantly. "Why, Beth and my wife talked during the previous week. We knew perfectly well she was coming. Wanted us to have time to make our plans," he said, looking down his nose as best he could at the man who was still several inches taller even while leaning back comfortably in a rattan chair. "A most considerate woman," said Mr. Morrison. "Wouldn't dream of simply forgetting about her old friends." As if to reinforce his argument, he turned in his chair and called loudly to the young bartender, who, surprised but still polite, was arriving with the required drink just as Chief Silva was walking away down the veranda.

■ ■ ■

Merrilee counted the balls of yarn, decided she had enough, and dropped the yellow balls one by one into a basket at her feet. Throughout the tedious work of rolling the yarn she had looked across the upstairs sitting room at her husband, who was lounging in an armchair, his feet flat on the pale white carpet, his hands resting on the arms of his chair, his head back, and his chin up. Every now and then he blinked furiously and then his face was still, until the next wave of blinking. Finally, as she dropped the last ball into the basket Merrilee could stand it no longer. Not only had Howard sought her out up here, a rare occurrence in pleasant weather, but he had then remained silent during the entire time he had been sitting with her.

"What are you doing, dear?" she finally asked. Since he failed to show any signs of having heard her, she asked again, the second time more loudly.

"Eh? Hm?" Howard said, looking around to see if he could identify what had interrupted his thoughts. "Ah," he said when he noticed Merrilee looking expectantly at him; he smiled back at her. She called out her question a third time.

"Thinking," he replied.

"About anything in particular?" she asked as she picked up a pattern book for a series of sweaters.

"Ah, well, yes," he said.

"That's nice," she said vaguely as she studied a pattern.

"Chief Silva is coming by in a few minutes," he explained.

"Really?" She put down the book. "Any reason or just—"

"Well," Howard said, uncertain how to proceed. "I think he wants to ask me something." He raised a pudgy hand to his tie, straightened it, and prepared to stand.

"Darling Howie," Merrilee began, startling Howard, who eyed her suspiciously. His wife was casually affectionate, not excessively so. "Dear" was normal, "darling Howie" was not. He waited.

"Howard darling," she began again after noticing him start suddenly in his chair, "haven't you already spoken to the police?"

"Yes," Howard said, after thinking this over quickly.

"So they're probably asking for minor details now, to fill in the gaps, so to speak," Merrilee said, all the while holding the pattern book firmly in her lap.

Howard blinked several times and finally acknowledged this might be true.

"Then that means," she said brightly, "that you don't have to trouble them with confusing old stories about other people. Isn't that right, darling?" She looked straight at him.

Howard blinked several times, failed to find a file in which to place this information, so he merely nodded in apparent agreement.

"Good," said Merrilee firmly as she returned to reading her pattern book. And so the two sat, in amiable but silent confusion, each puzzling over a personal problem—Merrilee, over translating the pattern into another size, and Howard, over his last conversation with his sister. No matter how he examined it, it did not point to impending murder. It had just been a typical conversation with his sister. And now, he cast a skeptical eye at his wife, for she too was beginning to initiate confusing conversations. Unfortunately for Howard, Merrilee glanced up at him at that very moment and caught the suspicion in his eye.

"Howard," she said sharply.

"Yes, dear," he said, jolted into rational awareness by her sharp tone.

"You're not going to start suspecting everyone in this house, are you?" she ordered him.

"No, dear," said Howard, now doubly confused.

"Good," said his wife as she returned to her pattern book. "We don't want to confuse the police with irrelevancies."

"Ah," said Howard, working hard to compute the conversation.

■ ■ ■

And so, in a frame of mind more distracted than even his usual state of distraction, Howard O'Donnell greeted Chief Silva and settled him in the living room. With his thoughts full of his wife's opaque advice and his sister's illogical last conversation about catamarans and fulcrums, Howard listened as attentively as he could to the chief's questions and attempted to answer them with a precision and succinctness that Silva rarely encountered. Indeed, so succinct were they that Silva was thinking of looking into Howard O'Donnell's background more closely.

"It's not clear to me, Mr. O'Donnell, where you were during the party," Silva said.

"I was here," Howard replied.

"How about at ten-thirty?"

"Hmmm," Howard said. "I was talking to someone, and then they left. I think I was also briefly speaking to Mr. Steinwell. He was just saying something to Mrs. Handel, and then she rushed off, and I guess I caught the end of one conversation and it turned into another one. Hmm. Ahh, and then Lee Handel."

"Anyone else?" Silva asked.

"No, just those people until Lee and Hannah left."

"I understand you gave Mr. Handel a bird feeder," Silva said.

"Ah, yes. I showed him the bird feeder out in the garden. Lee was most appreciative of the design, so I, ah, gave it to him." Silva had to strain to hear the last few words, which Howard mumbled.

"Did you meet anyone else out there?"

"No, no. Most of the guests were gone by then. There was no one around at all," Howard said.

"Are you quite certain? This could be very important, Mr. O'Donnell."

"Yes, I'm certain. I saw Mrs. Handel in the side hall as we went out, and of course we passed Frank, my son-in-law. He was in the hall too. There was no one else there. And no one outside."

"How long were you out there?" Silva asked.

"Not long. Let me see. Perhaps five or ten minutes," Howard estimated after scanning the ceiling for guidance. "Closer to five minutes."

"What did you do then?"

"Well, we came inside, and Hannah and Lee left, right after Mr. Steinwell. Do you know him?" Howard asked. "Interesting man. Fabrics," he said as much to himself as to Chief Silva.

"And after everyone had left?"

"Afterward?" Howard said. "Well, I watched the caterers for a while. They have a system for collecting and washing glasses; we discussed it, so to speak. I don't think I quite understood. Hmmm. I watched Merrilee. She fell asleep in the living room. Hmmm. I went upstairs. To bed. It was late," he concluded, bringing an end to the evening and his recital of it.

"Thank you, sir. That's very clear," Silva said. "What about the book your sister was writing?"

"Book? I never heard about a book," Howard said, genuinely stumped. He cast about in his mind for some clue to the answer that he assumed must be hidden in the question, but he found none. He was about to dismiss the very idea of a book when Silva moved ahead.

"Someone overheard your sister talking about it," the chief said.

"I know nothing about this," Howard said at a loss. "But it is entirely possible, I suppose." He thought for a moment, then added, "It's not like her, but it is possible."

"I suppose she would be writing about New York social life?" Silva suggested.

"I suppose so," Howard agreed skeptically. "To tell the truth, I don't know." He blinked furiously, but nothing popped up on the screen of his mind. "I don't recall any-thing so noteworthy in her letters that would be worth a book."

"But she knew a lot of important people?" Silva asked.

Howard admitted this might be true, but could add noth-ing to it. As he pondered the fact of her murder, his sister took on the cast of a stranger, a person now described by others in alien terms from alien perspectives. He was becoming aware of just how little attention he had given to her life. His reasoning behind his responses to her had always been in part that she had never sought his attention and in part that he was reluctant to engage a life so inimical to his nature. And now he felt a twinge of regret for failing to listen more closely to her. She was turning out to be a woman of surprises, and Howard was not comfortable with surprises.

"That would explain her connection with Mr. Handel," Silva said. Howard started, then shifted in his chair but said nothing. Silva continued, "It seems the obvious solution, if your sister wanted to write a book, to get an offer from a friend who was a publisher." Howard moved further back in his chair, rapidly scanning his earlier conversation with Merrilee for a clue to this series of questions. "Would Mr. Handel make an offer just because she was the sister of a friend?" Silva finally asked outright.

"No, no," Howard replied after finding no explicit instructions from Merrilee to cover this topic.

"So it would have been a legitimate offer?" Silva probed.

"Ahh, well . . ." Howard hesitated.

"Well?" Silva prodded.

"Well, I doubt Lee Handel would make an offer for a book by my sister," Howard finally replied, his tone of voice suggesting that he now felt in command of the conversation. "Not his sort of book, anyway," he explained.

"But there is talk that she had an offer from Chambers," Silva pushed on.

"She did? Then you'll have to ask Mr. Handel. I know nothing about it."

"So your sister could have worked something out with the Marine Press without your knowing about it," Silva suggested.

"She could have," Howard admitted, "but it would have been unlikely. You see, Mr. Handel did not care for my sister."

"Any particular reason?" Silva said as innocently as he could manage.

Howard thought for a moment and replied, "Yes." Silva waited, but when Howard failed to continue, Silva prompted him. Howard sighed. "Handel associated her with a business loan that became difficult. His business was in jeopardy for a while and he felt Beth had something to do with it. The man who made the loan was a friend of Beth's and made a great deal of money."

Silva said, "I can see that would prevent Mr. Handel from wanting to do business with her again."

"He's over it now," Howard said in a hurry to squelch any suspicions that might be forming in Silva's mind, his wife's advice finally becoming clear to him.

"No grudge? No resentment?" Silva asked.

"Resentment, yes." Howard nodded, hoping Merrilee

was not listening nearby. "That's only natural. But he's put it behind him. After all, it was almost four years ago, Chief."

Four years ago, Silva thought, as though four years were a lifetime apart. Beth O'Donnell almost ruined Lee Handel, but according to Mr. O'Donnell, he's over it now. Silva thought back to all the rumors about the hard times endured by the Handels, how tough things had been, how worried their friends had been. Was four years really long enough to get over something like that? Lee Handel wouldn't be human if he didn't carry some resentment still for what she did to him. Howard might want to remove his friend from the list of suspects, but Silva couldn't. Not yet.

But Lee Handel wasn't the only person who had a grudge against the victim. He tried to recall exactly how Mrs. Miles had put it. What had she said? Every year Beth had another victim. Four years ago Lee Handel; two years ago, Medge Vinton; and this year, who?

8

TUESDAY EVENING

*T*HE GATEHOUSE that was now the Vinton home had been separated many years ago from the rambling summer estate for which it was built, the main house of which Medge's parents now occupied. Over the years the gatehouse had been modified, modernized, renovated, rehabilitated, restored, and revived, depending on the mood of the owners and the fashion of the times. When the Vintons had taken it over, they had settled on restoration, and so unsightly modern appendages had come down and historically accurate and tastefully designed extensions had gone up. When the interior and exterior work had been completed, Medge Vinton turned to the grounds.

The various yards had been landscaped to suggest a small French cottage in the countryside, replete with pebbled walks through artfully planned flower gardens and arbors. The mild disarray of the spring garden had taken two nurserymen, one gardener, and Medge Vinton three years to perfect. Three bright red tulips spoiled the intended effect, but cheered Silva, who liked flowers he could name. He wondered how long they would last before being pulled up by a zealous gardener.

Silva liked to glean what he could of a person's character from browsing through the man's or woman's surroundings, but he was stymied for the second time by a setting that was in the best of taste, obviously well cared for, but in no way personal. Where was the person behind the design, he idly wondered as he made his way to the front door. Where was the part of it that made it Medge Vinton's, that made it her garden rather than anyone else's? He looked back at the red tulips and wondered briefly if Medge Vinton left them there as a sly act of rebellion against the demands of her class. With that thought tickling his imagination, the chief rapped lightly on the front door. He was soon admitted by a woman whom Silva knew to be the part-time housekeeper; she left him briefly in the living room, where he could look out on the field that separated the gatehouse from the O'Donnell home, and returned a few minutes later to tell him that Mr. Vinton would be with him shortly.

"Did you know Miss Beth O'Donnell?" Silva asked before the woman could leave the room. Silva knew her name was Em and she worked as a nurse on the weekend at a nearby nursing home.

"I only knew her as an occasional houseguest of the O'Donnells. She was here off and on for lunch when she visited them," Em said as she straightened a pair of embroidered cushions on the sofa. Having taken the job five years ago when she was already in her early forties, Em had remained the casual middle-aged housewife. She declined to learn the rules governing housekeepers and would have been offended by the suggestion that she was a servant. She was not the housekeeper Mrs. Miles had expected Medge to hire and she knew it. Now, whenever they met, Em and Mrs. Miles eyed each other speculatively and maintained a polite distance.

"She was here for lunch, was she?" Silva asked offhandedly. "Whenever she visited?"

"She came for lunch last time she was here, two years ago," Em said. "Actually, she came a couple of times."

"Were Mrs. Vinton and her aunt close?" Silva asked.

Em laughed. "No. Miss O'Donnell was probably just bored. I don't recall her coming around other than for the lunches. She seemed to notice Mrs. Vinton for the first time during the second luncheon."

"I suppose that was nice for Mrs. Vinton," Silva said.

"Mrs. Vinton didn't really care from what I could see. No reason why she should," Em said.

"No family feeling at all?" Silva prodded.

"Not for her aunt," Em said. "Miss O'Donnell didn't show any special interest in her niece until two years ago and by then it was too late. Mrs. Vinton had already decided how she felt about her aunt and her behavior toward other people. So her aunt's new interest didn't sway Mrs. Vinton. She seemed more annoyed than anything else at the new attention." Em straightened a pile of art books and pocketed a few loose threads she gleaned from the carpet.

Silva picked up a photo of Medge and her mother. "They're a lot alike, aren't they?"

"They look alike," Em agreed. "But Mrs. O'Donnell had a harder time coping with Miss O'Donnell's visits. Mrs. Vinton was really quite separate from the problem."

"So you think Beth was a problem?" Silva said turning to her.

Em smiled. "Everyone thinks she was a problem, and she was." She walked to the hallway and turned back to face him. "Mr. Vinton will be with you shortly," she said and left the room.

■ ■ ■

"Good evening, Chief Silva," Frank Vinton said as he came in, extending his hand and smiling warmly. Unconsciously, Silva touched his back pocket, where he kept his wallet. This was the man, Silva reminded himself, who could entice thousands of dollars from the pockets of strangers during five minutes on the telephone. The job of a stockbroker made Silva instinctively uncomfortable.

"I can't help admiring your garden," Silva said as the two men shook hands. "It must have taken a lot of work."

"It did, and money." Frank smiled indulgently after the obligatory firm handshake.

"It doesn't look like you've missed anything."

"We haven't," Vinton said as soon as the words were out of Silva's mouth.

"The best of everything," Silva said.

"Of course," Vinton said, forgetting for a moment who Silva was. He recovered himself and said, "In this neighborhood people like to show off what they can afford as long as it's the best. It's part of the game we play."

Silva nodded. "I suppose every neighborhood is the same."

"We end up spending a lot of money on things that are more than a little foolish."

"Like doorbells," Silva suggested.

"Like doorbells, garage doors, shelves for cellar storerooms."

"And raincoats and bird feeders," Silva said.

"And raincoats and bird feeders," Vinton repeated with a laugh.

"There are some who would really envy you things like that," Silva said, "especially the bird feeders."

"I suppose so."

"I was talking to Mr. Handel recently," Silva said, "and he has an odd collection of contraptions hanging around the house. He seems to love bird feeders that work differently; he judges them like an engineer would judge a bridge."

"So I've heard." Frank laughed without any warmth in his voice. "He's getting to be famous for bird feeders around here."

"Have you ever seen them?"

"No, just heard about them." Vinton's face creased into a perfect smile, but there was only mild boredom in his eyes.

SUSAN OLEKSIW

"They look fragile. Some of them look like a small pigeon could knock them down," Silva continued.

"Probably could," Frank said.

"I have to wonder what happens in a storm? They don't look very strong. They look like they'd blow away."

"They probably do," Vinton agreed.

"Now where does that leave the birds? What do they do in a storm? Seems like all that effort at taking care of them would be wasted. Or worse. Misleading," Silva said.

"They hide in the brush until it's over," Vinton said briskly. "Then we all go out and dig out the feeders." They both laughed. "Why don't we go into the library, right here," Vinton said, leading the chief down a short hall. "My wife is out right now, so we can talk undisturbed."

Silva appreciated the calculation behind the remark—the call for a certain allegiance between men and an unspoken suspicion of the relatives of the deceased. Silva could easily imagine this man moving quickly up the ladder of any company.

Vinton led Silva into a room decorated in black and red, with bookcases lining one wall. The shelves were full of expensively bound series of Western classics, small statues, and four small trophies that appeared to be for baseball. Silva got only a quick look at them before Vinton ushered him to one of two leather chairs. Vinton sat down next to the chief, rested one leg on the other, leaned one arm on the back of the chair while clasping his hands in front of him, and said, "I've put my business phone line on the answering machine, Chief, so you can take as long as you like."

Silva calculated the number of points Vinton had managed to make since their handshake and how important it seemed to him to score in a competitive conversation. Some people competed as naturally and as devotedly as breathing, unable to let attention slide away from them, and unwilling to let another score any points, no matter how unimportant the contest. Silva listened to the smooth voice, wondering how much the man had changed since he and Medge had first met. The idle comments he and Vinton had passed back and forth here and in the living room told the chief nothing; Frank Vinton seemed to have less to reveal—other than a distaste for self-revelation—than anyone else the chief had spoken to so far. When he finally turned to the purpose of his visit, he felt almost defeated.

"I'm just checking some of the statements from people who were at the party Saturday evening," Silva explained. "I hope you don't mind answering some of the same questions again?"

"Not at all, Chief," Vinton said with a smile that would have pleased his dentist but no one else. "We are all aware of how serious this business is and your burden is certainly onerous." Silva gave him another three points for courtesy, condescension, and patronage, and wondered what business school he had attended.

"Could you tell me again what time you arrived and when you left?" Silva asked as he opened his notebook.

Vinton settled into his seat, recrossed his legs carefully, and nodded agreeably. "I'd be glad to help if I can. Let me see. I had to work this past Saturday, which you probably already know. I got home late so I was late for the party. The evening was in full swing by the time I got there." He smiled the smile of the urbane and successful. "My mother-in-law likes a good party, and I must say I do appreciate hers."

Silva gave him another point for charm and asked, "What time did you actually get there?"

"About eight o'clock, I think," Vinton said immediately, apparently not requiring any time to recall the evening.

"How long did you stay?"

"Till eleven or so," Vinton said, still smiling.

"And when you left the party?"

"Straight home, Chief. I just walked out the front door and across the field. I was in bed before eleven-thirty."

"You're sure you left by the front door." Silva studied him before recording his answer.

"Positive, Chief. It's the shortest way home."

"I just wondered. Someone reported seeing you by the door to the garden when Mr. O'Donnell and Mr. Handel went out."

"I think I did see them, but they went out. I didn't. Now that you mention it," he said, broadening his smile, "I think I opened the door for them. Don't tell me I'm going to be in trouble for taking the time to be courteous?"

"Not at all." Silva began to feel foolish. "I just want to make sure I know where everyone was."

"You're quite right, Chief. Quite right. Let's see. I was at the party from eight until eleven. I was there the whole time, and then I went home. I didn't see anyone out front when I was on my way home who shouldn't have been there. I'm afraid that's not much, but it's all I've got."

Silva dutifully recorded the information. "Mrs. O'Donnell said she saw you going home across the field."

If this corroboration startled Frank, he didn't show it, but his voice was brittle when he said, "I'm surprised she noticed. It'd been a long day for her."

"And you." Frank nodded, and Silva continued. "You must have been glad after working all day not to have to help your wife and mother-in-law clean up. You were able to leave along with the other guests."

"That's right," he said. He looked puzzled by the question. "In this family, we always hire people to do the boring work. Was there anything else?" He managed to inject into the phrasing of the question the mildest note of justified impatience. Silva gave him another point.

"When did you last see Miss O'Donnell?"

"It must have been some time during the party. I certainly don't recall seeing her around after the guests had gone."

"Can you be any more specific? Nine or ten, perhaps?" Silva suggested.

"Possibly. I really couldn't say, Chief." Vinton continued to smile, every inch of him the perfect executive. This, thought Silva, is what Bob Chambers aspires to be.

Aloud, Silva said, "So you spoke to the victim during the party, but you couldn't say what time?"

Vinton became a little more openly impatient, then generously laughed it off. "It must have been when the party was in full swing," he said, and Silva gave him another point.

"Was your wife close to her aunt?"

"No. She saw her occasionally over the years, but Aunt Beth was never more than formally an aunt to Medge," he said. "She isn't someone Medge talked about or wrote to. Beth was just a fact of life," Vinton said, and the boredom in his voice was evident.

"You seem pretty sure of their relationship, and yet you never saw them together until Saturday night. You never even met Miss O'Donnell until that night. Isn't that right?" Silva hoped he wasn't pushing the other man too hard; there was nothing he could do if Vinton pushed back.

Vinton laughed, a harsh rough sound. "Absolutely, Chief. But I have been listening to my wife for fourteen years. And make no mistake about it. Medge did not care for Beth. She was, as I said, a fact of life."

"Fourteen years. In all that time you never managed to be around to meet her." Silva's statement was not a question until he let the pause lengthen, forcing Vinton to speak.

"I'm a busy man, Chief. Besides, why should I make time to meet someone my wife doesn't particularly like anyway? In my business I spend a lot of time talking to people I don't like personally; it's part of the job. I don't have to start doing it on weekends, too." Silva had to admit that this was a fair explanation, but he wondered how his in-laws felt about it.

"Does that mean there was animosity between your wife and her aunt?" Silva said, switching direction.

"Not at all, Chief. We were used to her ways, that's all."

"How do you mean?" Silva still hoped the man was ready to give in to the vanity of confiding personal knowledge to the police.

"Just that she came up here every couple of years and her presence was unsettling," Vinton said.

"How long has she been doing that?"

"I really couldn't say, Chief. She's certainly been doing it for as long as Medge and I have been married."

"How long is that?" Silva asked, giving the man two points for concealing what must be real annoyance by now.

"Fourteen years in June. And the visits were taken for granted the first time I heard about them after we were married," Vinton said.

"What do you mean?" Silva asked, knowing how the repeated bland question could wear down the nerves of even the most resistant.

"The family just seemed to take it for granted that Aunt Beth would appear whenever she felt like it. And she did," Vinton replied stubbornly.

"Do you mind if we go back to the party for a minute?"

"Not at all. Go ahead," Vinton said, his posture unchanged but his smile waning.

"Do you recall anything in particular that Miss O'Donnell talked about?"

"Such as?"

"New York, fashion, the weather?" Silva was surprised at the fleeting reaction to his question, and wondered if he had imagined it. For a second he was sure he had seen a flash of intense anger in Vinton's eyes, but it passed too quickly for Silva to be certain. It could have been no more than annoyance at the irritatingly petty questions Silva was repeating.

"Let me see," Vinton said. "She was talking about writing a book, I think. At least, she was answering questions about it from Bob Chambers. He seems to have some connections in New York, or at least he tried to get her to think so."

MURDER IN MELLINGHAM

"How do you mean?" Silva asked.

"He hinted that he could get her a big advance."

"What did she say to that?" the chief asked.

Vinton's smile grew and he said, "She made a comment about little boys playing in the big leagues and finding out they're little boys." He flicked a piece of lint from his pant's leg and smiled broadly at the chief. "Yes, in answer to the obvious question, it made Chambers very angry."

"What did he say?"

"He asserted his integrity as an editor, reminding her of his current position," Vinton explained, "but she wouldn't let him out of it gracefully."

"How do you mean?"

"She kept reminding him that she knew he was trying to look like something he wasn't and she enjoyed seeing him brought down." He smiled condescendingly at the chief as if to say it couldn't happen to Frank Vinton.

"How did it end?"

"He told her he'd contact her when he made it to New York," Vinton said. "Neither one of them wanted to give in."

"But you don't think he has any connections in New York?"

"Would he be working here if he did? If Chambers had connections, he'd be working in a major publishing house instead of working in a place that hobbles along and prints travel diaries that no self-respecting publisher would touch and ad books for small-machinery companies."

Silva hadn't expected such venom against Chambers or Handel or anyone else except the victim, perhaps, and wondered how Vinton's view of Handel and the Marine Press had developed. Everything Silva had ever heard about Frank Vinton had tagged him as an aggressive, determined salesman who had little or no contact—other than social—with the local business people. What he was hearing now was an anger that spoke of an experience long buried, and an experience completely unknown to Silva. The chief wondered if Vinton's animosity to Handel might in any way be connected to the murder and made a mental note to poke around in Handel's past connections with the Vintons—if he could find any.

"Do you remember anything else about Chambers's conversation with Beth O'Donnell?" Silva asked.

"No," Vinton continued, unaware of how venomous he had sounded. "She talked about her book, told stories about people she knew in New York, and generally made herself the center of attention."

"You said you left around eleven," Silva said, switching direction. "What time did the other guests leave?"

"People started to leave after ten o'clock, and most of the guests were gone by ten-thirty." Vinton now had little interest in the conversation. "The few remaining guests were people the O'Donnells knew well."

"And you didn't happen to notice what time Beth O'Donnell left?"

"No, I didn't," he said, sitting up in his chair. "There really isn't anything else I can tell you, Chief."

"Actually you've been very helpful," Silva said, taking the hint and giving the man two points for seizing the initiative to control the length of the interview, and still thinking he could. As the two men walked to the front door, Silva said, "You've worked for Mr. O'Donnell for some time now, haven't you?"

"Over fifteen years," Vinton said as he opened the door for Silva. "I have the best of all worlds, Chief. I live out here with a lovely wife, enjoy a good business in Boston, and get along with my mother-in-law." He laughed easily. Silva gave him another point for ending on a note of gentlemanly courtesy.

"I noticed you had baseball trophies in your library," Silva said. "Yours?"

"Nice little things, aren't they. Remind us when we were young enough to think we could do anything. I guess that's why I keep them here. I confess to being a sentimental man, Chief," Vinton said.

Sentimental, Chief Silva repeated to himself as he turned down the driveway. "Competitive" is the word I would have chosen, he said to himself. And far too competitive to have won a special award for good sportsmanship. Silva recited the few words of the inscription he had been able to read and ruminated on the kind of character a young boy must have to earn such an award. He consoled himself with the thought that the real winner, his engraved name long destroyed by a careful hand, had probably forgotten about his missing trophies years ago.

■ ■ ■

The low green mounds dotted the dark brown dirt, promising a full and bright garden in the weeks ahead, but for now they were only a promise, and Hannah Handel had her back to the border while she arranged pots along the brick terrace behind her house. Silva watched her work for a few minutes, enjoying the light turning gold and red as it splashed off the pots onto the bricks. He appreciated the sheer physical strength that must have gone into digging up the lawn and laying out the gardens, and the careful movement that must be required to work among the closely packed but delicate spring and summer blooms that surrounded her home. This was the woman, he reminded himself, who had been able to come up behind him without warning during his first interview with her husband, Lee. That was worth remembering, he said to himself before stepping forward to call out hello and announce his arrival. Mrs. Handel stood up slowly and looked around at him, and Silva had the sense he was encountering something far more elemental than mild curiosity. He had never before wondered what the self-contained Mrs. Handel might also carry in her reserved soul. She stood still, waiting for him to approach.

"All the same questions again?" she asked, keeping her eye on him, her powerful, gloved hands still holding the terracotta pots.

"Well, no. Just a few, to help me get some details straight," Silva replied. She lowered the pots, placed them, then stepped back to see how they looked.

"Well, go ahead," she said, "unless you want me to stop work completely while you talk." She turned back to her pots without waiting for an answer.

"This is a murder investigation, Mrs. Handel," Silva said. "Could we sit down. I'll try not to take up too much of your time."

She straightened up again and looked him over with a light smile on her face, then pointed to two metal chairs nearby. When they were both settled, she said, "Well?"

"I want to go over the end of the party. Where were you from, say, ten-fifteen to eleven-fifteen."

She pulled off her gloves, folded them neatly in her lap, revealing the strong hands of a laborer. "As I recall, at ten-fifteen or thereabouts I was talking to my hostess. Then she went off to say good-bye to some people who were leaving."

"Do you remember who that was?"

"Yes," Hannah said, keeping her eye on him. "The Morrisons."

"Were they the only ones at that time?"

"No, there were several others," she said, and listed guests already interviewed.

"What about Beth O'Donnell? Did you see her around ten-thirty?"

"Yes," she said, pausing. "Yes, she was seeing the Morrisons to the door. That's why Merrilee went off and stayed at the door until everyone had gone." Hannah delivered this in such a flat tone that Silva had to think twice about the implications of her reply.

"The Morrisons seem to be special friends of Miss

O'Donnell, if I've got that right." Silva hoped this might get Hannah to talk.

"I guess so. They grew up around here, both of them. Lived here when they were first married; that's how they know Howard and Merrilee. But they moved away, and then met Beth, but I don't know where. The Morrisons come back for a visit every year, but they don't have many friends around here anymore. With Beth as a friend, it's little wonder." The last comment brought a sigh. "That sounds terribly cruel. They were quite nice when I first knew them, but that was years ago. I suppose that's why I still send flowers up to the Agawam when they come."

It might be useless information, but Silva was glad of the softening he saw in Mrs. Handel and of her effort to be kind about two people that he, too, found unattractive. He returned more gently to what he really wanted to know.

"Mrs. O'Donnell stayed at the door until you left. Which was when?" he asked.

"Eleven o'clock," she said.

"And where were you between ten-thirty and when you left?"

"Right in the front of the house with Merrilee. I got waylaid by Mr. Steinwell, and then when I managed to get away, I sort of walked around so no one else could corner me. I'd had my fill of idle talk by that time."

"You didn't talk to anyone else?"

"No. I hid in the powder room for a while when I thought Mr. Steinwell was coming back and I didn't want to get tied up again. It was getting late. As it was, Mr. Steinwell started into one of his long stories just as I was ready to grab my husband and leave."

"What time was that?"

"Eleven o'clock, Chief Silva. And it's going to stay eleven o'clock no matter how many different ways you ask the question. If you don't believe me, you can ask Frank Vinton. He didn't like getting stuck talking to Mr. Steinwell any more than I did. But we both managed. And then Lee and I left. We came straight home, we didn't stop, we didn't go back."

"Like Bob Chambers?" he said.

Hannah glared at him.

"Did you see him come in a second time?" he asked.

"Yes. I saw him leave with Lisa and I saw him come back alone. He must have forgotten something."

"Did you talk to him?"

"No, and I may not talk to you anymore if you don't come up with anything better to ask than the same old questions about time."

When Silva thought about this interview later, he was surprised he hadn't felt any need to correct her attitude, to remind her again that he was conducting an important investigation. At first he wished he had, because it seemed to mean that he was now thinking of her as a suspect to be studied carefully, for she had given him much to think about. And then he realized that her hostility burned away the mists of his prejudice and he had an inkling of the identity of the murderer.

■ ■ ■

Mellingham offers little for those who want excitement, even activity, in the evening; the two small restaurants concentrate on food rather than atmosphere. Mellites have accepted this, but tourists are often confounded, unsure of themselves in a restaurant unleavened by subdued lighting, original art, and the other accoutrements of a sophisticated meal.

The Harbor Light, located on Pine Street and facing the harbor across the road, was originally billed as a diner owned and operated by Mr. Hight. Mr. Hight had wanted to run a restaurant, but hadn't wanted to compete with old friends (the Torreys, who operated the Family Café), so he settled on opening a diner. Unfortunately, there were no diners in Mellingham, so Mr. Hight bought an old shed (long and narrow like a diner) and a few old booths and other suitable appointments, and went into business. Occasionally he tried to dress up his establishment, but each time he knew he had failed halfway through, leaving the interior with three incomplete decors—one for the booths (art nouveau), one for the counter (Victorian), and one for the rest rooms (colonial). Then Steve Badger, a tourist, bought the diner in the 1970s, and instead of fixing it up, he accepted the mélange of styles with good humor and let time wear down the rough edges of the decor until the interior finally had a uniformly worn appearance.

The food was excellent, partly because Steve was lazy and rarely performed his duties of assisting the chef. Though he liked to cook, and looked it, he liked to talk about it even more, which meant that his waitresses often had to step in to help the chef, or the patrons would get nothing to eat for hours. Chief Silva felt at home in Badger's diner, because when he had first arrived Steve Badger had sat with him for two hours on a Sunday morning explaining life in Mellingham. Badger, for his part, thought he was explaining the summer recreational program he helped run.

Silva parked in the small lot behind the diner and went in through the front door. He was greeted by the smell of deep-fried scallops, reminding him that he and Badger were among the few left who still ate fish on Fridays. Popular demand had forced Badger to offer fish every day of the week, but his waitresses claimed fish was still the main item on the menu on Friday because Badger was too lazy to think of something else to serve. Badger himself refused to eat it on any day except Friday. He also considered it his duty as a man who "remembered" the Church before Vatican II to offer his customers an opportunity to restore honorable practices to their lives.

Silva waved to Badger, who stood at the far end of the counter surveying his success, his blond hair slicked back, a clean white apron draping him from chest to knee, his eyes staring into the distance. Badger nodded and slowly drew his eyes along the booths lining the wall to his left until he spotted a half-empty one. Silva followed Badger's eyes, recognized Bob Chambers in the chosen booth, and moved to join him.

"Are you working or relaxing?" Chambers asked after they had exchanged pleasantries.

"I could ask you the same thing," Silva replied, nodding to a stack of envelopes on the bench beside the editor.

"Fair enough." Chambers agreed.

It took the men a few minutes of desultory conversation before they finally found a topic they both enjoyed, and the time passed pleasantly while they discussed the intricacies of dredging harbors, their occasional comments punctuated by crockery hitting the Formica tabletops, doors slamming, and sudden bursts of laughter.

With coffee, Chambers became direct. "Are you allowed to tell civilians what kind of progress you're making in your investigation?"

"There's nothing very interesting to tell so far," Silva said. "Except about the victim. She seems to have been a consummate artist in handling people." Silva watched Chambers to see how he would respond to a police officer making what should be considered an unprofessional comment.

Chambers nodded in agreement. "We usually call them master manipulators, and you're right. She was good at it." He sipped his coffee and relaxed on his side of the booth, apparently persuaded that he and Silva were of one mind where Miss Beth O'Donnell was concerned.

"I've been collecting examples of her artistry all day," the chief said as he poured milk into his coffee. "I'm surprised anybody would even want to try talking to her," the chief concluded. "Would you have bothered if you knew what she was like beforehand?"

"I did know," Chambers said. "So I was ready for her."

"How do you get ready for someone like that?" Silva asked. A man of quiet reserve and deep convictions about the proper conduct of police officers, Silva had reservations about initiating an intimate conversation with a suspect in the hope of leading him to a confession of useful information, or anything else, but he was willing to prompt the other man to talk up to a point. If nothing else, the surroundings—other diners in the adjacent booths and waitresses passing by—should remind the suspect that what he was saying would be public knowledge. Thus consoled, Silva said, "How do you steel yourself for someone like that, particularly in your line of work?"

"I planned my approach," Chambers said. He gazed out the window, then turned back to Silva and said, "I remember I was standing behind some people near the window facing the garden. Lee Handel was nearby, but I don't think he was talking to anyone. I think he was just standing there, listening to people. That seems to be his usual way," he said. "Anyway, I was moving clockwise through the room, just chatting with people, and I must have approached Beth by eight-thirty or earlier. She was standing near the front window. Most people come into a room and move right. She positioned herself to be seen and to be in the middle of the traffic flow."

"Is this hindsight?" Silva asked, impressed with Chambers's careful observations of his quarry and forthright description of his own behavior.

"Hardly," the editor replied. "I asked some people in New York about her. From what they told me, I knew that someone with her background is going to know every trick in the book, and use them all, too." As though to underscore his judgment, the waitress slapped down two checks on the table and walked on.

"How did you know she would be coming to the party when her brother didn't even know until the day before?"

"I've heard this is a real mystery to the O'Donnells, which

tells you something about the O'Donnells." Chambers laughed and shook his head. "Merrilee sends out invitations and she always includes people who know Beth just because Beth knows a lot of people after all these years. Beth probably calls them around the same time every year just to get the date right for the party. It can't be hard if you're shrewd and pushy. And Beth was both."

Silva had to admit that it made sense. After all, the O'Donnells assumed, naively, that no one would come unless invited, and, of course, they were wrong. The Morrisons just got their invitation from Beth. Silva filed this information, wondering if it meant anything that Chambers understood Beth O'Donnell so well.

"You said you finally met her by eight-thirty. How?" Silva asked after he had looked at his dinner check.

"I just walked up and introduced myself," Chambers said. "She seemed to be glad to meet me." He paused slightly, then said wryly, "I've since concluded that being welcomed by Beth O'Donnell was not auspicious."

"How so?" Silva asked, pretending a lack of interest he did not feel.

"I had the feeling she was lying in wait for me." He shifted on his side of the booth. "She started right off with a standard anecdote about an actress in a flop in New York."

"A good story?" Silva asked, stirring his coffee.

"So-so."

"Was she alone when you approached her?" Silva asked.

"No. She was talking to Frank Vinton. Actually I thought he was going to drift off while she was talking. He didn't seem interested in what she was saying, but she made some comment to him about not hearing it last time she was here. So he may have felt he had to stay and be polite." Chambers smiled at the recollection.

"Did he react at all?"

"He looked angry," Chambers said as he recalled the

scene, "but everybody usually does after talking to her for any length of time and then he was so excessively polite to her that it was hard to know how he felt about her."

"And she just went on talking," Silva commented.

"She got on to when she was here during the blizzard of '78." He scowled. "She likes to make us sound like hicks up here, which is a bit much." It was probably as well that Chambers was facing the front with his back to the kitchen door, where stood the owner, Mr. Badger, who would never be confused with a New York restaurateur.

"Did anyone else comment on that?" the chief asked.

"No. Frank moved on then, and I later heard her repeating the same story to someone else, a little loudly I might add," he said.

"Did you talk to her later in the evening?"

Chambers looked over at Silva, as though finally realizing who he was. "Briefly."

"Did you talk to Frank later?"

"No, only in passing."

"What do you mean?" the chief probed.

"I just nodded to him when I came back later. I saw him in the side hall when I was leaving the second time. Lee and Howard O'Donnell were just going out into the garden and Frank was holding the door for them."

"About what time was this?" Silva asked.

"Late. Almost everyone was gone by then, so it must have been well after ten-thirty. Maybe ten forty-five."

A new wave of dinner guests had arrived, and the quiet that had descended as several groups finished and left was now replaced with the calls and laughter of new people. Couples took the booths on either side of the chief and Chambers, who inspected the pair taking their seats behind Silva's back and then turned his attention to the waitress passing by.

"You seem very concerned with my return to the house, Chief."

"It's unusual, don't you think?" Silva suggested.

"Maybe. I didn't think so at the time."

"You said you went back to see Beth," Silva said. The waitress behind him was loudly explaining the menu to a younger couple.

"Yes," the editor admitted. "I wasn't comfortable with how I'd left things with her."

"Exactly how had you left things with her?"

"I wanted something a little firmer," he said.

"Such as an agreement to publish with you?" Silva suggested.

Chambers was taken aback by Silva's question. "Just something firmer."

"You could have called her the next day," Silva said.

Chambers glared at the chief.

"Let me guess what happened," Silva said. "You learned everything you could about her from contacts and friends in New York, made her an offer here or even while she was in New York, and she turned you down. Maybe with a few insults thrown in. Am I right?"

Chambers was silent.

"Well?" Silva said, pressing him.

"All right," Chambers said. "Yeah, basically, that's it."

"Basically?" Silva said. "What part did I leave out? Did she just hint she might take you up on your offer?"

"Hint?" Chambers said in an explosion of anger he quickly swallowed. "She practically agreed in a phone call we had."

"So you'd talked to her before?"

"Okay, okay," Chambers said. "Yes. I talked to her before."

It was plain to Silva that something had happened prior to the party. "Let's hear the whole story, Mr. Chambers. It'll be easier all around in the long run."

Chambers hunched his shoulders, then took a deep

breath, and began. "I'm looking for another job. That's no secret. There's not much future here for me. Anyway, I called some people in New York, just trying to make contacts, find out what was possible, who I should meet, that sort of thing. Well, I got talking to one guy who had met Beth O'Donnell at a party and heard her talking about her family up here. I realized who that had to be. I knew she came up here every couple of years so I figured she was due. Anyway, this guy said she was joking about writing a book about her life in New York. He didn't seem interested, but I thought—" He stopped, perhaps ashamed now of his earlier behavior. "Anyway, after a few more phone calls, I got her number and called her. She was the quintessentially charming lady on the phone. Wanted to know all about me, who I knew in the business, what I wanted to do for the future. I felt I was really onto something. Then at the O'Donnells' party she made it clear that it was just a game," he said. "She just wasn't interested. Didn't want to bother with me after a few minutes."

Silva considered what Chambers had said before asking, "And you thought you could change her mind if you spoke to her alone?"

"She seemed to play to an audience," he explained, "and I thought I might have a better chance with her alone. I had to try."

Silva agreed that this was a reasonable approach for Chambers to take. The chief stirred his coffee. "Had to?" Silva finally said. "I guess that explains what one of the caterers overheard."

Bob Chambers shifted in his seat and said, "How do you mean? I told you, I didn't find her when I went back."

"I was thinking of earlier," Silva explained. Chambers pushed back against the seat. "One of the caterers overheard you and the victim arguing," Silva said. He stirred his coffee, gratified to see the effect his words had on the other man.

"So?"

"So she was kind of rough on you, that's all," Silva said, watching Chambers.

"A big talker, that's all," Chambers said with a shake of his head. "Like any woman, jumps right into ultimatums and threats. All talk."

"What did she threaten you with?" Silva asked softly and Chambers recognized where he had placed himself. "It'll confirm what we heard," Silva added.

"Nothing, I told you," Chambers replied. "She just wanted me to think she was someone big, that's all."

"Someone who could wreck your career by a few well-placed phone calls?" Silva said, hoping he had guessed correctly.

"I told you," Chambers said, grabbing his check with a hand clenched tight, "just like a woman. Idle threats. Ultimatums. All talk."

With an unexpected roughness, the editor pushed out of the booth and lurched to the cash register, his dinner bill crushed in his hand. Silva watched Chambers pay his bill and leave, going over in his mind the reported nastiness of the man's encounter with the victim, wondering if a threat to ruin a career barely off the ground were sufficient motive for murder. He thought back over the cases he had handled in his career and marveled at the petty grievances that could erupt into a fatal passion, destroying other lives forever. Beth O'Donnell, Silva concluded, seemed to have easily provoked such passion in Bob Chambers.

■ ■ ■

Mr. Badger was still standing at the end of the counter when Silva was ready to leave after a second cup of coffee. "A good crowd tonight," Silva observed as he walked back to greet the owner.

"Always is. Only on the television do families stay home for meals," Badger replied without looking at Silva. People often remarked on how accurately Badger could recall their physical appearance though he never seemed to look directly at them.

"I suppose people have their favorite nights and favorite seats," Silva said.

"Favorite nights," Badger agreed, "but I can't always give them the same booth every time."

"He'd have to clean it himself to do that," a middle-aged waitress said as she emerged from the kitchen with a tray held high. Silva leaned back to avoid getting hit in the head.

"I heard that, Clara," Badger said. "Pay no attention to her," he said to Silva. "I always take care of my regulars. Good for business," he said as he suppressed a yawn. "Besides, people like to be remembered."

"Not that they expect it from him," Clara said on her way back to the kitchen, her tray now empty.

"I always remember," Badger said. "You can test me if you like." He turned to Silva and gazed directly at him, waiting for the chief to take up the challenge.

"This I have to see," Clara said, turning back from the swinging door into the kitchen.

"Who's your oldest customer?" Silva asked with a smile.

"Mrs. Linley." Badger looked around as though she were there hiding from him.

"Mrs. Hight," Clara contradicted him. "When her husband was ready to open this place, she came in to see if the food was any good and he made her a sandwich. She said it was good enough to charge for, so he charged her. She wouldn't come back till Steve bought the place."

"I was just going to say that," Steve said, not in the least ruffled by Clara's ready memory.

"Let's see," Silva said, ready to continue the game. "How long have the Hunts been coming here?"

"Since three weeks after it opened," Clara said, jumping in. "And they've never missed a Sunday supper." She glared at Steve, who said, "Never, quite right."

"How about the Handels?" Silva asked.

"Fourth Thursday of the month since it opened. Never missed." Steve smiled smugly at Clara.

"Yes, they did, you idiot," Clara said.

"No, they didn't," he shot back.

"Yes, they did, almost four years ago," she said as she stepped forward. "No one saw them here or anywhere else for six months," Clara whispered loudly.

"Quite right. I was just about to say that myself," Steve insisted.

"I don't remember their going away then," Silva said innocently. Badger cast a curious eye at him, but Clara fell for the chief's ploy.

"They didn't," she said. "Didn't anyone ever tell you the story, Chief?" She went on without waiting for his answer. "They had so little money then that they couldn't even afford to eat out once a month. My sister works at the bank. Mr. Handel really had to scramble to save his business—and everything else he owned. Not that he owned much." She glanced at Silva and then nodded toward Badger as if to say her boss would never scramble more than an egg, then went back to the kitchen.

"Must be nice to have them back again," Silva said conversationally.

This prompted another long look from Badger. "Yes," he finally said, "it is."

"Thanks, Badger," Silva said with a smile. "I'm always glad to have your opinion." The chief left Badger gazing over the end of the dinner crowd, counting receipts in his head, and planning to fire Clara, which he did on alternate Mondays.

9

WEDNESDAY
MORNING

*F*OR AS LONG as he could remember, Joe Silva loved the morning. This was when he did his best thinking, when he set the rhythm of his day and the tenor of his work. In this he was no different from generations of Silvas before him, and he often thought of them as he drove to the station. As a boy in the summer, he had accompanied his father and uncles out to sea with the fishing fleet, and heard the stories, some true, some not, all exciting, of ancestors long gone. It had taken him only a few trips as a youngster to learn that the stories people on land told about heroic deeds and survival on the raging Atlantic weren't originally meant to entertain; they were meant as warnings of what you could expect if you took one too many risks, got sloppy, or lost interest in what you were doing for a second. And some were just reminders of the insignificance of human beings. He had forgotten a lot of the tales until he met in Mellingham men who had worked as boys on boats in his father's fleet. Listening to them some summer mornings brought back the songs and stories, the voices rising from the machines and nets, like whales rising and dipping in the sea. Perhaps that was why he had always thought it odd that landlubbers expected listeners to look the storyteller in the eye and watch his face while he spoke.

Whenever he caught himself thinking like this, he remembered how long it had been since he had walked out before dawn with his father. Now his brothers and cousins took their sons as his father had taken him. He did not regret stepping out of the line of men walking to the docks, but he thought of them in the morning, when he could smell the incoming tide or hear a small boat put-putting slowly out of the harbor. Sometimes, while standing in the parking lot by the harbor on a windy day, when the wind mixed the exhaust of a car with the salt of the ocean mist, he forgot for a second where he was and sent his thoughts to test his feet, finding where they were and how they felt. He even once caught the last turn of a horn far away as he stood near an open window in a cold snap and heard his unconscious report aloud, legs okay, feet okay, toes okay. But he never tried to unlearn what had been for his people a survival skill and he wondered at how his mind worked even now, on and on, along the first path his training had cut for him as a child.

Chief Silva pulled into his parking space behind the station, watching the sun wash into the corners between the houses across the harbor. The fleet had left two hours earlier; six-thirty in the morning wasn't early for a fisherman. He listened to the gulls squawking overhead; dirty birds, he thought to himself as he walked up the steps.

Silva recited the names of the suspects to himself as he let the screen door of the station slam behind him. He was glad to see Dupoulis already in his office, hunched over his desk. The younger man sat with a pile of statements in front of him and made an occasional note on a sheet of paper beside him. When he had finished, he scanned his notes and sat back. He again looked over the list and checked off several items. After considering these he stepped into the chief's office and explained what he had been doing.

"You asked me what they talked about at the party," Dupoulis said. "I went through the statements, jotting down whatever was still in the formal statement, and people mentioned the usual things." He held up the sheet of paper.

"What did you come up with?"

"Well, as I said, the usual," the sergeant replied. "Who's doing what to their home, who changed jobs."

"All normal," Silva said. "No gossip you hadn't heard?"

"Just about the woman who wants to open a Bible school," Dupoulis said.

Silva raised an eyebrow and Dupoulis said, "She's been saved three times according to one of the guests."

"So?"

"So nothing, sir," Dupoulis said. "But usually she wants to open a day-care home, then she gets saved and wants to open a Bible school."

"I got it," Silva said. "That's why she keeps withdrawing her application and then resubmitting it." He shook his head and smiled. "What else?"

"Lots about bird feeders," Dupoulis said. "Mostly when Mr. Handel was around, which probably explains it."

"Have you seen any of his contraptions?"

"No, sir, but I've heard about them from the neighbors. You sent me out on a few calls when a neighbor complained that Handel's yard was so ugly it was lowering all the property values on the street."

Silva laughed. "I remember. I suppose we shouldn't be surprised if the subject comes up when Mr. Handel's around." He chuckled, then said, "What else?"

"The weather."

"Really?" Silva said in mock surprise, then looked at his sergeant more carefully. "Why does that matter, Sergeant? What exactly were they talking about?"

"Mostly about the blizzard of '78," the sergeant replied.

"Hmmph," said Silva, unable to think of any reason to find this suspicious. "What else?"

"The tax rate," Dupoulis said, "and some of the guests

thought the police would like to know in detail how they felt about it." Both men smiled. Silva was warned when he first resigned in favor of a small-town force that he would have to listen to a lot of talk about property values. The better off the town, the more they talk about taxes, his supervisor at the time had told him. And he'd been right.

"What's next?" Silva asked.

"Mrs. Vinton's anniversary came up a few times," Dupoulis said. "And I do find that strange. It's not as though she's an old townie having her fiftieth wedding anniversary in the next few days."

"You're right," Silva said, thinking this over. "Maybe we should bring it up and see what people say about it spontaneously. What else came up?"

"The new men and women's clothing shop," Dupoulis said. "Apparently the clothes are very high priced and no one likes that but they like the clothes."

"You must have really enjoyed reading those statements. Give you a chance to improve your sartorial knowledge," he said, alluding to Dupoulis's well-known penchant for day-glo T-shirts, which had become his off-duty uniform. His fellow officers never resisted making a comment when they saw him thus attired.

Dupoulis looked down at his chief and said, "Right, sir. You want to hear anything more?"

"Go on, Sergeant," Silva said, amused at his sergeant's thin skin.

"A book," Dupoulis said obliquely, glaring at the chief.

"All right, Sergeant, no more comments on your taste," Silva said pacifically. "What book?"

"The victim's."

"Really?" Silva said, swiveling his chair so he faced Dupoulis directly. "Several other people were discussing this?"

"Yes, sir," the sergeant said. "At least, they remembered it when we questioned them about the evening."

"That's interesting," Silva said, recalling his conversation with Bob Chambers.

"Maybe the victim kept bragging about it. That would explain why everyone remembered it."

"Or maybe she just wanted someone to think she had a book in progress," Silva said, thinking this over quietly.

"It sounds pretty definite, according to some of these statements," Dupoulis said. "At least, the party guests took the idea seriously."

"I got a different impression from Bob Chambers." Silva told Dupoulis about his conversations with the editor.

"Could she have had someone else interested in it?" Dupoulis asked.

"Maybe, but I got the feeling from all of this that all her talk about a book may have been a ruse," Silva said.

"A what?"

"A ruse. A trick," Silva said absently, his mind now moving in another direction. "Check with the caterers and see how many of them can confirm Chambers's story about going back and waiting in the living room."

Silva stretched out his hand for Dupoulis's notes and looked again at the list, envying those on the force who felt they could tell intuitively who was guilty and who was innocent, although those people tended to think everyone was guilty of something. He might promote the role of logic as a tool in police work, but he often wished there were an easier way. He copied the list of topics into his notebook.

"Got any ideas yet or is that off-limits for now?" Dupoulis asked.

"Not off-limits. What've you got on your mind?" Silva asked.

"The murderer. It seems to me we can narrow down our list of possibles to Howard O'Donnell, Frank Vinton, Lee Handel, Mr. Morrison, and Bob Chambers."

"That's all?" Silva asked.

"Well," Dupoulis said, pausing. "You're right, Chief. You think I'm assuming that the person in pants who followed the victim to the guest cottage was the murderer."

"Are you?"

"I guess I am," Dupoulis admitted, "and I'm assuming that it's a man."

"You're leaving out a few other women who wore pants," Silva replied.

"We checked with the caterers. All the women wore skirts. In addition to Mrs. Handel, only three women guests wore pants. But there's nothing there. We've checked their background and their connections with the victim," Dupoulis said, "and we can't find anything linking Beth O'Donnell with any of them, except Mrs. Handel."

"Okay," Silva said. "Any chance, in your view, of any of the other women guests changing clothes and coming back?"

"You mean a guest who left early, went home, changed, and then came back? Someone who didn't expect to see Beth O'Donnell at the party and then decided to take advantage of her being there?" Dupoulis said, trying out this new idea. "Doesn't sound realistic," he said after thinking it over. "But I suppose it is possible."

"A woman could have gone home and come back and waited for the victim to leave the party," Silva speculated.

"But she still would have had a hard time getting around the house without being seen," Dupoulis said. "That side of the house was under the eyes of the caterers the whole night. Anyone who had wanted to sneak back in would have been spotted. She would have had to hide in the bushes somewhere on the chance that the victim would come out alone and walk to the cottage."

"You're right," Silva agreed. "It's not a strong possibility, but it is still a possibility. And we have to check out everything."

"Okay," Dupoulis said. "I'll check the people who left early and see if there's anything there."

"Good. Now let's go at it from another direction," Silva said. "Suppose we leave out the person in pants. Who else becomes a suspect then?"

"Lisa Hunt, Merrilee O'Donnell, Medge Vinton, Hannah Handel, Mrs. Morrison, Mrs. Miles, and the caterers. It could get to be a long list."

"The Morrisons are probably out of the running," Silva said.

"Did you interview them yesterday at the inn?" Dupoulis asked. He had been leaning against the doorjamb inside the tiny office, but with Silva's contribution he eagerly stepped into the room. Silva moved the folders that had been piled on the second chair and Dupoulis sat down.

"I thought I'd take your advice about seeing them separately," the chief said, "since you were sure they were hiding something."

"I was," the sergeant said. "But I couldn't tell what it might be. What did you find out?"

"Talking to Mr. Morrison in the lounge at the Agawam Inn reminded me that people live on different levels, Ken," the chief said. "You were right about their hiding something, as much from themselves as from us."

"What exactly?"

"Gate-crashing," Silva said with a smile. Dupoulis stared at the chief, then repeated the unfamiliar phrase. "That's right, Ken," Silva said, "the greatest social transgression of them all—gate-crashing."

Dupoulis leaned back and laughed. When he stopped, he asked, "Did Morrison tell you that?"

"He did in a manner of speaking, and I believe him. The Morrisons' names were added in pencil on the guest list Mrs. O'Donnell gave me. They were invited by the victim when she decided to come up for the weekend, which, by the way, was several days before she called her brother and informed him of her plans. She called the Morrisons during the previous week." Silva opened a file and pulled out the sheet of paper Mrs. O'Donnell had given him.

"Bob Chambers pointed out that Beth knew when Merrilee and Howard usually held a party in the spring and who they probably invited. Beth just got on the telephone—I think he's right about this—after the invitations would have gone out and tracked down someone who got one. After that she probably called around to make sure she'd have friends at the party, someone to talk to, like the Morrisons. The last people she bothered to talk to were the O'Donnells."

"But why be so secretive about it? The Morrisons, I mean," Dupoulis asked.

"The O'Donnells had figured out years ago that one of their guests was telling Beth O'Donnell what the party plans were every spring and the victim used that information to time her congenial visits. Finally annoyed enough to do something about it, the O'Donnells dropped their prime suspects—Mr. and Mrs. Morrison. They may have made a good choice, but the Morrisons certainly weren't the only ones in touch with Beth O'Donnell. So Beth showed up anyway, but first she checked with her friends, the Morrisons, found they hadn't been invited, and invited them herself."

"And they just came, without an invitation?"

"Of course, they did," Silva replied. "From what I can tell, the point of all this isn't to be friends with the O'Donnells; the point is to be seen at their parties and meet other people. Some of the guests would expect to see the Morrisons, since they've seen them there every year, and others would figure the Morrisons must be worth knowing if they're guests of the O'Donnells."

Dupoulis swore mildly as he listened to this, and Silva chuckled.

"The real point, Sergeant, is that the Morrisons were very embarrassed not to have been invited and so they went when their friend, Beth O'Donnell, invited them. They knew what they were doing, I guess."

"And that's what they were hiding from me when I talked to them?" Dupoulis asked skeptically.

"They were hiding it from each other as much as from you," Silva said. "They didn't want to have to face exactly how badly they had behaved socially, since that seems to be one of their major concerns about other people. As it was, Mr. Morrison blamed his wife and the victim, the 'girls will be girls' kind of explanation," he said, closing the file on his desk. "Saving face can be very important, and some marriages can't go on without their masks."

Dupoulis listened to the last without interruption. "That's pathetic," he concluded. "Well, that's that. So you're ready to cross them off any list of suspects?"

"Yes, unless we find out something else about them," Silva said. "They were friends of Beth O'Donnell and there was no sign of any trouble between them at all. We can come back to them if we learn anything else about them. Right now we have other people we have to look at more closely."

"Okay," Dupoulis said, effectively dismissing the Morrisons from his consideration for the moment. "Are you eliminating anyone else?"

"Yes," Silva said. "So far several people have said that Merrilee O'Donnell was at the front door from ten-thirty to eleven o'clock, and then in the living room until eleven-thirty, relaxing while the caterers cleaned up."

"So she's out of the running if the murder was committed between ten-thirty and eleven-thirty," the sergeant said.

"And then she and her husband say they were together upstairs for the rest of the night."

"And the caterers and Mrs. Miles seem to have no motive and vouch for each other," Dupoulis added.

"Right," Silva said.

"What about Lisa?"

"No one saw any sign that someone went to the cottage

SUSAN OLEKSIW

from around the house, but that's no reason to exclude her. Right now, we have nothing either way, so we'll just set her aside for a while, but we can't eliminate her entirely."

"So where does that leave us?" Dupoulis asked. "We have the Vintons, the Handels, Bob Chambers, and Mr. O'Donnell, unless the caterers cover all his time after eleven o'clock."

"Right," Silva said.

"Were you thinking of one of those in particular?" he asked, certain the chief did have someone in mind.

"Yes. The Handels, first of all," Silva said. "We need to know a lot more about them."

"You've mentioned them several times, but you still haven't said why," Dupoulis said.

"I'm not sure why myself," Silva commented, "but there is an undercurrent where Lee Handel is concerned."

"You think there's something we're missing about him?"

"Yes," Silva said. "I'm not sure about the details yet, but a little over four years ago, Lee Handel wanted to expand his business. The victim heard him talking about this and told a friend in New York. This man probably presented himself as a venture capitalist with lots of money to spend on businesses like Handel's. The money was just what Handel wanted and it came through someone he could trust, presumably—a friend's sister. The Handels were not likely to know about the problems in the O'Donnell family. And how many people would expect the O'Donnells to know someone disreputable in business? There was no reason for the Handels to suspect anything."

Dupoulis listened impassively and asked, "Just how bad do you think it was?"

"I'm not sure," Silva said, "but the investor called in his loan less than a year after he made it. That left Handel scrambling for money, particularly since he had very little he could use as collateral for another loan without giving up his business entirely."

"They did seem hard up back then," Dupoulis said.

"They almost went broke," Silva went on. "If the grape-vine is correct, things were so bad they didn't even go out for a cup of coffee. That's pretty bad for a middle-aged couple that's spent over twenty years building up a business."

"But he never shut down, Chief," Dupoulis pointed out. "He survived."

"That's right. Somehow he survived. And the question is, How much did it cost him?" Silva rifled through his note-book. "The bank manager can tell us more about that," he said as he made a note, "when the time comes."

"Do you think he could hate Beth O'Donnell so much for giving him a bum investor that he would murder her?" Dupoulis asked, trying out this new idea.

"He might. Some people carry a grudge all their lives, just waiting for a chance to get even," Silva said. "Those are the ones who worry me. You never know when they're going to explode in rage."

"He's never seemed like the type to carry a grudge," Dupoulis said, still trying to cast Handel as a murderer in his imagination.

"No one ever seems like the type until they actually do something," Silva pointed out. "Suppose he saw Beth O'Don-nell and just seeing her brought it all back, all the struggle, all the frantic calls to find cash to bail him out, all the stress that can break men at his age." Silva knew better than he wanted to admit how Handel must have felt during those times. "Just seeing her could have triggered a return of the worst moments of his life. Or suppose he thought she was about to pull another job on him or on his business."

"Another investor?" Dupoulis asked, starting to take Handel seriously as a suspect.

"No, probably not," Silva said. "This time she might have been more subtle."

"The book," Dupoulis said, and Silva nodded. "I don't

get it, Chief. How do you think it would have worked this time?"

"I'm not sure, but suppose Handel saw his editor, Bob Chambers, chasing after a woman whose meddling almost cost him everything," the chief said. "To her it's just a game she plays while she's here, but to Handel it's his life, it's years and years of work."

Dupoulis looked skeptical, but he listened. "He might get desperate," the sergeant finally agreed. "He might think that if he had another bad streak he would really go under. But he's not the only one who could have killed her."

"I agree," Silva said, nodding and brooding in silence for a moment.

"You included Mrs. Handel in your list," Dupoulis said. "So you think it's possible for Mrs. Handel, too."

"Yes, it's possible for her, too."

"That's the one I find the hardest to consider," Dupoulis said. "From what I know of her, she never gets angry about anything. I don't think I've ever even seen her angry."

"You can't rely on what she's been like in the past, or in times we might consider normal. Murder means that someone has been pushed to the edge—and gone over. The murderer, man or woman, may think the murder brought safety, but it didn't. It never does," Silva said philosophically. "And our job is to consider everyone, even the ones who seem impossible as suspects. Hannah Handel is a quiet, reserved woman who went through very hard times with her husband."

"—and never complained," Dupoulis commented.

"Which only makes her less likely to be noticed by the ordinary person. It doesn't make her any less dangerous. The most dangerous person can be the one who never complains. They act."

"And the kids?" the sergeant asked, referring to the two boys who had seen the victim only moments before she went into her cottage.

"They saw two pants legs. That's all," Silva said.

"And Mrs. Handel always wears pants," Dupoulis said.

"Always. Now, suppose Mrs. Handel saw a new threat from the victim," Silva elaborated, "one that could finally destroy her husband financially and personally. What would she do? It was her idea to buy the Marine Press years ago, and she worked hard along with her husband in the early years. Do you think she could watch her life fall apart from the machinations of a woman like Beth O'Donnell and do nothing?"

"And she's a determined person," Dupoulis added. "She would be hard to intimidate."

"Both Mr. and Mrs. Handel had a chance at the end of the party to be alone with the victim, and both had reason to dislike her."

"We could say the same thing about Chambers and Lisa Hunt," Dupoulis went on.

"We could," Silva replied. "Lisa and Mrs. Handel could have very similar motives. And we know Lisa was left alone in the car for almost twenty minutes after the party was over. Right now we're assuming that the man or woman in pants was the murderer. But if we find out otherwise, Lisa will start to look attractive again."

"No one's come forward in the interviews, Chief. No one has admitted going out to the cottage with the victim, even for a second," Dupoulis said.

"Lisa had the opportunity," Silva reasoned, "to go back to the cottage, kill Beth O'Donnell, and return to the car before Chambers got back. The snag there is that she had no idea how long Chambers would be, and she couldn't be sure that the victim had gone back to the cottage."

"What about Chambers? It wouldn't have been as easy for him," Dupoulis said, "but still possible."

"He had the better opportunity," Silva said. "He admits going back to the house and waiting around for almost twenty minutes. And the motive for him gets stronger the more I poke around. Beth O'Donnell did a lot more than lead him on and bruise his ego. She threatened to ruin his career, and for a young man like him that could be—"

However Silva meant to qualify this last comment was lost with the arrival of an officer in the doorway. He handed in a number of letters and announced that Daley was now making coffee, and withdrew. Dupoulis said he'd follow up on what he still had to do and followed the other officer out.

■ ■ ■

Daley watched the gas flame flicker under the coffeepot. A large man with an expressionless face, he watched the coffee on most mornings, and pronounced judgment firmly on the day's brew. He disapproved of instant coffee, as well as most commercial brands, and often brought his own ground coffee to the station. He was determined to make connoisseurs of the rest of the force, but it was slow going. They were appreciative but uninformed about the merits of various blends. Even worse, they were uninterested. Nevertheless, the small force had come to expect the aroma of coffee at a few minutes after seven whenever Daley was on the morning shift, and Silva for one was glad of the ritual.

He sorted through his desk in the early hours, and was especially grateful for the time this morning. Talking through the list of suspects with Dupoulis was as much for his own benefit as for his sergeant's, for he was now reaching the stage when he had to add up what he had and define specific hard questions about each suspect. He could hear the scratchy sound of bubbles starting to form and rise in a pot of water set to boiling and let his mind drift comfortably away to his work. He looked over the notes of his conversation with Bob Chambers the night before and made a list of items to check. Then he turned to the autopsy report, which had been in the pile of papers just handed him.

The chief had never learned to tolerate an autopsy, the act of calmly and scientifically dehumanizing the body, and had been glad to find among his men in Mellingham at least one who had no qualms about watching the operation. He was profoundly grateful for Maxwell as he imagined the medical examiner's hands deftly probing the brain mass, or so the report indicated he must have done. Silva moved quickly to the conclusions, nodded in silent agreement, and slipped the report into his desk.

Putting the report out of sight had always made it easier for Silva to speculate on the problems still unresolved after the operation: death was the result of a blow from a blunt object to a part of the skull that Silva knew he would never be able to pronounce. Death occurred between 10:00 P.M. and 3:00 A.M.

Silva recalled to mind a picture of the cottage and the victim slumped in the wing chair, her feet resting on a footstool. She had been still in her evening dress and looked at first glance like any hostess at the end of a party, tired, relaxing for just a minute before going to bed.

"I'll just take this, sir," Maxwell said, breaking into Silva's thoughts and taking his coffee mug. In exchange he dropped a parcel on the chief's desk.

"New York?" Silva asked.

"Yes, sir. Very cooperative and very quick," Maxwell replied. "But nothing on your other questions. If she had any enemies down there, the police can't find them. People didn't especially like her, but there wasn't anything that pointed to murder. They weren't at all unhappy to suggest we keep our murders to ourselves." He grinned as he handed over a thick envelope.

Silva had directed Dupoulis to get the victim's diaries as expeditiously as possible, and had been relieved to have the ready cooperation of Howard O'Donnell and his attorney in New York. But he had been careful not to let his hopes rise for a solution from the journals. Now as he looked over the package of diaries he realized that unconsciously he had let his expectations grow. Silva opened the parcel and counted fifteen volumes covered in fabric with different patterns. Each volume was approximately five and one-half inches by eight and one-half inches, with two hundred pages of good-quality paper.

"I never understood the attraction of these," Silva said. "How about you?" he asked Maxwell, who was standing in the doorway watching.

"There's a course my wife took on using journal writing for"—he paused in midsentence—"for writing," he ended uncertainly. "Well, she took it. Said she liked it." He went back to his desk, leaving Silva with his pile of journals. Silva's youngest sister had once kept a diary: for seven or eight months she carried it with her everywhere. During those months she had peered at, studied, and watched the family, rarely engaging in conversation but always on the edge of the family circle. She had refused to share it with anyone, and was barely willing to acknowledge that she even had the thing in her hand, several times actually sliding it behind her back while her eldest brother stood before her, asking conversationally how it was going. And then, just as suddenly, she had put it aside, and after that she talked at every one of her turns at the dinner table and at every other gathering, a full and eager member of the large, often loud family. The experience had left Silva with what he was willing to admit was an unreasonable suspicion of the writerly instinct.

The chief had requested the journals for the years 1977 to the present. He flipped idly through a few of them. Beth O'Donnell had not made an entry for every day, but she had noted people she had met, letters and pictures received from family and friends, menus from dinner parties, places she had visited, and her income for every month. He settled down to a closer inspection. On the first of every month was written a dollar amount. The amounts varied from month to month, but generally by not more than a few dollars. Howard O'Donnell was a generous man.

He next turned to the volume for the year 1977 and began at January 1. Beth O'Donnell was methodical—a new volume for a new year. He had fifteen volumes, one for each year from 1977 to 1991. That meant, if Beth O'Donnell had held to her pattern, that the journal Mrs. Miles insisted had to be out there in the cottage was for 1992. The coffee perked and Silva read on. He was glad when the coffee finally arrived, as he moved into July. And he was wide awake by the time he reached October. He skimmed forward to February in the following year, and then turned back to reread the winter months. On the first of each month in this period, the figure for income was followed by a question mark. The figures were about a thousand dollars less than the figures in the early months of 1977. Silva flipped ahead, but there were no more question marks. There were none in the volumes for 1979 or 1980. He made a note of the months and years. Among all the talk and gossip he had listened to, he had never heard any rumors about money problems in the O'Donnell family. Nor had he heard any talk about windfalls. The family had lived consistently and quietly on a certain level for all of his time in Mellingham and for as long as he had heard about from others in the town. It was possible that Howard O'Donnell had had a bad period and had kept it quiet, keeping it from everyone except his sister, who had to know. Silva went back to October 1977 and read to the end of the year. By the end of January 1978 Silva was losing any sympathy he might have felt for the victim. Revealed in her journal, Beth O'Donnell was a whiny, selfish, greedy person.

Silva moved into February 1978. He remembered the storm of that year, and how hard it had been on those who could barely afford heat in the winter. He had been temporarily detailed to Boston then, and remembered it all too well. For some people it had been fun to have a week off with pay.

For others it had been a nightmare to have no work while the state shut down under thirty inches of snow. It had become the shibboleth of the New Englander—Where were you in the great storm? No one had expected it, least of all Beth O'Donnell, who had arrived, uninvited as usual, on Monday evening, February 6, 1978. Hers must have been one of the last flights into Logan Airport. And she hadn't made it to Mellingham. Like a lot of travelers and even commuters, she had been caught unprepared for the suddenness and swiftness of the storm. She had been lucky to make it to a hotel in the city; hundreds of commuters had been stranded in their cars on the highways, waiting to be rescued by DPW trucks. The taxi driver who had refused to drive her the thirty miles to Mellingham from the airport knew what was coming. It must have been one of the few times when Beth O'Donnell hadn't been able to buy whatever she wanted.

Beth got as far as the Parkland Hotel, and there she sat— for six days—until Monday, when she apparently managed to get a flight back to New York in the afternoon. Used to getting her own way, Beth had come north determined to see her brother and only the blizzard of the century had been able to stop her. Silva noted that once again, she had come without an invitation and without giving reasonable notice of her intent to her brother and sister-in-law.

Silva turned to the entry for February 6, 1978, the day the snow began, and read through the notes and comments on the hotel. By now, he knew what to expect. Some would call her exacting, demanding; others would call her chronic complaints something else. She liked her room at the hotel, but not some of the staff. She liked some of the guests but not those who had been forced in off the streets by the snow. Silva remembered the frustration of the manager of a small independent hotel who had tried to balance the demands of his guests with the obvious needs of the two derelicts who regularly slept in a nearby alley and had not at all surreptitiously insisted on moving inside. The same dilemma had faced the manager of the Parkland, but Miss O'Donnell made no mention of how the matter was settled. Instead, she recorded in detail the problems with the hotel service, cataloguing every failure of the staff to attend adequately to her needs. After eventually finding congenial companions, she and they had watched from the bar as stranded travelers mingled and meandered through the lobby. Those who reappeared regularly received nicknames, unimaginative but telling. There was Hugo, Ichabod, and Jezebel, and the Kissing Cousin, the Granbabby, and the Stupid Prince.

Mostly Beth had been frustrated at not discovering old friends even here. Each day brought fresh complaints against the hotel, the staff, and the residents of Boston for their deplorable weather. By Thursday she was angry about everything and it showed in every word, though she paused to record that she had seen her beau. She gave not another word to what should have been the most pleasant part of her stay, and Silva decided it was another sarcastic reference.

By late morning, Silva had read to 1986 and was fed up with all keepers of journals. He had concluded, before ten o'clock and his third cup of coffee, that if Beth had a reflective moment, a generous thought, a kind feeling, she hid them all. He couldn't claim to be surprised, and kept on reading. In late spring 1988 she met Lee Handel and made detailed notes about his business, but thereafter, in New York, she made only one reference to him, in a statement that she had mentioned his name to KM. There was no indication of the identity of KM and Silva found no more on this. He reread the relevant passages and then all the months in the period following but still found nothing. It was evident that she didn't personally care for Lee Handel, but there was no overt animosity and no repetition of his name to indicate an obsession. The chief recollected Mrs. Miles's comment that the victim could put someone on the path to trouble even if she didn't walk along with her target, and noted how little interest she had in someone after she had set them up for what she must have known would be trouble. It was as though having put a train of events into motion, she no longer had to wait and watch at each crossing.

Silva moved into spring 1990. In May she had called from New York on a Friday evening and arrived on a Saturday morning. The chief had already noted that in most years her arrival coincided with news from friends near Mellingham that her brother had scheduled a late spring party. There was no mystery to how she managed to arrive for the party without an invitation from her sister-in-law. It was a wonder, Silva thought, that anyone put up with it.

In 1990 she had stayed less than two weeks and had seen as many people as she could. He stopped at the last note on her last day. "No FV. Can't wait." He flipped back to the day of her arrival. Again the last note on Saturday read "No FV." He turned back to 1988, 1986, 1984, 1982, and 1980. There was no other visit in 1978 after the snowstorm. The last volume ended in December 1991.

"A great book, is it? A best-seller?" Dupoulis had come to the doorway and watched the chief read through the last few pages.

Silva sighed from weariness. "Not this one. If this is what she was thinking of selling as a book," Silva shook his head and left the sentence unfinished.

"Some people like that sort of thing," his sergeant said. "They like reading about the rich and famous. And they like knowing them and knowing people who knew them."

"I never knew you had a psychological bent, Dupoulis," Silva said with amusement.

"I don't," Dupoulis said. "I just think people are interesting."

"She doesn't say that much about people," Silva said, still wondering about the value of the diaries. "It reads more like an office diary or a timetable of events."

"You were hoping for a really solid clue?" Dupoulis said. "Maybe an idea about who hated her?"

Silva laughed. "I have to admit, yes, I was hoping for something more. I thought at the least there would be something about one of the suspects, some information we didn't have already. But it really isn't much more than a calendar or a listing."

"My mother used to do that," Dupoulis said. "She used to keep a record of everything she did and everyone she saw so she could remember who to send thank-you notes to, and cards for birthdays and such like."

Silva nodded, now only half-listening as he flipped back through the notebooks.

"Kept it next to her cookbooks," the sergeant continued. "I asked her about it once. Asked her if it was a diary." He looked at Silva briefly, then said, "She said she wasn't foolish enough to keep a diary in the kitchen where everyone could see it and read it. She said it was—" He stopped to think. "Like an—ah—aide-memoir," he said, stumbling over the unfamiliar term. "I think that's what she called it. Anyway, she never forgot a birthday."

Silva stared at his assistant, repeating the term that had unexpectedly fallen from his lips.

"Of course, she did," Silva said to Dupoulis's surprise. "Of course, she did." The sergeant looked hard at the chief, mouthing again the unfamiliar word that had provoked such a strange reaction in him. But Silva was no longer paying attention to him. Intent now on another idea, Silva looked through a few pages, then said, "She refers to some people by nicknames and some by initials. Make a list of all of them and check as many as you can against the guest list for the party." Silva handed over the stack of volumes and then said with a satisfied grin, "I'm going out to lunch." So saying, he stuck his hands in his pockets and sauntered out the door.

■ ■ ■

Medge added another photograph to the pile nearest Mr. Campbell, which she had designated the most tasteful selections of the photographs taken at various times of the hotel. When she had first considered Jim Kellogg's offer to join his Kitchen Cast Caterers, she had thought of the freedom to dress in old clothes with no makeup much of the time, present clients with choices rather than a hard-core sales pitch to a senior vice-president, and sit outside on a lovely day like today, if she felt like it. She tried to tell herself that such thoughts were unprofessional, and completely unworthy of someone with her experience and training, but that only made the rhododendron flowers seem larger and whiter and the breeze softer and more sensuous. She reminded herself that this was supposed to be work and poked her finger at the pile of photos closest to Mr. Campbell.

"These are sure to attract a nice clientele," she said.

He nodded and sighed, looking over the golden hair and lightly tanned limbs, thinking how much more effective a photograph of Medge might be. Unfortunately, he thought, as he looked down at four photos spread out in front of him, she seemed to have a penchant for scenery and elderly guests.

"How about some with young people?" he asked.

"Children? I don't think there are any of children," she said, flipping through one pile of photographs.

"I was thinking of older young people," he said hopefully.

"Teenagers?" Medge said aghast. "You want teenagers to advertise your hotel?" She looked around at the subdued elegance of the veranda. "It would change everything."

"I was thinking of even older," Mr. Campbell said, making another futile effort to be understood.

"I'm lost, Mr. Campbell. What young people?"

"Young couples in their twenties and thirties or so," the owner finally said.

"I'm not sure we're a tea-drinking crowd," she said skeptically. "We're more the type for sunset suppers on the roof deck."

"That's it!" Campbell said. "That's perfect." He clapped his hands together. "Sunset suppers! On the roof deck! We'll get double the use out of it. Lots of young couples up there for romantic suppers, champagne under the stars. Wonderful!" he almost shouted.

Medge scribbled ideas as he talked, trying to keep up with the rush of words from a bubbling, excited Mr. Campbell, whose eyes got brighter as he speculated on the receipts his new idea would generate.

"And photographs," he finally said. "Nice young couples leaning against the railing on a terrace with a sunset behind."

The man thinks he's selling the Bahamas, she realized with a shock. "Are you sure about all this?" she asked tentatively, wondering how safe it would be to have a bar on the roof looking over the harbor. She was glad the permits weren't going to be her problem.

"About the dining room," she said, trying to get a grip on the planning again. "The roof is good for afternoon teas as long as the weather is nice—"

"We'll get an awning. That deck will make this place," he said enthusiastically, rubbing his hands together. "Work up some menus. I'll tell the cook we're going to keep the dining room a regular restaurant. This could be great." He jumped up from the table and went off gleefully.

"Great job you're doing," Mr. Campbell said to Jim Kellogg as they passed in the doorway. "Great job!"

Beaming from the unexpected compliment, Jim sat down beside Medge and smiled broadly at her. "He must have really liked what you showed him." He turned to the stack of photographs nearest him and looked through them, hurrying through the pile to the one that must have delighted Mr. Campbell. "Gee," he finally said, "I wouldn't have thought these would have made him quite that happy."

"Actually, it isn't the pictures he liked," Medge began.

"That's good. Some of these are awful," Jim said without looking up. "You need to take lessons, or get someone to come over here to take them. You're a terrible photographer."

"Thanks a lot," she said, not the least bit insulted.

"What did he like?" he asked, finally looking up.

"Nothing of what I tried to sell him." She sighed and said, "He's on to sunset suppers on the roof."

The color slowly drained from Jim's face and when he pulled up his jaw, which had dropped a good four inches, his mouth set in a tight straight line. "Now look, Medge," he said with his teeth clenched. "We agreed. You help with the menus and the brochure. Nothing else. I do the setups. I pick the spots. That was our agreement."

"I know, I know," Medge said in an effort to calm him down. "And I'm really sorry, Jim. Things just got a little out of hand," she said, reaching out to pat his arm and soothe her new business partner.

"That roof is no place for regular dining," Jim said.

"He's really hooked on it, Jim," she said, wondering if she should be concerned over how worked up he was getting.

"We'll have to talk him out of it." He pushed away the photographs.

"I don't think we can," Medge said. She scrambled for some of the photographs as they flew to the edge of the table.

"We have to," Jim said, rocking the table on its legs as he jumped up to go after Mr. Campbell.

10

WEDNESDAY
AFTERNOON

*T*HE GROWTH of a town is often recorded in the shifts in
the location of the center, from the first crossroads, then to
the first town green with a church, and on to the first park.
These spaces are not always distinct or separate or even maintained, but in Mellingham each site continued to fulfill a role
and therefore to be kept up. The park, though small, continued
to host once a year a small Independence Day carnival and
other occasional events, ensuring that the grounds would be
cut and trimmed, the road gravel raked, and the benches re-
paired. The last received the most general use, since they faced
the harbor and attracted the retired men in the morning, the
office workers nearby at noon, and young mothers with their
children in strollers in the afternoon. If any crime were ever
committed in the harbor, the police knew they could always
find a witness, but so did the criminals apparently, for the
harbor was consistently uneventful throughout the year.

Lisa Hunt was a regular in the lunchtime crowd in the
fair weather, and in the spring invariably sat facing the harbor,
with her legs stretched out to the sun. It was not, therefore,
serendipitous that Chief Silva, with a sandwich in one hand
and a cold drink in the other, should stroll along the dirt path
through the park to a group of benches facing the harbor

and encounter the one person he had hoped to casually bump into.

"Mind if I join you?" he asked Lisa as he came up behind her, aware that his shoes crossing the gravel walk had already announced him.

"Of course not. Have a seat." Lisa smiled at him.

"You picked a nice spot," he said, looking around to reassure himself that no one was close enough to overhear them. "Do you have lunch out here often?"

"You see me here every day in warm weather, Joe." She took a delicate bite from her sandwich and looked at him expectantly. Her nonchalance didn't mean a lack of interest in the stilted conversation coming out of Joe Silva.

Silva laughed. "I've wondered about that," he said. "Why don't I see you having lunch with some handsome young man?"

"Who did you have in mind?" she asked.

"No one in particular," he replied, uncomfortably reminded that Lisa always held her own in any conversation.

"If you think you know someone suitable, give me his name sometime."

"You could get your friend Medge Vinton to fix you up with a blind date," he suggested.

"I could, but almost everyone she knows is married, except me," Lisa replied.

"How about Frank's friends?" Silva asked. "He must know a few bachelors."

"If he does, they're all hidden in Boston," she said. "Out here his friends are Medge's friends." She chewed her sandwich in silence, pondering the chief's interest in Frank. "Now that I think about it, I don't think he's ever brought friends out here for a visit or even for a party."

"Not even a business friend?" Silva asked. "Seems hard to believe."

"I know. More's the pity," she said with a sigh.

Silva smiled at Lisa's parry, and asked, "How about some friends from his bachelor days?"

"I don't think he had any then either," Lisa said unselfconsciously as she checked the angle of the sun as it shone on her not-yet-tanned legs. "Even before he met Medge, when he was first working for Mr. O'Donnell, he was known as a worker. He wasn't in with any crowd I ever heard of."

"We'll have to look elsewhere then," Silva said. "You used to work in Boston too, didn't you?"

"Yes, but that was several years ago." She examined the interior of the second half of her sandwich, found it acceptable if uninspiring, and took a small bite.

"Do you ever miss it?"

"No," she said. "Lee Handel has always been good to me. He's a good man to work for."

Silva waited a few seconds in honor of the passionate tone in which this evaluation was delivered before saying, "I thought I heard some years back that you were thinking of leaving." He casually inspected the end of his sandwich and wondered how long he could keep this up. The various ploys he had learned to adopt to appear uninterested, even bored, while surreptitiously interviewing a witness were increasingly an irritating collection of habits he longed to drop and never have recourse to again. He had little doubt that Lisa saw right through him.

Lisa turned to him. "Leaving? Me? You never heard any such thing."

"I thought I did," he said, ignoring her tone of voice. "I thought Lee was thinking about shutting down the press."

"Not exactly," she said. "The press almost went under." Lisa sat up straight, wrapped the end of her sandwich in the paper bag, and tossed it into a trash barrel nearby.

"Do you mind telling me what happened?" Silva asked, dropping his appearance of casual indifference as he turned to look directly at her. "If you don't mind talking about your boss."

"You must know most of it—especially if you've been looking into everyone's past for a motive for murder."

"I'd like to hear it from you." He smiled encouragement. "It was probably the worst time of my life—and theirs. The Handels," Lisa explained after studying the chief for a few seconds. She took another sip of her soft drink. "Lee was doing well and I think he started to get restless. When I say he was doing well, I mean in a modest sort of way. Anyway, he got this idea about expanding his business. After twenty years, he knew his market, he had a lot of steady sales, and the time seemed right. He had even been talking about it with some bankers and they had liked some of what he had to say, so he'd gone as far as a formal plan for expansion and inquiries about loan applications. A lot of people knew about it, and he talked about it to Beth O'Donnell and some others at one of the O'Donnell parties a few years ago. Then one day he got a call from a man who said he had invested in some related businesses—one was a bookstore, I think. Anyway, his businesses were thriving in New York and now he was looking for another investment. He said Beth O'Donnell had given him Lee's name."

"What was the man's name?"

"I only heard an initial, K, for his first name. I never got the whole thing. He was just K. Martin in the office. Anyway, Lee told me that the name didn't mean anything to him and Beth hadn't said anything about an investment company." She continued in a softer, more thoughtful voice. "It was all so casual. He didn't expect anything to come of it, but the man called again. He said he was interested and wanted to come up for a visit."

"And did he?"

"Yes. First, Lee sent him some reports and prospective budgets. Then he came up to look over the business. And then, before I knew it, Martin had made an offer and Lee had accepted it. They settled it right away, just the two of them." In that moment Lisa's polished persona of the light and calm heart adrift in a crazy world fell aside, and Silva glimpsed the worry and care creeping up to her eyes, a deeper level than he had ever before seen in her, though he had long suspected it was there.

"How long did the whole thing take? The paperwork, everything?" Silva asked, trying to keep the information flowing.

"About a month. We should have known," she said bitterly. "It was too good to be true. And too fast. A lot of money for a small business, control stays with the current owner. We should have known."

"What happened after that?" Silva asked, now genuinely curious.

"Nothing for a few months. Lee brought in more manuscripts, gave out some large advances, hired two more people, paid for a big advertising program, ordered some big printings, did a lot of market research for a new line of books he wanted to do." Lisa rattled off each item as if she had been reading them from a sheet of paper.

"In simple terms, he spent all the money," the chief said.

"That's exactly what he did. Lee paid out every cent over the next five months. That's not bad; that's exactly what he meant to do," she said quickly. "That was the problem."

"How much money are you talking about?"

"Well over half a million dollars," she said.

Silva whistled. It was more than he had expected. The Handels lived modestly and raising such a sum on short notice would have meant hardship. Their friendships with people like the O'Donnells were based not on money but on mutual respect and shared interests. Silva began to understand the crisis that had faced the Handels a few years ago. "Then what happened?" he asked.

"Then Martin called one day to say he was calling in the loan. And that's when we discovered what Clause 3 in Section d meant. That's d for destruction," she said. "Lee had to pay a hefty percentage of the interest in addition to the principal.

I guess that was for the privilege of borrowing the money in the first place."

"Was this a legitimate loan?" Silva asked, unable to resist.

"I have no idea, Joe. All I know is that Lee signed a contract and he thought it was valid. It does sound fishy, doesn't it? Anyway, Lee said he didn't have the money and the guy said he'd take the business and everything else—house, car, all of it. It amazed me that he could be so pleasant, so personable, and so brutal. All in one phone call. He never budged one inch—not on the money, not on the time. He did not want to negotiate.

"Lee called Beth O'Donnell, thinking she could remind Martin that it wasn't the end of the world, but all she said was tough luck." Lisa tossed her empty soda can into the trash barrel. "Lee was shocked. He went back to Martin, who had a lawyer write to him spelling out what steps they were now taking. That was even worse." Lisa took a deep breath before continuing. "So Lee made up his mind that no matter what he would get out of that mess."

"And has he?" Silva asked.

"He's in debt for at least thirty years. He'll never be able to retire. And he doesn't fully own anything, not even his household furniture. But he's not drowning."

"He mortgaged his house again?" Silva asked.

"His business, his furniture, his insurance, his pension plan. You name it, if he owned it, he mortgaged it. Or sold it. Or cashed it in."

"That must have raised everything he needed," Silva said, calculating what he might have received for the two-wing colonial a few years ago, when the real estate market rose to unexpected, even delirious heights.

Lisa watched him as he figured in his head, then said, "You're making a big assumption, Joe."

"What's that?" Silva asked.

"About what he owned."

"What, exactly, did he own?" Silva asked.

"Only the wing of the house that the press is in, which is a fairly small piece of real estate. There's a fire wall between the two sections of the house. They rent the other part of the house," Lisa said.

"Rent?" Silva began to appreciate the magnitude of Handel's debt.

"Rent. When they bought the press, the wing was part of the deal, but Lee wasn't sure he wanted the whole building. When he finally decided to buy, the old woman who owned it no longer wanted to sell—at least that's what her lawyer says. But Lee just let it go until it was too late."

"Where does that leave him now?"

"He's okay. He has a rental agreement with the old lady that's good for him but the lawyer can't stand it," Lisa explained.

"How is the business now? Safe?"

"Not very, but it's much better. We won't go under," she said, the relief evident in her voice.

"And Lee?" Silva asked, watching her closely for a reaction.

"He's all right."

"Just all right?" Silva repeated.

"Well, he went to the party and talked to people and acted almost like his old self," she said.

"It sounds like you watched him most of the evening."

"I did," she replied, her vehemence startling the chief. "I suppose that sounds strange, but I kept my eye on him most of the evening just to make sure nothing upset him. I wanted to make sure he was okay. It meant I had to maneuver Bob around and then leave him a few times, but I was determined to keep my eye on Lee. I didn't want him running into Beth O'Donnell."

"Did he?"

"No," she said, turning to watch a car driving down the street by the park. "Almost, but not quite."

"You must have been relieved," he heard himself saying,

wondering when the interview had slipped away from him. "Maybe in time he'll be back to normal."

"No," she said again, shaking her head. "He's not the same anymore. He'll never be the same again. The whole thing really took something out of him," she said, putting her shoes back on. "Can't blame him. It really scared him—the idea of losing everything at his age. Hell," she whispered, "it'd scare anyone."

■ ■ ■

The sun was warm on their backs as they walked along the harbor on the way back to the press. Silva had followed up Lisa's unexpected information with a few unimportant questions about peripheral matters while he assimilated what she had told him. He had expected details about Lee's debt, but he hadn't expected it to be so serious. At first, he had taken the view that Lee Handel had exercised bad judgment, perhaps led on by Beth O'Donnell, but now it looked more as if Lee Handel might have been taken in by unscrupulous investors. If that were true, and his financial condition had been as precarious as Lisa described, then any approach by Beth could have been viewed as a direct threat to everything Lee and Hannah Handel still had. This, considered Silva, gave Lee and Hannah a far better motive than he had estimated.

"The Handels had to raise an awful lot of money fast," Silva said as they came to the sidewalk. "How did he manage it?" Silva tried to sound casual.

"He managed it, Chief," Lisa said politely.

When they came to the street, he took her elbow as he waited for the traffic to pass. "Did you think of asking Mr. O'Donnell for a loan? Just as a point of general information, could he personally manage that big a loan?"

"Yes," Lisa said without hesitation. When they reached the other side of the street, she said, "I'd rather not say anything more than that."

"How about Frank?" Silva asked. "Could he have helped out Mr. Handel?"

"I doubt it, but he wouldn't have had any reason to anyway. They weren't friends. As for money, he only has what he earns. If Medge wanted money from their investments, she'd probably just take it."

"Sounds like she runs things," Silva said.

"She does," Lisa said as they walked down the street toward the press.

"Probably even proposed," he said lightly.

"She did," Lisa said, now taking her turn to watch for a reaction.

"He's not from around here, is he?" Silva asked.

"No. Midwest somewhere."

"Where'd they meet?" he asked.

"Here. Medge met him after he started working for her father," she said, beginning to lose interest.

"When was that?" Silva asked. "Do you know?" They turned down the small side street on which the press was located.

Lisa thought before replying. "Back in 1977, I think. She fell for him right away. She dated him all fall. Sometime around Thanksgiving she seemed to make up her mind. She told me then she was probably getting married in the summer. I asked if Frank had proposed and she said not yet. I think they were engaged by Christmas."

"You women sure take a lot for granted," Silva said ruefully.

"Maybe she's just perceptive," Lisa countered. "Anyway, she wanted to let her parents have an idea of what was coming so they wouldn't upset anything. After all, Frank was working for Mr. O'Donnell. I guess Medge wanted to make sure he wasn't fired."

"Was there any chance of that?"

"I doubt it. I think Medge was just playing it safe."

"Did she have any other reason to worry?" Silva probed.

"No, she was never worried about losing him," Lisa said, once again startling Silva with what he regarded as a brazen attitude. He had never accepted the bold lack of sentimentality he found in women, and wanted to tell Lisa to be less cynical, if only to humor him.

"No other worries?" he asked. "Money might have been a problem."

"Frank made very good money then. Still does," she said.

After adjusting as much as he could to her unromantic attitude, he said, "You don't seem to think very much of him one way or the other, or are you just being discreet?"

"He's all right," she said.

"That's not much of an endorsement, Lisa."

Lisa was quiet for a few minutes. "He's different—at least from his in-laws. I don't think he cares very much about anything or anyone." She paused. "He plays a lot of golf."

"And?" Silva prompted her.

"And nothing. Medge and Frank are having the usual problems right now," she confided unhappily. "They're like any couple their age, but they'll probably work it out. At least, I hope they do," she said with more sadness than hope.

■ ■ ■

Ken Dupoulis looked down at his sandwich, one of Steve Badger's weekday specials at the Harbor Light restaurant, and wondered why food just didn't have much of a taste these days. Robust and optimistic, he had never thought of a meal as anything other than a sensual pleasure, but now he felt almost physically unsteady as he wondered where that feeling had gone. He chewed vigorously, deep in thought, as Jim Kellogg skipped in through the screen door. When Jim saw his friend in the booth, he offered the police officer a big grin and folded his long limbs onto the seat opposite.

"Hey, Ken," Jim said as he leaned back in the booth and grinned. Ken nodded and continued to chew. "Boy, is it good to get out of there," the caterer said. Ken stared, but since his mouth was still full, he said nothing. "The inn," Jim said by way of explanation. "I mean, it's a nice place," he said, "but I've been there for days, and I'm really getting tired of it. You know what I mean?" Ken nodded and chewed on, his mind recalling the pleasure of a hot roast beef sandwich with gravy he had enjoyed a few days ago, before he had seen his first corpse.

A waitress walked by and dropped a menu on the table without looking at either occupant or stopping to address them. "Boy, what a relief," Jim said again as he opened the menu and read it quickly. He looked around for a waitress and when he caught sight of one, waited for her to look his way. Clara finally noticed him and he called out his order to her while she stood behind the counter.

Ken took another bite of his sandwich and Jim launched into an emotional tale of the hardships of the catering business and then abruptly changed pace. "Hey, what does it matter? It's a good business and we're doing okay." He looked around at the other people in the diner and seemed content to watch in silence while Ken ate.

"So how're things on your end?" Jim finally asked Ken when the policeman was through with his sandwich.

"Okay," Dupoulis replied, finishing up the remaining french fries. "We're still checking out statements, asking questions, that sort of thing." Even the french fries, he thought miserably, tasted like cold, wet mashed potatoes.

"Oh, yeah?" Jim said with childlike interest. "So do you really look for people who could've murdered her?" Ken looked at him but did not reply, which Jim apparently didn't notice, so entranced was he in watching a new couple who had just settled down at the counter. "Gee, this place is okay, you know?" he said to Ken. "It's been ages since I've been in here," he explained. "So how's it going with you?" he said again.

"Okay," Dupoulis said as Clara put a sandwich in front

of Jim. The young police sergeant eyed the sandwich plate wistfully, recalling a hot pastrami on rye he had enjoyed just last week at a drive-in on Route 1.

"I've got to admit, Ken—but don't tell anyone, please— I really love this kind of food, the greasy spoon stuff," Jim said with a smile. "But no one would ever pay me to bring this to a party." He took a large bite of his hot pastrami sandwich and munched happily.

"What would people say if they knew?" Dupoulis said genially. "And why don't you eat at the inn?"

"Have a heart, Ken," Jim said. "I feel like I'm there all the time now as it is. I don't have to eat there, too." He took another bite and avidly inspected the insides of Badger's pastrami sandwich, one connoisseur enjoying the work of another.

"People seem to really like that place," Ken said. "Somebody said they overheard you planning to cater a party there for Beth O'Donnell."

"Not exactly," Jim said with his mouth half-full. He continued to chew, but his face became pale. Finally he swallowed and said, "She just asked in passing about holding parties at the inn. She wasn't serious." He chewed more slowly now, watching the policeman.

"Jim," Dupoulis said carefully, "someone overheard her asking you about holding a party on the roof deck and later they heard you arguing about it with her. What was it all about?"

Jim swallowed hard. His face was still pale and his breathing was growing heavier. He still held the sandwich in his hands, the bread falling apart under the pressure of his fingers.

"Can you tell me what it was all about, Jim?" Dupoulis asked. He waited while Jim stared back at him, unable to make up his mind how to answer. "Jim—"

"It was nothing," Jim said. He dropped the sandwich on

his plate and stood up in the aisle, pulling out his wallet from his back pocket and ripping out a five-dollar bill. "I told you, it was nothing," he said as he tossed the bill onto the table and rushed out of the diner. Ken Dupoulis sat very still, thinking that this was the first time he had ever seen his childhood friend angry.

■　■　■

"And this is the new logo for the Kitchen Cast Caterers," Howard O'Donnell said proudly to Chief Silva as the older man picked up a large color drawing that had been propped up on the sofa in his living room. "We were looking over several choices last night, but this is the one they've picked." Silva looked down at the drawing as Howard again propped it up on the sofa and nodded an approval he didn't feel. Every time he entered the O'Donnell house he was alerted to his own limited appreciation of the world of art and its objects. He had become used to the gawky wooden statue in the front hall— a chubby little boy wearing an excess of jewelry and holding a ball in the palm of one hand. He never knew what to make of it when he saw it, but he could tell the carving was good, a skill he had learned as a child from his grandfather. His thoughts returned to the several drawings on the sofa, and he was glad he didn't have to choose among them.

"This should give them a good image to begin with," Howard said. "Jim and Medge want to get the new partnership off to a good start. Even though so many small businesses fail every year in this country, they are still such an important part of the economy. Actually, I prefer the small business." He went on to list several reasons for his views, which Silva guessed were probably worth several thousand dollars, if he knew what to do with them. "So I always look for the small business to invest in," Howard concluded.

"Is that why you decided to invest in Lee Handel's business after the investor pulled out?" Silva asked.

Howard looked away. He rearranged a mock-up of a brochure beside the drawing of the logo before turning back to the chief.

"Certainly such an investment would conform to my general principles," Howard said amiably.

"Are you the credit behind the loan to Mr. Handel?" Silva asked even more directly.

"Does this have a bearing on your investigation?"

"Yes, sir, it does."

"All right." Howard nodded. "Yes, Chief, I am." He motioned Silva to sit down as he subsided into a wing chair. "How did you figure it out?" he asked out of curiosity. "I have at least ten layers of bureaucrats and managers between me and the loan."

"I don't believe in miracles and I don't believe in kind-hearted bankers," Silva replied as he settled into his chair. "It had to be a friend. And the Handels know very few people with that kind of money." Silva had decided on the short drive over to the O'Donnell house to speak candidly, judging that the best approach to Mr. O'Donnell. Silva was relieved when Howard nodded in agreement with his guess.

"Yes," Howard said, "to your eye it had to be me, I suppose."

"I don't want to know the details of the loan."

"Good," Howard commented.

"But," Silva continued firmly, "I want to know what Mr. and Mrs. Handel know. Do they know that you're responsible for the loan?"

"Lee knows," Howard said, turning directly to Silva. "You must understand, Chief, that all of this was handled discreetly. I suggested that Lee talk to a certain loan officer. Lee would have understood from that what was going on behind the scenes. But in explicit terms, I have nothing to do with any of it."

"So he's in hock but safe for thirty years?" Silva asked.

Howard paused, tapping an antique crystal box on a side table.

"This is a murder investigation, Mr. O'Donnell," Silva reminded him.

"Yes, of course," the businessman said.

"Mr. Handel would appear to have a very strong motive for murdering your sister. Does he, in fact?"

"Lee?" Mr. O'Donnell said in surprise. "Oh no, not Lee. There isn't any financial motive, if that's what you mean."

"What are the terms of the loan?"

"He's free and clear after ten years, ummmh, ah, regardless of what's left unpaid."

Silva whistled. Howard laughed. "I agree," he said. "I wouldn't mind getting a loan like that for myself someday."

"That's unusually generous, Mr. O'Donnell, if I may say so," the chief said, unable to suppress his amazement. "You've effectively given him his business back."

"Ah, well, yes," said Howard, withdrawing again into the shell through which he viewed the world.

"Or is there more to it?" Silva asked, suspicious as he watched Howard look restlessly around the room.

"Oh well," Howard said. "I do hold a very nice equity position." Howard explained the terms to the chief, confusing him on everything except the substantial sum both Lee and Howard might make in fifteen years. Two things were now clear to Silva: Mr. O'Donnell was very generous and very rich, and Mr. Handel would probably end up better off through this arrangement than anything he might have worked out with Mr. K. Martin or anyone else.

"Who else in your family knows?"

"No one. No one. Too risky," Howard said rapidly with embarrassment. "Can't have people talking about something like that. Much too risky."

"Why too risky?" Silva genuinely wanted to know.

"Destabilizing," Howard said. "Destabilizing. It's not

good for a small business to go under in a small town, and it's just as bad for people to do too much speculating about it. Not good."

"So you never told your wife or daughter." Silva was surprised that Howard thought he could suppress the information about the press and its financial condition, particularly in a small town like Mellingham.

"No. I never said a word. But Merrilee, Mrs. O'Donnell, probably guessed. She would," he said. "But not Medge. And there was no reason to tell her."

"Could she also have guessed?"

Howard repeated the question softly to himself. "No," he finally replied. "I don't see how. The people in Lee's office probably haven't figured it out yet."

"How about Frank?" Silva asked, setting aside for the moment that Lisa seemed to know the general truth about how Lee had survived, if not how generous the terms were.

"Frank?" Howard considered this. "No, never told him either. No reason to."

"Could you have let anything drop when you were talking about something else?"

"No, no." Howard was adamant. "I never let anything drop," he added, and Silva had little trouble believing him.

"He might have guessed."

"No." Howard grew firmer. "I don't talk about my personal business with my son-in-law. Business in general, certainly, but not personal business."

"I see." Silva closed his notebook, and rose. He was beginning to see his way now. "I'll have to confirm this with Mr. Handel, of course, but I appreciate your being so open with me."

"Not at all, Chief. Glad to help." He followed the other man to the door. "Are you getting any—any ideas?" he asked diffidently.

"Yes and no," Silva said. "I'm sorry to sound so unhelpful

with that kind of answer. What I mean is I've had a few ideas, but I've had to discard them one by one. Such as the Morrisons," he explained to Howard's obvious embarrassment. "They were very uncooperative during our first interview," Silva said, watching Howard's reaction, "so we had to look more closely at them."

Howard plainly didn't know what to make of this development and opened and shut his mouth twice before he finally found the words. "They were among the few genuine friends Beth seems to have had," he finally said.

"And since you didn't want her to arrive during this particular weekend, you didn't invite them."

"Ah, yes," Howard replied, his face turning pink. "I see you figured that out. Yes, my wife had hoped to avoid Beth's unexpected but suspected arrival this spring by not inviting the Morrisons, but someone else must have told her about the party because she called anyway, as you know. And then she said she had talked to the Morrisons and invited them, so of course Merrilee added their names to the list. She told me she had to add them for you."

"That's what I figured," Silva said. "Well, I'll keep you informed," he said as he stepped outside, despising the meaningless phrases that fell from his lips so easily at times like this.

■ ■ ■

By late afternoon Silva was tired of talking and listening. He had questioned, speculated, read, and questioned some more all over again. He had listened to just about every angle of the murder and its investigation, and the hazy outlines of the murderer were getting no sharper. In his weariness he recalled a sergeant he had worked under years ago who had once said, the problem with most people is not that they don't understand what they hear; it's that they don't hear what is said. People tell you everything you want to know; it's up to you to hear it. The warning came back to Silva as he climbed the stairs to Lee Handel's office.

Lisa Hunt and Bob Chambers had gone for the day, leaving only the owner in the building. Lee stood now in the quiet of the white-painted room, the late afternoon sun shining through the newly washed windows and glinting on the gold letters embossed on the spines of old books in the bookshelves that lined two walls. On the radiator near the window sat four purple African violets in bloom. On the floor was a braided rug. Lee's desk, a large wooden desk with drawers and a lamp with a green glass shade, sat in the middle of the room, giving Lee a limited view of the street in the front and the garden at the side. Behind him on the floor were arrayed several piles of papers and books. Lee Handel filed on the floor only; there were no filing cabinets in the room. Dressed in slacks and a cotton shirt with his sleeves rolled up, he ushered Silva into the room, smiled kindly at him as the police officer settled into a chair, then seated himself at his desk. He was in the middle of a sentence inquiring about the purpose of the chief's visit when the answer came spontaneously to mind, and his smile flagged, then dissolved. Silva stepped into the silence, outlining what he had learned about Lee's financial difficulties without mentioning any names, and asking Handel to confirm, deny, or clarify the information. Lee confirmed everything.

"It's not something I want to talk about," Handel finally said. "Some people don't mind the adventure of taking financial risks, but I'm not one of them. I prefer something steady." As he spoke he moved the brass lamp so that its rectangular base was in perfect alignment with the top left-hand corner of the desk.

"It must have been quite a shock when Mr. Martin first called in your loan," Silva commented, probing for a deeper reaction from the publisher. "Did Beth O'Donnell offer any help?" he asked, watching him closely.

"Beth O'Donnell is very different from her brother," Lee said.

"Did you call her more than once?"

"No. It was clear that she had no interest in my troubles," Lee said bitterly, relaxing his hand on the lamp.

"How about the next time she came here for a visit? Did you speak to her when you saw her up here?"

"No," he said.

"When did you see her again to speak to after the loan collapsed?"

"I saw her two years afterward and no, I didn't speak to her again. I was too angry," he admitted, though he spoke less passionately now.

"And this time? Saturday evening?"

He hesitated slightly, then said no.

"Not at all?" Silva prodded gently and waited.

"You're right, of course," Handel said, relaxing his grip on the lamp still more. "I meant to. I was going to say hello, just to show there were no hard feelings. Or maybe to prove that I had survived. I saw her talking to Chambers alone in the hall and I started to go over. But when I heard what she was saying to Bob, I backed off." He stared down at the top of his desk, the flesh of his face suddenly flaccid and old.

"Do you mind telling me what she was saying?"

"Enough to make me realize that she didn't care if I survived or not," he said, his anger returning. "To her it was just a game. She liked to wreak havoc just to see what people might do."

"That's pretty harsh, Mr. Handel."

"I'm not exaggerating," he said as he shook his hand at him. "She liked to make trouble."

"What did she say to Chambers?" Silva asked again.

"She was telling him, 'You're not going to offer me a big advance, not with Lee still running things. He can barely keep the business going.'" Lee imitated a woman's whiny voice. "How do I defend myself against something like that?" he asked plaintively, shaking his head. "It made me so angry, I—" He glanced at Silva and stopped.

Neither man spoke; Lee glared at Silva and the chief sat very still.

"How angry, Mr. Handel?"

"Not that angry," Lee replied. "Not so angry that I had to do anything," he said in a calmer voice. "I was angry. I admit it. I was so angry I couldn't speak to her, but that's all," he said, letting his hand rest on the base of the lamp. "And now—I'm only sorry for Lisa's sake."

"Lisa? Why?" Silva asked, surprised at this turn in the conversation.

"Because she was standing nearby and she heard it all," Handel said, his hand trembling slightly as he held onto the base of the lamp. "She thinks I didn't notice her, but all evening she was there whenever I turned around. I knew what she was doing. I knew she was worried I might say something to Beth, but I didn't mind her watching me. Not till the end, not till Bob Chambers went off to talk to Beth alone. I guess we were both avoiding Beth O'Donnell, but near the end we tripped up. I came out in the hall and there they were, talking as though no one else was there. And this time Lisa heard all of it."

"Are you sure about that?"

"Yes, I'm sure. She didn't see me, but I saw her. I wish I hadn't." Silva was struck by how much his expression softened as he said, "It must have hurt her. She was very proud of how we pulled the business back together."

And that, thought Silva as he walked to the cruiser, was what Lisa Hunt had on her mind that night as she sat in the car.

11
THURSDAY AFTERNOON

*T*HE STATION HOUSE sat in the quiet of midafternoon, the time after the lunch hour and before the changing of shifts when office workers and others got most of their serious work done. No matter how important or serious a morning meeting, no matter how pressing the deadline before lunch, Silva still looked to the hours of midafternoon as his most productive time. It was a quiet time that hung between two busy, bustling periods, and Silva was grateful for it.

The chief settled himself at his invariably neat desk. He had learned to keep a desk clean in the room he had shared as a boy with his two brothers because seeing young Joe's books and papers spread out around the room had made his father uneasy, not because Joe's father was a tidy man, but because the books told him that this boy was different. Young Joe was the only one in the family who had wandered off for an afternoon with a book, who had studied people as well as history. People, his father had once said, were not to be studied. They were to be enjoyed. Like your relatives, his father had said one afternoon at a large family picnic. But Joe had studied, and kept his desk clear when he wasn't there using it. It was a habit that he had never given up. The desk might be messy while he was working, but it was neat and almost bare if he was leaving the room for more than a few minutes.

Silva spread his notes on the murder out on his desk blotter and stared at them. In the last several days he had managed to settle in his mind who had not killed Beth O'Donnell. And now he had an idea of who may have done it, but he needed more than an idea. Much more. He listened to an officer answer the telephone and explain the parking regulations to a town resident who must have just received his first parking ticket and thus learned that parking regulations in Mellingham were written without a loophole for the locals. The town fathers were considered alternately remiss, inflexible, selfish, vindictive, and so on when the rules finally sank in. The strict parking regulations had already led one man to threaten to turn his backyard into a parking lot and make some real money at home. First, people laughed; then later someone would be shocked at the mere thought of a parking lot in Mellingham. And then someone would suggest it for real, and by then the idea would have filtered into the consciousness of a few people and come to sound reasonable. All for want of a few extra spots of parking downtown near Town Hall.

The chief turned back to his notes and began making a schedule of events, placing an asterisk by key figures and key actions, as he had come to see them. He stopped for a few minutes to review the list of speeding tickets issued to Mellingham residents while driving in other parts of the state and the names of those Maxwell would grant waivers for appearance in traffic court, and then signed the speeding citations. Then he went back to his notes for the investigation. The next time he was ready for a break he leaned back in his chair, far enough along in his thinking to let his conscious mind play with what he had.

Dupoulis must have noticed this, for he came to the door of Silva's office and said, "Is that the story as you see it?" He indicated the schedule lying on the desk.

Silva nodded and said, "I think I'm finally where I want to be on this thing. Almost, anyway. How about you? Who do you think did it? Got any ideas you want to test before we commit ourselves."

"We're really getting down to it now, aren't we?" Dupoulis said, shaking his head. He stepped into the room and sat down. "I do have a few ideas, actually."

"Go ahead," Silva said.

"Well, at first I thought it had to be the Handels, since the victim had almost ruined Mr. Handel," Dupoulis said cautiously. "He seemed to have the strongest motive."

"A reasonable view," Silva commented. "I thought he was the most obvious choice, and then a serious possibility—for a while. But . . ."

Dupoulis waited for the chief to finish his sentence. When he didn't, the sergeant picked it up and said, "But I had trouble working out how either one of them could have done it," Dupoulis said. "According to the O'Donnells, the guests, and the caterers, the Handels were always there in the house, except for the one time when Mr. Handel and Mr. O'Donnell went into the garden together. And came back together." He crossed his legs and went on. "The Handels were there all evening and I suppose they could have come back later, after everyone else had left. They both know the house well and the grounds, and either one of them could have come back later and murdered her. But that still leaves whoever followed the victim to the cottage after 10:30 unaccounted for and it places the murder maybe as late as 1:00 A.M., after the caterers had left. And we have nothing pointing to so late a time for the murder."

"Agreed," Silva said. "Anything else bother you about the Handels?"

"I think if either one of them had meant to kill her, they wouldn't have waited so long," he said. "They could have done something two years ago, when they were still close to the edge."

"That's not good reasoning, but it's good sense as far as

it goes. You're right about the timing. It doesn't quite work for the Handels," Silva said. "For a while there I began to think Mrs. Handel was a possibility; she had a strong motive in her husband's near bankruptcy, and she certainly has enough passion to be capable of murder. She's also strong, so being a woman, and an older one at that, has no weight in her case. She could easily have murdered Beth O'Donnell with a single stroke; she has the hands of a strong man. When I couldn't place her for the entire crucial period, only part of it, I began to think seriously about her, but the time available to her is just too short. She was with Merrilee when the Morrisons left, after the victim brought them to the door to say good-bye. The victim left, going back to her cottage, and Hannah was immediately cornered by Mr. Steinwell and remained talking in the hall for at least ten or fifteen minutes. No one saw Beth O'Donnell after she said good-bye to the Morrisons and went back into the living room. That's when she must have gone back to her cottage, and Mrs. Handel couldn't have followed her then. Whoever was a few steps behind her, so close that the two boys thought it was her husband just following her to the cottage, it wasn't Hannah. When she finally got away from Mr. Steinwell, she hid in the powder room, I guess they call it, until she thought she was safe from him again."

"That all adds up to eliminating her completely," Dupoulis said, with some disappointment in his voice. "Any other reasons you didn't mention?"

"Yes," Silva said. "She talks to me like a woman who knows she is innocent, the belligerence of the safe. I don't think she means to do it, but she does. She probably talks to everyone that way, but it's not the attitude of a murderer."

"So the Handels are out of it, in your view," Dupoulis said.

"Afraid so," Silva said as he swiveled in his chair. "Who's next? What about Lisa Hunt?"

"We have the same problems with Lisa," Dupoulis began.

"She could have gone back alone after the guests and caterers were gone, after one, or she could have gone back to the cottage between ten-thirty and eleven, when Bob Chambers left her in the car. That would be very risky because she couldn't know how long he would be gone or even where he would be," Dupoulis said, speaking in a low voice. An occasional citizen wandered into the police station for assistance or information, and all of the officers had learned to modulate their voices accordingly.

"She had something else on her mind," Silva said, relating his conversation with Lee Handel. "She overheard Chambers and the victim arguing, but what she heard hurt her feelings more than it made her angry, so she had reason to brood but not to kill."

"That leaves the family and Bob Chambers," Dupoulis said.

"Agreed," Silva said. "How about Chambers? What do you think of him as a murderer?"

"Not much," Dupoulis said. "He seems to be the weakest choice so far, since he only met the victim for the first time this year. All we've really found there is a hustle that didn't work," the sergeant said, and Silva nodded, recalling Chambers's lost dream of a hot property that would carry him to success in the big world of New York.

"What about the threat to ruin his career?" Silva asked.

"It might work as a motive if he'd had a good opportunity but between ten-thirty and eleven-thirty he's pretty well covered from what we know now."

"Agreed," Silva said, thinking of how dangerously close the editor had come that evening to leaving himself open to a murder charge.

"What about the staff?"

"Jim Kellogg has no secrets that we could find and no hidden connection with the victim. The same goes for Mrs. Miles," he added.

"Okay. So that leaves the family," Silva said. "And once we look just at them, and what they did during the party, we can see how it was done."

"So now we look at who did what during the party?" the sergeant asked.

"Right," Silva said, handing him the schedule he had been making and watching while the sergeant read it twice. The second time he read it slowly, pausing at the end of each line as he let it play out in his mind.

"I see," the sergeant said. "It was really that simple."

"I think so," Silva said. "The why is starting to come to me out of the morass of chatter we've been creating with these statements," the chief said as he glanced at a tall stack of folders.

"How're we going to prove it?" Dupoulis asked.

"By finding two pieces of evidence that I am convinced exist," he said, turning to another sheet of paper.

"Two?" Dupoulis echoed, hoping the chief would not stop now.

"Two," Silva repeated. "The first is the journal for this year. Mrs. Miles insists that the victim always had one with her, but the volume for this year was not in her New York apartment and not in the cottage. The New York police sent me fifteen journals, one for each year from 1977 to 1991."

"So?" Dupoulis asked. "Oh," he said as he understood. "So you think she must have told the murderer that she had incriminating information in it."

"Exactly," Silva said.

"And the second piece?" Dupoulis asked.

"Half of the murder weapon, you might say," Silva explained enigmatically.

"Half? That may not be very useful, Chief."

"It will be," Silva reassured him. "We'll get the other half from the cottage."

"We will?" Dupoulis said, feeling like a parrot. "Sorry, sir, but you're way ahead of me. You're sure we missed it in the cottage the first time but that it's still there? And this time we'll find it?"

"Yes, Sergeant, we will. This is what you need for the application for two search warrants," Silva said as he handed a sheet of notes to the other man. "I want two search warrants. For tomorrow."

"For the O'Donnell and Vinton places," the sergeant said as he looked over the notes. "How many men do you want for the search?"

"Six. That should do it," the chief replied. "You must be just a little relieved," he said in an even lower voice.

"How do you mean, sir?"

"That it's the family and not the caterers, specifically, your friend, Jim Kellogg," Silva said.

"Yes, I am, but there's still something wrong there. It may be nothing to do with the murder if what you have in mind is right. I questioned the caterers carefully, and Jim Kellogg was always there; he is fully accounted for from ten o'clock to after eleven o'clock, and later," Dupoulis said.

"So what's the problem?" Silva asked.

"Jim's the problem. Whenever I talk to him about the crime or the victim, he flips out as though I were accusing him of the murder."

"Hmm." Silva considered this. "But the schedule puts him out of the running unless we're way off in our calculations, and I don't think we are."

"I don't think we are either, sir," Dupoulis said. "And it's not just my imagination, sir. There is definitely something Jim's not telling us, but I think I know what it is."

"A mini-mystery, as it were," Silva said.

"Yes, sir, and it has nothing to do with the murder, if I'm right."

"So how are you going to find out what it is?" Silva asked. "Are you going to come straight out and ask him?"

"No, sir," Dupoulis said with a smile, "I'm going to ask Mack."

■ ■ ■

Mack reached into the weeds surrounding the rose of sharon and pulled out the remnants of a newspaper and a squashed soft drink can. He dropped these into the black plastic trash bag he was carrying and leaned over again to peer into the brush. Seeing nothing more to collect, he looked back down the cliff path to the bathhouse, where a few bathers could be seen sitting on the front benches. A police cruiser pulled up to the stone wall that edged the beach and parked. The beach guard swung the plastic bag briefly and estimated its weight, guessing how much in total he had collected, and concluded that life in Mellingham, at least at the beach, was getting cleaner. Pleased with his work, Mack walked back along the cliff to the bathhouse. August would be especially beautiful this year when the hibiscus-like flowers at the far end of the beach came into bloom, lining the path with a curtain of pink flowers. The odd forsythia had come and gone, and there would be no more color among the greenery for two months at least.

Mack waved to Ken Dupoulis as he approached and went off to dispose of his trash bag. When he came back, he found Ken waiting for him near the door to the lifeguards' room. Mack had always considered any man (or woman) who chose to work inside a bit strange, so he accepted Ken's request to talk privately in the lifeguards' room as no stranger than Ken's other choices in life, and agreeably unlocked the door. When Ken asked him to keep the conversation confidential, Mack concluded that Ken was either practicing the jargon of the police or was taking his job much too seriously; but being an agreeable soul, Mack promised to do as Ken asked. Mack was therefore surprised (and perhaps doubly convinced in his estimation of his friend) when Ken began to talk about their high school days and their scores on the basketball team. There had never been any secret about how they had played—badly.

"Gee, Ken, I don't know about my senior year," Mack

said, thinking hard about a year he had endured with good grace and an iron will. "I couldn't play most of the time because of my grades and then when I could play the team didn't need me."

"You must have played a few times," Dupoulis said. "Didn't you spend the summer raising money for uniforms and traveling?"

Mack made a face and drew his brows together as he thought hard, a burden he had hoped to leave behind after senior exams. "I don't remember making any money," he finally said.

"You guys were asked to play in Maine or Vermont or somewhere out of state and you had to raise the money over the summer," Dupoulis said, urging on his old friend. "Think hard, Mack."

"I am, Ken, but I don't remember making any money." He paused to think. "I don't think we made any money at all that summer," he said as his memory came into focus.

"You didn't?" Ken repeated eagerly. "Who was we? You said we."

"Jim Kellogg," he said, still frowning and thinking hard. "I know he didn't. I remember now. He twisted his ankle every other week, that was it."

"Every other week? Tell me what happened exactly?" Dupoulis leaned forward in the rickety beach chair.

"He twisted his ankle, that's all," Mack said. "We were supposed to raise money, but we didn't make much."

"What happened, Mack?" Dupoulis asked again, trying to get Mack to open up.

"I'm not sure. Why don't you ask Jim?" Mack suggested reasonably.

"Because you worked with him, didn't you?" Ken said just as reasonably.

"Oh yeah," Mack agreed. "I thought you wanted to know how much—"

"Tell me what you did?"

"We painted houses," Mack said. "Or at least we tried to."

"Was it hard work?"

"No," Mack said, "but Jim just didn't seem able to finish one house without getting hurt. As soon as we got started, he hurt his ankle. I don't know how he ever got strong enough to play that winter," he said, wondering why his friend was now nodding and grinning. "What's so funny?"

"Nothing," Dupoulis replied. "Jim's ankle. Did it keep him out of work for long?"

"Most of the summer, but he was really fair about it. He didn't keep any of what we earned, and he even gave me the ladder his dad bought him for the job. I offered to pay him for it, but he said no," Mack explained. "Jim's okay."

"He certainly was lucky to have you for a partner," Dupoulis commented.

"That's what his old man said," Mack replied, more convinced than ever of the dangers inherent in a job that kept a healthy human being indoors through much of the year.

■ ■ ■

"I'd like to confirm a few points, if I may," Silva began. He rested his hand on his notebook, ready to drop the tip of his pencil onto the page at the sound of the voice of the man sitting opposite him. Comfortably settled in the O'Donnell living room, he wondered what Mr. Howard O'Donnell would think if he knew what steps Silva had recently taken and where his conclusions were leading him. "Your sister was a regular visitor?"

"Yes, every two years," Howard answered. Mr. O'Donnell had assured Silva on his arrival that the house was empty and they could speak undisturbed.

"Everyone we've spoken to has remarked on her regularity," Silva said. "She never deviated, did she?"

"No, at least not during the last several years."

"Except for once, I guess," Silva said as he made a show of flipping the pages of his notebook.

"Once?" Howard asked. "When was that?"

"Let me see—1978 I think it was," Silva said.

"Oh," said Howard, gazing at the far wall as if the answer hung among the pictures. "1978," he repeated.

"She seems to have come during a snowstorm. Is that correct?"

Howard was silent, then said, "I don't think I remember." He stared hard at a small covered basket containing potpourri and Silva waited. "Oh yes," Howard said, finally looking up. "I believe she did come then. During that huge snowstorm."

"Why was that?" Silva asked. "Another party?"

"No. A financial matter, I believe."

"Would you mind telling me about it?"

"Not at all if you think it's important," Howard said, speaking slowly.

"I do," Silva assured him.

"My sister received a payment every month from an account—similar to a trust fund—and she was concerned about it."

"Was there any reason for that?"

"There might have been," Howard said, and again cast his eyes to the ceiling in search of a reason, seeing before him an invisible ledger of payments to his sister. After several moments, his eyes still on the ledger only he could see, he said, "She was troubled by three or four payments back then. Maybe more. I don't recall the details, but I sent her some additional funds." He looked back down at Silva.

"Concerned? That's about all there was to it?"

"Well, no. Actually, she was very upset. She came up here to talk about it, I think."

"In 1978," Silva reiterated.

"Yes. We had that big storm that everyone remembers,"

Mr. O'Donnell said. She called the week before to ask about the money, tactfully, of course, but she was upset and said she'd be up the next week to see me. Seemed to think I was in money trouble." He added the last as an afterthought.

"Were you?" Silva asked, almost certain of the answer.

"No," Howard said, almost blustery. "I explained that to her. I told her everything was fine, just fine, but she didn't seem satisfied. Then she seemed to think I was no longer fond of her, started talking about how much she had helped me in the early days." Howard shifted in his chair. "I reassured her that all was well, that I would still handle everything for her, but at the end of the call she was just as determined to go over her financial matters in person."

"So she came up here, arriving before the storm," the chief said. "Did you go over the account with her?"

"No. When I heard about the storm, I assumed she wouldn't get out of New York, so I went home early, like everyone else. I overlooked how, ah," Howard searched for the right word, "determined Beth could be. She arrived in the late afternoon and made it as far as a hotel downtown."

"The Parkland Hotel."

"Was it?" Howard asked.

"That's what she says in her journal," Silva explained.

"Yes, that sounds right."

"Then what?" Silva asked.

"Nothing really. She couldn't do anything because of the storm, and I couldn't do anything either. She couldn't even reach me by telephone at first. When she finally did get me, all I could do was reassure her that I would see to everything," Mr. O'Donnell said in a voice that had soothed the anguished mind of the insecure rich for decades.

"Did that satisfy her?"

"No, actually it didn't. It was most distressing," Howard said, put out that his sister had resisted his best effort. "I had to promise her repeatedly that she had nothing to worry about.

She still didn't believe me, but after a week of being confined to a strange hotel she was ready to accept what I said. She left as soon as she could. She wasn't happy in the hotel."

"Too bad she wasn't caught in a ski resort," Silva commented.

"Now that's exactly what Beth said." Howard was intrigued at the coincidence, and he spoke excitedly. "Said we all should have been caught in a ski resort up north. Of course, she knows we don't ski. Frank and Medge ski, but they weren't married then. Actually, Frank was caught in a ski resort, in New Hampshire."

"Lucky man," said Silva.

"Now, that's what Beth said." Howard was again intrigued at the coincidence of their comments. "Frank left around noon. We all told him he probably wouldn't make it, but he did."

"So he unexpectedly got a week's vacation and Beth unfortunately got a week's confinement. She must have wanted to forget about it as soon as possible," the chief said.

"I think she was just glad to get out. I told her just before she left that I'd look into the condition of her fund and not to worry."

"And did you? Look into the fund?"

"Yes," he said frowning. "I did so just so I could reassure her that I had checked everything out. I only meant it as a formality; I didn't expect to find anything."

"But you did find something out of order?" Silva asked the question, but it was obvious from Mr. O'Donnell's expression that he recalled the problem in detail and had in fact discovered something very wrong.

"Yes." Howard continued to frown. "Her checks for several months were definitely incorrect; they were far too low, lower than they'd been for years. But the figures in her portfolio were correct. I spoke with the woman who wrote the checks and she couldn't explain it. It didn't make sense. She'd been with us for several years and I had no complaints about her otherwise so I let it go. Normally, we'd fire someone if they made that sort of mistake."

"Had you ever had that problem before with any other account?"

"No. We'd never had any problems. We're a relatively small firm, Chief. It's easy to keep an eye on everything and resolve little things before they develop into problems."

"Including discrepancies in accounting?" Silva asked.

"Yes," the older man agreed. "But it never happened again, so I just forgot about it."

"Did you ever figure it out?"

"No. I did some checking, but not very much," he admitted. "It just seemed a fluke, an accident, so I put it aside. But it did bother me." Silva saw a flicker of deep concern flash across the other man's face, and realized that for Howard business was a very personal matter.

"Did you talk to anyone else about it?" Silva asked.

"I may have mentioned it casually to my partners. I certainly talked to the man who handled the account. He's gone to another firm now."

"Did you mention it to your family?"

"Possibly. They knew Beth was here and I probably indicated it was more of a business visit."

Silva flipped a page in his notebook. "You said that in 1978 she called the week before to let you know she was coming. This year she called the night before to tell you she was coming. Did she usually do either one or the other?"

Howard cleared his throat. "Beth had gotten into the habit of calling the night before she planned to arrive." He locked his fingers together as he spoke.

"Did that present any problems for your family?"

"No, not really, Chief. Mrs. Miles always seems to be in complete command of the situation," Howard said, to Silva's tacit agreement.

"And Mrs. O'Donnell?"

"No, no problem there, Chief Silva."

"Your wife didn't mind the sudden arrivals?" Silva asked.

"Mind? Yes, I'm afraid my wife hated it. Got worse every time," he said in what Silva regarded as the man's first real confidence. "But Merrilee was always nice to Beth. Never refused to have her. But it did start to bother her more and more over the last few years."

"How about your daughter? How did she feel about suddenly having her aunt arrive?"

"Medge? I don't think it really affected her." He seemed surprised at the question, but continued, "Beth never took on the role of the affectionate aunt and Medge never seemed to want her to."

"And your son-in-law?"

Howard blinked in puzzlement. "Frank? No effect at all," he replied, then added, "They never even met until Saturday."

"Never?" Silva repeated.

"Never," Howard repeated.

"That seems hard to believe," Silva commented. "You had a party every year she came, and there were several other social activities while she was here, plus the Vintons live just down the road. There must have been plenty of opportunities when Beth was sure to be around."

"That's true, at least as far as it goes," Howard replied. "I guess the problem was that she came so suddenly. She knew when we were having a party. Her friends told her," Howard said. "But that was no guarantee that Medge and Frank would be there."

"Did it ever bother her? Did she ever ask about that?"

"Yes, she did. Every now and then she called him my invisible son-in-law. Of course, I saw him all the time. At work. I told her once that if she wanted to meet Frank, she could plan her visits to accommodate that, but she never did."

"I suppose she wasn't pleased at that," Silva said.

"I'm afraid she had little faith in her ability to plan such things. Surprising when you think about it."

"Yes, isn't it," Silva said.

"She said that no matter how she arranged her schedule, the result would be the same. Frank would be busy with business and we would have a heavy schedule of social activities," he said.

"Is that why Frank was never here to meet her? Business?"

"Mostly. He gets out a lot on weekends. He plays golf a lot."

"It's interesting what we choose for relaxation," Silva said. "Mr. Vinton plays golf, your daughter plays tennis, Mr. Handel tends bird feeders."

"Oh yes, Lee loves birds," Howard agreed.

"He was hanging a new feeder when I talked to him recently, a very fancy one."

"Ah, yes," Howard said, like a child unable to conceal his pride.

"I understand it was a gift from you."

"Just a small one; I gave it to him Saturday night just before he left."

"That must have been pretty late."

"I suppose it was, maybe ten of eleven or so. We just slipped out to the garden for a few minutes."

"Did you pass anyone?" Silva asked.

"No one outside," Howard said. "We passed Frank in the hall by the door as we were going out but there was no one outside."

Silva stood up and shut his notebook, thanking Mr. O'Donnell for his time as the other man showed him to the door. "Your sister seems to have been a very popular woman in New York, but she never married," Silva commented.

"No, she never did," Howard said. "I sort of assumed she would at one time, but she never did," he repeated, a trifle wistfully it seemed to the chief.

"Did she ever mention a special gentleman friend in the last few years?"

There was no mistaking the shock on Howard's face. "Beth? A gentleman friend? Of a personal sort?" he inquired. "Oh, my. Oh no, no. She never said a word."

"She never said she had a beau at any time in the last fifteen years or so?"

"She never said a word," Howard repeated with even greater amazement.

12

FRIDAY NOON

MR. O'DONNELL had been surprised when Chief Silva had asked to search his home and the Vintons' property, but he had agreed immediately, and Silva had discreetly left the warrants on the coffee table. Howard had collected them and tucked them into his pocket. Medge Vinton, in contrast, had snatched up the warrant, read it through, and stared in disbelief at Sergeant Dupoulis. But like her father, she had not said a word. After a few seconds the magnitude of the request had sunk in and she had abruptly slammed out the door, leaving the sergeant and another policeman alone in the house, ready to begin the search when Silva signaled.

Silva had warned both Mrs. Vinton and Mr. O'Donnell that the searches would be thorough and therefore time-consuming. Indeed, this could take the better part of the day if his men followed his instructions to be careful as well as thorough. The chief had spent some time preparing his men, making it clear what he was looking for and advising them on how not to overlook it. To himself he admitted that he was using the preparation time to prime himself to recognize something he couldn't identify precisely even now. Nevertheless, Silva was determined that if either of the two items in question were in either home, as he had good reason to believe they were, his men would find them. The younger men had taken their chief's warnings to heart and were now meticulously working their way through several piles of junk and trash in the cellars and toolsheds.

■　■　■

The warm rich smell of the freshly cut lawn enveloped Jim Kellogg as he breathed in deeply and exhaled slowly several times. When he opened his eyes to the bright sun glinting on the lawn furniture in front of him, he felt much better. He leaned back on the wooden bench set on the edge of the lawn behind the inn and felt on his neck and shoulders the cooling breeze coming through the shrubs behind him. The placid setting of the white wicker tables and chairs was calming to his nerves.

He unwrapped his lunch and began to eat. Peanut butter and banana sandwiches were not his favorite meal, but he had not wanted another encounter with Ken Dupoulis at the diner—or with any other policemen in any other place. He had brushed off his argument with Ken on Wednesday, chiding himself for overreacting to the sergeant's mention of Beth O'Donnell, and had spent most of the rest of the afternoon longing for his unfinished hot pastrami sandwich. Jim took another bite and wished he'd ordered a sandwich from the Harbor Light on his way to the inn this morning. Sometimes he even wished he'd opened a deli.

The problem with Ken, Jim mused, was that he was a policeman now; he went around suspecting everyone. That wasn't the Ken he had gone to school with, Jim admitted to himself. The guy had to take everything so seriously now. Jim shut his eyes again and willed himself to be calm. It wasn't that he didn't trust Ken anymore, Jim reasoned; it was that Ken didn't trust him, Jim Kellogg, his old friend from child-hood, someone he had known his entire life.

The lanky young man winced as he recalled the shock of

SUSAN OLEKSIW

his conversation with Mack yesterday evening at the beach when Jim had stopped by just to say hello. It was frightening now to think how his world was closing in on him. The beach had always been the one place on earth where he felt completely safe, a place of solitude, firm white sand, and immovable revetments, a place where he could find a friend to talk to and a sanity that sometimes seemed to elude him in other places—until yesterday. He couldn't bear the thought of losing his safe haven. He had tried to appear uninterested when Mack told him that Ken Dupoulis seemed to have a strange idea about how to go about a police investigation, asking questions about the basketball team and how they had raised money for their equipment, just to test a guy's memory. Really odd, Mack had said. But then, Mack had babbled on, Chief Silva had even questioned Lisa Hunt, of all people. Mack had seen the chief talking to her at the park. Jim had frozen in fear as Mack had rambled on and on, wondering how their old friend had turned out to be so boring and uninteresting, so suspicious of his old friends. Jim nodded and listened but he was nearing hysteria inside. Mack had concluded philosophically that it couldn't be helped, that people were as they were meant to be, and he and Jim just had to accept Ken Dupoulis as he was even if they didn't particularly like him anymore. And with luck, he might change back into his old self.

Jim had disagreed, but not aloud, and had made up his mind to take action. He wasn't certain what the action might be, but he was determined just the same. He knew that if he didn't do something, his life would be out of control. Ken might have been a friend at one time, when they were both students, but that was many years ago, and Jim knew as well as the next man how little weight that carried with someone who had taken an oath to serve with the police. No, Jim swore to himself, he could take no chances, put no faith in old friends, or old habits. He had to block Ken and anyone else who got too close.

242

Jim's resolve of Thursday evening was fortified the following morning, only a few minutes ago in fact, when he saw a parade of police officers in cruisers and unmarked cars drive by the inn. Just the sight of them reminded him of Dupoulis's insistence on knowing about Beth O'Donnell and her questions about a party on the roof deck. No matter what the obstacles, Jim had to act. He could feel the sweat beading on his forehead and at his temples, slowly falling in rivulets down the side of his face, the same soft drops that had combined in another place at another time to cut through stone to create the Grand Canyon. The same quiet, relentless determination now cut through Jim's heart.

Jim took a tearing bite out of his sandwich, looked across the lawn to the Victorian inn and up its sweeping porch lines, up to the gables, and then to the weather vane swinging lightly in the breeze. He would do it today. But first he needed a plan.

■　■　■

Officer Maxwell had never expected the cellars of the rich to be any different from his own and he was not disillusioned today. He had searched through boxes of old pictures and frames, cartons of broken toys, boxes of pieces of furniture—slats, legs, arms—even paper bags of broken dishes and dented pots and pans. Why did people bother, he wondered. Why didn't they just toss them out? He looked over the woodpile he had just inspected, dusted off his pants and shirtsleeves, and turned to the brick chimney. He could hear the chief's footsteps in the kitchen above him, though, to be honest, he knew he was hearing only a slight creaking where, he presumed, Silva was walking. Maxwell opened the door to the incinerator and poked through the coals with a long prod, wondering if his partner at the Vintons had found their incinerator warm from recent use. Whenever the town's environmental group pushed to have all incinerators in private homes shut down, he was glad he could say officiously that he couldn't take a stand because of his job on the force. It wasn't true, of course, but between his mother's old house out on a back road where no trash truck would go and his wife's insistence on doing their part to clean up the environment, Maxwell felt more than stymied. The two women were pushing harder and harder for their own positions, and he wondered sometimes if he could survive standing neutrally between them. So far their fondness for each other had kept their debates polite and sometimes even humorous, but Maxwell no longer looked on the convenient cellar incinerator in quite the same way.

Silva had been certain that of the six officers, one would find at least one of the items he was looking for, and he was right. Sometime during the next hour a large hand poked a stick deep among the smoldering ashes and pushed to the side a burned fragment of a book that had once been covered with a red plaid fabric. Only a few burned pages, still entangled in threads singed brown, clung to the woven binding. Fused to one edge was a large, white linen handkerchief. The fabric was too badly burned for anyone to make out the once neatly embroidered initials, but the quality of the linen was still evident. One corner was even still whole, the imperfections in the thread giving the fabric its distinct texture. The officer was quick to salvage what he could and report his find to the chief.

■ ■ ■

As soon as she had assimilated the information in the warrant, Medge Vinton gave in to a strong impulse to have lunch in the town. As she drove toward the center of Mellingham, she gave in to another impulse to eat with a friend. She collected Lisa Hunt from work, telling her to save her sandwich for tomorrow and carting her off to the Harbor Light.

"I just felt I'd rather not be there while they searched the house," Medge explained after Clara left the menus. For once the waitress found herself dealing with a customer who ignored her as much as she ignored the customers. It confirmed Clara in her commitment to her own personal brand of service, but left her wondering about Medge Vinton, who had always seemed oversocialized in Clara's view.

Medge cringed in the corner of the booth, wringing her hands in her lap, her shoulders hunched over so that they almost touched the Formica tabletop. "I took the week off to help my parents and work out some things with Jim Kellogg, but now I think I should have gone to work." She glanced wildly around the diner. "I should have gotten away, somehow."

"Who's at the house now?" Lisa asked, her mood unruffled, her curiosity subdued.

"The police," Medge replied. She had ordered for both of them, not asking Lisa what she preferred, and even now seemed unaware of her lunch partner. Lisa quietly studied her friend's face, after making no objections to the order.

"I'll bet you think I should have stayed," Medge said.

"No," Lisa replied.

"That's all? Just no?"

"That's all. They're not going to find anything to incriminate you, are they?"

"Well, no. Certainly not," said Medge, nonplussed at her friend's attitude.

"Then why worry?"

"Lisa, are we talking about the same thing?" Medge asked, rattled by her friend's calm. "The police are right now searching my house for God knows what."

"Probably a murder weapon," Lisa said calmly, refusing to be stimulated into distress by her friend's anxiety.

"That's right," Medge said. "A murder weapon. My God, Lisa. Think of it."

"I am."

"Well, you're certainly very calm about it, Lisa Hunt.

How can you? How can you be so calm? I thought you'd be concerned. I guess I misjudged you," she said, talking herself into a squall of fear and anxiety.

"It must be going around," Lisa said.

"What's going around?"

"Doubt, suspicion, fear," Lisa said matter-of-factly. "It must be the tension of the murder investigation."

Medge watched Lisa eat for several minutes, willing the angry silence to press against her friend enough so that she would have to look directly at her, and she could then confront her with her callousness at this awful time. But Lisa was unperturbed and continued to munch quietly. She looked up briefly with a smile when Badger came by, commented on the good fortune that brought him such lovely customers in the middle of the day, and asked Medge how she liked her lunch. Getting no answer from Medge, he posed the same question to Lisa.

"It's fine, and so is hers."

Satisfied, Badger walked off, never one to question a compliment.

"Lisa, the police are searching my house, but you sit there eating liver and accepting compliments as though today were an ordinary day. What's wrong?"

"What do you mean, 'What's wrong?' " Lisa replied. "This is a murder investigation and I'm bothered by it like anyone else. But I am not going to let it disrupt my lunch."

"How about your afternoon, then?"

"Steady on, Medge," Lisa said. "I'll deal with the afternoon when it gets here." She returned to her lunch.

"There's something else, isn't there?" Medge said. "The police questioned you on Sunday, didn't they? Silva told you something, something you're not telling me. Didn't he."

"I'm trying to remain calm so you will too," Lisa said.

"Thanks a lot."

"Because I feel guilty," Lisa continued.

"Guilty?" Medge was thrown off balance by this admission.

"Yes, guilty. I feel guilty for being relieved that it's not Mr. Handel's home that's being searched right now," Lisa said. "I'm sorry, Medge, I really am," she added in tones that pierced Medge's wall of anxiety.

Medge took a deep breath but instead of challenging her friend's admission, a shuddering sigh broke through and tears welled in her eyes. "It's too real for me," Medge said.

Lisa nodded in sympathy. "I know. It wasn't so bad while the police were investigating everyone equally. But now it's getting—" She paused; unable to find the right word, she finally said, "personal. Really personal. They're going to point to one person, someone we know. And that one will be pulled out of our lives forever. And even after it's all over, we're never going to feel the same way about each other again, no matter what. And we're just going to have to accept it."

Medge listened and nodded. "No matter how unpleasant Aunt Beth was before, we could just forget about it after she left, but not this time."

"No, not this time. She always wanted the last word."

"And this time she's going to have it with a vengeance," Medge said.

■ ■ ■

The cottage, closed to everyone except the police since the discovery of the body, was cool inside. The draperies had been drawn and the doors locked, and the small hideaway had been closed up just long enough for a heavy stale smell to begin seeping out of the carpeting and the corners of the two rooms, filling the cottage with the unmistakable smell of the absence of life. Chief Silva had ordered everything opened up, at least for while he was there, so he stepped into a freshly aired room. The police had been over the room twice, but still had not found a murder weapon. This rankled Silva, who was certain that the critical part of the weapon was somewhere in the cottage, so certain in fact that he was going to search the cottage again himself. He looked around the room and at the chair where Beth had died, recalling the smashed skull and the autopsy report.

"Dupoulis," he said, "unless our murderer came armed to the party or went home for a weapon, the weapon had to be something found right here or in the house." Silva stepped slowly to the center of the room. "But this was a spur-of-the-moment crime," he said to himself as much as to his sergeant.

"Is there any chance that it was planned?" Dupoulis asked even though he knew the answer.

"No, I don't think so. Everything we have so far adds up to an impulsive act. The victim calls the family the day before she plans to arrive, shows up and settles in by midafternoon, talks to her brother by early evening, and is upset and on edge by the time the guests start arriving. During the party she follows her usual pattern of insulting people. She goes after Chambers, not because he was her chosen victim, but because he makes it easy for her. He keeps putting himself in her path, trying to get some kind of business agreement out of her. She treats him the way she treats anyone she doesn't want to deal with. But she has her eye on someone else. She goes through the evening playing on people's fears and weaknesses, but only one is special. She picks on one who takes what she says seriously and when she leaves the party a little after ten-thirty, that person follows her. Beth O'Donnell dies here in her cottage, killed by something the murderer found here." The more intensely he rethought this, the slower he spoke, until the last few words of his sentence came out of his mouth at intervals of a long, deep breath.

Dupoulis looked around him, his hands in his pockets, his head cocked to one side. "I can see that it has to be something the murderer found after getting to the party. But couldn't it be something from the main house?"

"Is anything missing from the main house?" Silva asked.

"Well, no, sir, not that we can find," the sergeant said. "Mrs. Miles insists nothing is missing from the kitchen, no hammers or anything like that. We also went through all the tools in the garage, and both she and Mr. O'Donnell insist again that nothing is missing. But it just seems so much more likely that the murderer would find something there."

"Perhaps more likely, but I don't think that's what happened. The murderer came out here after the victim left the party, following her on the spur of the moment. That person had to use something that was available here."

Silva ran his eye over the room. "It must be here." He turned back to the door and slowly walked around the periphery of the room. "Somewhere in this cottage is a weapon; it doesn't look like one, but it is one. Something the murderer would recognize at a glance as just the thing." Silva turned to the sergeant. "Go through the bedroom once again; I'll do this room."

"Yes, sir," Dupoulis said, then added under his breath, "but I don't know what I'm looking for."

"You'll know it when you see it," Silva said.

Silva moved methodically around the perimeter of the room. He searched the writing desk and the built-in bookcases. He noted everything he saw, passing his eye from object to object. He noted the first end table and its lamp, the bud vase and the small tray holding three china pill boxes, the drawers filled with coasters and cocktail napkins and extra light bulbs, the love seat, the second matching end table with a lamp matching the first one, the deck of cards tied with a ribbon and the small glass bowl holding three marble eggs, two empty drawers, then the leather wastebasket, lined with silk and empty, the french doors with sheer curtains, the mantel over the fireplace, with two candlesticks (already tested by the lab), three small figurines (valuable, Silva had been told), three now-dead irises draped dramatically (Silva had been told) on the

SUSAN OLEKSIW

mantel, a small framed watercolor propped on a miniature easel, an imitation Fabergé egg, and a tall Chinese vase; another set of french doors and a secretary with a small china lamp, a glass inkwell (also tested), several pieces of stationery, three pens, and a clean blotter. The fireplace had a number of loose bricks, but none loose enough to remove. In the center of the room were two armchairs and a small coffee table, on which sat a delicate enamel bowl, a vase of dead flowers (Silva remembered them fresh), three coasters, and four heavy art books. In front of the chair in which the victim had been found was a caned footstool with a pillow on top. The rose of the pillow blended with the pink silk of the sewing bag. Sticking out of the bag were two pieces of needlepoint canvas, the first a nearly finished, delicate design of flowers. The second piece, pushed deeper into the bag, was a larger-sized mesh, with less than a third finished, producing a rough boxy picture, Silva noted, not at all like the delicate work of the first piece, or the work he had seen several times in the O'Donnell living room. On the walls beside and behind him were several oil paintings. With his arms akimbo, Silva slouched, frustrated at his blindness. It is here, he said to himself, and began his item-by-item review of the room again. And then he saw it.

"In here, Dupoulis."

"You found something?" the sergeant asked as he came in from the other room.

"This is it," he said, pointing to the bright bauble. And he was right.

250

13

FRIDAY EVENING

*T*HE BALMY HEAT of the day had lifted and a breeze chilled by the water had slipped in, lightening the land and reminding people along the coast that it was not yet full summer. The nights would still be cool and the warmth would come slowly in the morning. Even now a light mist hovered over the field between the Vinton and O'Donnell houses, the light from the windows playing on the edges of the gray mist. Silva was glad for the stillness though it made him and his men more noticeable. The evening air sharpened the sound of his footsteps as he approached the small blue car from the back. He caught the officer's eye in the side mirror and sensed the young man relax once he recognized whose footsteps he had heard.

"Anything?" Silva asked the officer, who had been watching the houses since the late afternoon.

"The Vintons walked over to the O'Donnell house at 6:09. They're still there. No one else has been in or out, either house."

"Thanks," Silva said. "When I go in, you drive up closer to the house and get a good view of the living room."

"Yes, sir."

"Dupoulis will be in the side garden," Silva explained.

"I've sent Frankel and Maxwell to the other side." The chief explained briefly what he expected to happen before he walked up to the O'Donnells' front door.

■ ■ ■

Mrs. O'Donnell greeted him and showed him into the living room, where his unexpected appearance brought a lull to the conversation. Three heads turned toward the chief as their voices died, as though he were a magnet pulling the sound from their mouths and out of the room, leaving them only their silence. Medge and her father sat at either end of the sofa while Frank Vinton stood at the bookcase. Through the french doors, Silva could see Dupoulis step into the shadows of the side garden.

"Mr. O'Donnell kindly assured me this would be a convenient time to let you know what we've found," Silva said, letting the message take on the feel of a gesture of good will in the hope of avoiding any precipitous action.

"Does that mean you've found out who did it?" Merrilee asked, folding her hands into her lap. She had settled herself in her wing chair after directing the chief to a seat.

"I've identified the murderer," Silva answered, and noted the surprise on their faces. Three voices sounded at once, to which Silva replied, "I thought you might appreciate hearing what we know."

"That's very thoughtful of you, Chief," Frank said.

"Have you arrested the murderer?" Medge asked distinctly when there was a moment of silence.

"No," Silva replied. "I'm hoping the murderer will be sensible and surrender to us rather than wait to be arrested. It would make things easier all around. The evidence becomes more compelling the more we find."

"What exactly is the evidence?" Frank asked.

"Can you tell us that without endangering your case?" Howard asked.

"I propose to tell you everything," Silva said. This assertion stimulated Mrs. O'Donnell to pick up an empty cup, wave it lamely in the air for a few seconds, decide against filling it with the cold coffee still in the coffeepot and offer it to the chief, and finally replace it on the tray. The chief was glad to be, for once, spared the need for social niceties. She drew back into her chair and said only, "Well, well."

"You've been very efficient, Chief," Frank said. "I had no idea you could solve anything this serious so quickly."

"If it is solved," Medge said.

"It is, Mrs. Vinton," Silva said.

"I'm sure it is," Mrs. O'Donnell said with the maternal voice of encouragement.

"Perhaps we should just let Chief Silva get on with it. Eh, Chief?" Howard said.

Silva was glad to begin. "Beth O'Donnell's murder presented me with almost more than I wanted to handle. Mellingham is after all a small town, and we are a small-town police force, but there I underestimated my men," he said. "Probably the same mistake the murderer made."

"I suppose anyone who commits a murder might be said to underestimate the opposition," Merrilee said absentmindedly. Both Howard and Medge glanced at her, but quickly dismissed her comment.

"Do go on, Chief," Howard said.

"Thank you," the chief said, looking around at the group. "A New Yorker who rarely came to visit her brother and his family is murdered on the first night of her unannounced and unscheduled visit. It hardly made sense. But it had to, so I went back over the day and evening of the murder. What happened between noon and midnight? A party. I decided to operate on the premise that the answer to the murder was hidden in something that happened at that party."

Merrilee interrupted, "But nothing happened. It was one of the most ordinary parties we've ever had."

"Not quite, Mrs. O'Donnell," Silva reminded her. "Something did happen, to your sister-in-law and to one other person. And that's where I began. Beth O'Donnell, a society figure from New York, a sought-after guest for all social events, an important contact in the city. A woman with money and influence. That was how she saw herself. At least that was certainly how she presented herself. That was how she wanted to appear to people. Isn't that true, Mr. O'Donnell?"

"Yes, I suppose it is," Howard agreed.

"But is it accurate?" Silva asked.

Howard and Merrilee glanced at each other, then back at Silva. "My wife does have a less glamorous view of my sister," Howard finally said.

Silva nodded. "An older woman who never achieved any standing in a profession or business, never had a family, who early on chose to become dependent on her brother's generosity. A woman who began adulthood with prospects and intelligence, but who soon found that because of her brother, she didn't have to work; she could enjoy life as she wanted. She could entertain, travel, do as she liked, and so she did, leaving everyone with the impression that she was independently wealthy. In fact, she probably began to believe it herself," the chief said. "How long have you been supporting her, Mr. O'Donnell?"

"Over thirty-five years."

"And in all that time you never complained to her, never suggested that she should take care of herself?"

"No, definitely not," Howard replied, offended by the suggestion that he might abandon a financial obligation, or his sister.

"Of course not," Silva agreed. "You would never have suggested anything like that to her. And you never even suggested she watch over her own account at your firm, did you?"

"No," Howard paused. "The fund guaranteed that she'd always have an income as long as she lived. She didn't need to control the principal."

"No, of course not," Silva said again. "And she had relied on your word for years, and there had never been a problem."

"Never," Howard repeated.

"So imagine what a shock it must have been to her when her income was reduced," Silva said.

"Reduced?" Howard repeated. "Ahh, you're referring to our earlier conversation."

"It was never reduced," Merrilee broke in. "Howard never even thought of not taking care of her. I always knew where we stood with her, always."

"And you knew she would always have an income from your husband."

"Yes, always," Merrilee said.

"But Beth didn't know that," Silva said.

"What?" Merrilee looked around at the others in the room. "Of course she knew. Howard told her. Years ago Howard told her he'd always take care of her."

"And did he ever mention it again?"

"No, certainly not," Merrilee said. "There was no need to."

"Perhaps not in your mind, Mrs. O'Donnell," Silva said, "but your sister-in-law was never as certain as you are about it."

"What do you mean?" Medge asked. "She always acted as though she had the final say over everything."

"That may be," Silva replied, "but she took no chances. She kept a journal—she had for several years—and she noted every payment in it. She kept a close eye on how her income went—up or down. She knew when the check was due and about how much it should be each month."

"She had a journal for her finances?" Medge asked.

"She had a diary in which she recorded income, events of the day, general information," the chief explained. "So imagine her shock—and worry, too—if a check noticeably smaller than she expected should arrive, and with no explanation. What would she think? What would anyone think?"

"That Howard had fallen on hard times?" Merrilee asked perplexed.

"No, Mother," Medge said laughing, then sobered immediately.

"I think Chief Silva is suggesting something else," Howard said to his wife. "You're suggesting, Chief, that she would think I was cutting back her income, perhaps warning her to find some other means of support."

"She might very well," Silva said. "There's no longer any way to know for sure, but it is possible, isn't it, Mr. O'Donnell?"

Howard stared down at the tops of his shoes, frowning. "Yes, it is," he said. "She never did say when she came that one time in the winter," he said and stopped. "I'm sorry," he apologized to no one in particular, "I was just recalling an earlier conversation with Chief Silva."

"Perhaps," Silva said, "you'd go over what we discussed, for the benefit of your family."

"Of course," Howard agreed, stretching himself taller on his side of the sofa. "About fifteen years ago Beth's checks were smaller than they should have been, and she was very, ah, concerned." Howard halted and looked over at the chief, who picked up where Howard left off.

"Behind the charming hostess from New York was a less secure, less charming middle-aged woman dependent on her brother's generosity. She visited occasionally, every two years or so. She dropped in on parties—big ones or those that included a few people she knew—but she never dropped in on important events, at least not those important to you or your family."

"You're right," Merrilee said. "We often have Howard's business friends here in the spring, but Beth has never come when they're here." Merrilee paused to think this over. "I don't think I ever really noticed it before, because she's always been so aggressive about visiting us. I suppose that was very thoughtful of her." No one showed any surprise at Merrilee's random comments. "I thought she'd try to run everything when we were first married. I was surprised when she didn't interfere in our lives more. She didn't even come to Medge's wedding."

"I wondered about that," Medge said. "I thought she'd try to run the whole thing and make herself the center of attention. I was surprised when she didn't come at all."

"Instead," Silva said, "she came regularly to visit and attend a few parties." Silva took up his narrative again. "Her visit this year was just another of her regular visits. Only once did she do the unexpected—about fifteen years ago—and that was the beginning of an effort on her part to get control of what she must have come to consider as her money. She never forgot that she had faced a decline in income—a completely unexpected one even if it had been relatively small—and it gnawed at her. She couldn't forget it—everything about it was vivid: the shock of checks that were smaller than they should have been month after month, the brother who insisted there was nothing to worry about, the decision to break a pattern that had worked well and fly to Boston in the winter instead of waiting until the spring, the snowstorm that greeted her arrival, the hotel she managed to find, the frustration at not being able to reach her brother immediately, the other people forced into the hotel by the storm, the boredom, the uncertainty, the isolation. All of these details were vivid in her memory. But something else happened that week, something that probably never made complete sense to her because she could think only of herself and her own problems. But she knew it was important in some way and she held onto it, and at the party last weekend she used it." Silva turned directly to Howard. "Is it true, Mr. O'Donnell, that during every visit, you and your sister had a private talk?"

"Yes," Howard said.

"And during these talks Miss O'Donnell was asking you for control of her money?" Silva asked.

"Ah, well," Howard said, glancing at Merrilee. "If I had known that—"

"We only just figured it out, Chief Silva," Merrilee said with a smile.

"And after those talks, whenever they occurred, either at the beginning or much later in the visit, your sister was far less pleasant," Silva said.

"Ah, well, yes," Howard said after a look from Merrilee.

"In effect, whenever Miss O'Donnell tried and failed to persuade you to give her control of her money, as she saw it, she took out her anger on someone else? Isn't that about right?" Silva asked, trying to keep a kindly tone to make up for the nature of the question.

Howard nodded, then shook his head sadly, but it was Merrilee who answered, "Yes."

"Well, Saturday night before the party she tried and failed again," Silva said as Merrilee nodded. "It was early in her visit but she had already been thwarted. She was angry and frustrated, so she was ready to lash out in her own way. At the party she dropped a few hints gleaned from several years ago and unwittingly created far more trouble for herself than she could ever have guessed. This time she became enough of a threat to someone to force that person to kill her."

Silva recrossed his legs. "At first I thought I only had to identify the person she was hardest on, but that didn't work. She had a lot of harsh things to say to Bob Chambers, but not because she had settled on him as her victim for the year. He wanted something from her and kept putting himself in her path. He called her in New York, then made a point of meeting her at the party. He targeted her, but she wasn't particularly interested in him. Still, she wasn't going to pass up an opportunity to cut someone down to size. I'm afraid she enjoyed such encounters." The chief listened to his own words, wishing he didn't have to say these things to the O'Donnells.

"But my time investigating Chambers wasn't entirely

wasted; he said something that helped me in the end," said Silva, hoping no one would ask exactly what that was. "There were others at the party who did interest Miss O'Donnell."

"Why couldn't it have been someone she knew from New York?" Merrilee asked.

"That would be nice for everyone here, and we looked into that," Silva said. "But it's not what the evidence tells us. It's not anyone from New York. The murderer was someone the victim met here, at the party."

"One of our friends?" Merrilee asked, this time eliciting only a tolerant look from her daughter.

"Let's go back to the party," Silva said. "Your sister talked to just about everyone who came. Most she had met before, but not all of them. One of them she had seen before, but had never met. And she said so. She made it clear to this person that she knew the face. 'I never forget anything,' she said. And she said it loudly enough for people to hear and remark on. To most people it was just a loud comment at a party. To one person in particular, however, it was too close to a direct threat to ignore. Miss O'Donnell also made it clear that she remembered when and where she had seen that face. And that was the threat. Perhaps Miss O'Donnell thought she was telling this person that she knew a secret, but she was profoundly unaware of the significance of that secret. Unfortunately, there was no way the murderer could know that." Silva paused while he glanced through the french doors for a sign that Dupoulis had moved in closer.

"The murderer knew what Beth was hinting at even if she didn't," Silva continued. "This left the murderer with no choice but to get rid of Beth that evening. The murderer wasted no time. Beth left the party soon after ten-thirty. She went straight to her cottage. She probably went in, put her feet up, and relaxed. The murderer was right behind her. Two youngsters saw a person in pants following along on the path only moments after Miss O'Donnell. Once inside, talking to the murderer, Beth probably made a stupid mistake. Unaware of how much she knew, she may well have tried to sound like she knew far more than she did. She may even have hinted at other secrets. And that was her mistake."

"This is all speculation," Medge interrupted.

"Some of it is, Mrs. Vinton, speculation based on the logic of your aunt's established behavior. But not all of it," Silva said.

"And not inaccurate," Howard said. "For years Beth had been parlaying slight acquaintances into all sorts of contacts or whatever. It probably seemed natural to her to enhance whatever she knew."

"The fact is," Silva went on, "someone murdered her at that moment. Whatever she said or pretended to know was enough to drive someone to kill her."

Silva's listeners were now still, their objections only private thoughts. "Miss O'Donnell's tactics," he went on, "were deadly. The murderer was forced to choose right then. Desperate, the murderer must have looked around for something to use as a weapon. The poker in the fireplace must have seemed obvious, perhaps too obvious and too easy for the victim to avoid, giving her time to call for help," Silva said. "No, the murderer did not use the poker. The killer used instead a thing of beauty, you might say, a little thing there only for decoration—a marble egg. Lying in a small glass bowl were three marble eggs. One with a tiny crack in it, which has been analyzed by our lab." Silva heard Merrilee gasp. "Perhaps the murderer picked up the egg and pretended to polish it, or maybe just slipped it into a pocket and then walked behind the chair. Either way, the murderer wrapped the egg in a handkerchief and swung it down on the victim's skull." Silva stopped. Merrilee shuddered and turned away; Medge glanced at her father, who continued to stare stiffly at the floor. Frank Vinton never took his eyes off Silva.

"The murderer then cleaned and polished the egg and put it back in the glass bowl, arranged the body in the chair, turned down the lights, and went back to the party, which was all but over at that point," Silva said.

"Beth O'Donnell was dead by eleven o'clock."

■ ■ ■

"The question, then, is why?" Chief Silva asked, wondering if he sounded as pedantic as he felt. "Why was she killed? Who did she scare, and how did she do it?" Silva looked around at three open faces watching him. "Beth O'Donnell enjoyed the feeling of power, but she didn't have any, except that of a woman whose tongue can harm others.

"She liked unsettling people with hints of what she knew. But this time she did know something, as I said, even if she didn't understand what it meant. For once she had stumbled onto something a person needed to have kept quiet, but she made the mistake of bragging about it."

"She did talk as though she knew everything about everyone," Medge commented. "I sort of took it for granted that she would have something to say about anyone she met."

"Whatever she knew this time, she knew by accident, and it involved something she could mention casually at a party without drawing attention to it," Silva replied.

"But she didn't mention anything that I could hear," Merrilee protested. "It was a thoroughly ordinary party."

"So you said, Mrs. O'Donnell. And if someone had shown me a tape of the party, I would have agreed. So I took a closer look. Through all the reports of the guests for the evening, certain topics kept reappearing. None seemed particularly unusual, but all of them seemed to stand out in people's recollections."

"Such as?" Medge asked.

"Bird feeders, for one," Silva replied. "Your aunt spoke about birds and bird feeders to several guests. And several guests remember the topic from other conversations."

"Mr. Handel was talking about bird feeders," Howard said.

"He's always talking about them, Dad. It's Aunt Beth you would never expect to mention them. At least I never heard she had any interest in them," Medge said.

"Let's go over them one by one," Silva suggested. "Your anniversary was mentioned, Mrs. Vinton, several times."

"That's right," her father said, "Medge's anniversary is coming up." He smiled fondly at her.

"That's right," Medge said.

"Their fourteenth," Merrilee added.

"And your aunt made the point that this was the first time she had met your husband," Silva said to Medge. "Is that correct?"

"That's right," Frank answered for his wife. "We'd never met."

"But she knew who you were," Silva said. "She had a picture of you from Christmas 1977. She received it in a letter from her brother."

"She did?" Frank asked.

"I sent her Christmas photos every year. It seemed the thing to do," Howard said.

"Your sister recorded their arrival," Silva said to Howard, then turned back to Mr. Vinton. "Miss O'Donnell knew what you looked like in January 1978, and she brought that photograph with her whenever she came to visit."

Frank had listened to Silva's narrative silently, all the while leaning against the bookcase. He shifted his weight slightly, but continued to stand where he had been all evening. "My mother-in-law's a pretty good photographer," he said.

"I often wondered about that picture," Merrilee said. "I once asked her about it. She seemed quite sentimental about it. Whenever she came, I usually chatted with her in the cottage a few times, and the picture was always there. I thought maybe she was getting especially fond of Medge."

Medge gave her mother a quizzical look and suppressed a smile.

"There was more to it than affection," Silva said. "Her niece was married to a man Beth had never met, but she knew him well from his photographs, and she kept the earliest one, from December 1977, when Mr. and Mrs. Vinton became engaged. The picture was a record of how long Frank had been in the family."

"But why would she bother?" Merrilee asked, the direction of the conversation once again lost to her.

"She bothered because even though she had never met Frank, she had seen him early on. In fact, she had seen him soon after she got the Christmas photo." Silva looked at Frank and said, "That was a stroke of luck, bad for you, Mr. Vinton, and good for Miss O'Donnell, or so she thought at the time."

"That's ridiculous," Frank replied smoothly. "What does it matter how many pictures she had of me or anyone else?"

"It was the one thing that did matter," Silva said. "There were pictures of Miss O'Donnell all over your fiancée's home; you knew exactly what she looked like fifteen years ago, long before you met her. But what you didn't know was that she had a picture of you. She knew exactly what you looked like, too. You knew who she was the minute you saw her, and she knew who you were the minute she saw you."

"What?" Merrilee and Howard said aghast at the same time. "Frank?"

"But you didn't know that, Mr. Vinton. You could only hope," Silva went on, "that her first sight of you would blur over time. But it didn't, did it, Mr. Vinton?"

"What sight of him?" Howard demanded.

"The sight of your son-in-law in the Parkland Hotel during the blizzard of 1978," Silva explained. Silva noted that only two people in the room were stunned at the news; he would ponder Medge's stoicism another time.

"That's a wild idea, Chief. The very idea is preposterous," Frank said.

"Is it?" Silva asked.

"I assume you have sound reasons for your accusations?" Howard asked.

"Yes, Mr. O'Donnell, I do. In February 1978 Beth was worried about her account at your firm," Silva began. "She tried to call it her trust fund, her money, but it wasn't hers and that bothered her. Perhaps that was why she always kept such a close eye on her finances. She was never foolish when it came to money. She followed the investments you told her about and she knew what they should come to every month. She had more information than you might think. When she had several months of low checks, she got worried and came up to see her brother. She had the bad luck to arrive on the day of the big blizzard. She made it to a hotel and her brother made it home, but she wasn't grateful for her good fortune. Instead, it was all designed to frustrate her more, in her view. She was angry and bored in the hotel and it shows in her diary. She had snide comments to make about everyone, except one. At first I thought her single reference to this person meant something quite different. In one entry she says she saw 'me beau.' At least that's how I read it. I thought her handwriting was poor and she meant her boyfriend. Then I thought she meant it as another sarcastic reference. She didn't. She meant Medge's boyfriend. Perhaps she had forgotten his name so she couldn't use his initials or maybe she knew too little about him to invent a suitable nickname."

"That's ridiculous. I was in New Hampshire," Frank said.

"That's what you said, Mr. Vinton. And after fourteen years who would remember? Who would even care? I wondered why you hadn't been able to meet your wife's aunt in all those years, even if she did appear only once in a while with little advance warning. There had to be a reason you never met her. I decided to go on the assumption that you didn't want to meet her. Why? Because if she met you, she would know something about you that you didn't want her to know. So you stayed away, long enough for an ordinary person to forget a face she might have noticed only briefly so many years ago. But Beth wasn't ordinary. She recognized you the minute she saw you fourteen years ago and she made sure she remembered. She needed nothing more. She had an interesting habit: she only recorded once the information that gave her an advantage over someone. She made one note of when and where she saw you for the first time, and then she waited. Ironically, you couldn't be sure if she would remember you after all those years and it didn't really matter as much as you thought. You might have been safe if you hadn't insisted on lying about being up-country. She only expected to embarrass you with hints about an old affair or something equally minor but awkward."

Frank opened his mouth but thought better of whatever he was going to say and closed it.

"It was clear to Miss O'Donnell that you wanted everyone to think you were in New Hampshire during the snowstorm, but you were in Boston. She knew that. That was the point of her apparently idle references to birds and what they do in weather like that. She kept raising the question of birds in the wild snowstorms to make you uncomfortable. If you had been at a country inn, Mr. Vinton, it would have been obvious in whatever you said in reply."

"I don't see how it can matter," Frank said.

"By itself, it doesn't," Silva agreed. "It was just her way of hinting."

"That seems pretty thin, even as a hint," Frank protested.

"Maybe, but it got me onto the right track. Just as it got you to follow Miss O'Donnell to her cottage," Silva said.

"That's absurd, Chief Silva," Frank said, but Silva ignored him.

"Beth O'Donnell chose a victim," Silva continued, "every time she visited, and never the same person twice. This year, she picked her victim during the party, so it had to be someone she spoke to during the evening, someone she hadn't picked on before, and someone she did not consider a friend. At first I thought she had set her sights on Bob Chambers, but after listening to people who knew her methods, so to speak, I

SUSAN OLEKSIW

decided I was wrong. Chambers approached Beth, not the other way around, because he wanted something from her. He put himself in the line of fire, more than once, and she was glad to oblige, but he was unimportant, just target practice. I eliminated Bob Chambers and looked at the other possible victims. She had certain rules, too, and they helped. She never picked on her brother or his wife and she never endangered her friendships. She was always careful about the people she felt dependent on; she took only limited risks. On one end we worked on eliminating everyone who wasn't a possible victim; from the other end we looked for some sort of corroboration from her journals. It wasn't long before I knew what I was looking for—at least part of it," Silva said. "We have the last diary, or what's left of it." Silva watched Frank closely, but he didn't even blanch. "You know where we found it."

Frank said nothing.

"Did Miss O'Donnell hint that she had it all right there, in her journal?" Silva asked.

"You're building a case on nothing, Chief." Frank tried to sound casual.

"Did she guess that you were in Boston that week in 1978 for the same reason?" Silva asked.

"The same reason?" Merrilee parroted.

"The discrepancy in her account," Howard said without emotion, having followed the précis calmly.

"That's right," Silva said. "In 1977, Mr. Vinton, you were working for Mr. O'Donnell in a minor capacity. The O'Donnells had known for some time that Medge was interested in you, but you apparently took longer to figure it out. But once you did, you had to change your plans. Why bother embezzling a few thousand dollars when you could have far more and all of it legal?" Silva paused.

"Why would I bother embezzling even a few thousand dollars?" Frank asked.

"Greed, perhaps, or maybe just debts that built up. We can check into your past and your financial records as we go on,"

Silva replied. "I only know about the money taken from Miss O'Donnell's account. You may have taken much more. Or maybe you had plans for more and this was going to be just the beginning. I don't know. But you found out you didn't have to embezzle. You could marry money," Silva said, aware of the nature of this news and wondering if he dared look at Medge.

"And so, in early February, to make sure nothing went wrong to ruin this opportunity, you were straightening out the papers for Miss O'Donnell's account. That explains why when Mr. O'Donnell finally checked through his sister's account, he found that a trusted employee had carelessly written several checks in the wrong amount but that nothing was wrong with the account itself. Beth's account was fine, only the checks were wrong." Silva heard a gasp from Merrilee, but never took his eyes off Frank.

"When Miss O'Donnell heard later," Silva went on, "as she must have, how everyone spent the blizzard, she must have guessed that you were in Boston to hide something, but she may not have made the connection between your presence in Boston during that storm and the end to her financial worries. All she knew was that she saw you in Boston at the hotel when her brother said you were up-country at a ski resort. And what you didn't know then was that she had already seen a picture of you. She knew who you were the minute she saw you. You waited fourteen years before meeting her, thinking that in time a face she saw for a few seconds in a hotel would fade from her memory. And she waited fourteen years to meet you so she could tell you obliquely how clearly she remembered you."

As Silva reached the end of his narrative he rose from his chair and approached Vinton, who then also became aware of the second police officer standing a few feet away from him. Vinton was rigid with anger. Eyeing both policemen but saying not a word, he let himself be led away.

■ ■ ■

By the time Chief Silva returned to the house after sending Sergeant Dupoulis and Frank Vinton off in the squad car, Mrs. Miles had swept into the living room to remove Mrs. O'Donnell and Medge to the kitchen, giving Merrilee the sight of an unfamiliar room to occupy her thoughts while the housekeeper tended to Medge, who was slowly coming to realize the change in her life now wrought by the police.

Howard stood staring out the window at the crab apple tree while Silva supplied answers to the various technical questions still troubling the older man. The chief was as tactful as he could be about the autopsy report, and Howard sighed. He shook his head and turned around.

"It seems to have happened without any of us sensing anything was wrong," Howard said. "You're certain it's Frank?"

"Yes, sir. We looked at every possibility, even the chance that the person in pants following your sister was a woman."

"A woman?" Howard was nonplussed at this idea.

"Your sister left the party at ten-thirty or soon after that and went straight back to the cottage. The caterers and anyone else in the kitchen or any other rooms on that side of the house could see anyone coming around or going into the cottage. No one did. The only safe path was out through the side hall into the garden and down the path. The only problem with that was someone might see them in the garden. It was a risk but a risk any guest could take. No one would question a guest admiring your garden, not when you have lights and furniture inviting them out there."

"No, I see what you mean," Howard said.

"So we had to look at who was where between ten-thirty and eleven o'clock and who was a possible target for Beth and therefore a potential murderer," Silva explained. "Unfortunately, by the end of the evening, Beth had already been unpleasant to several people."

Silva paused, wondering if any of this was necessary, but

Howard looked at him expectantly and the chief continued. "Several people overheard your sister egging on Bob Chambers and then turning on him. She even threatened to ruin his career."

Howard nodded, and his face hardened. "I didn't know she would actually do something like that."

"Well, when Bob came back to talk to her, she was gone, but the caterers and other guests saw him here and saw him leave. He didn't go around back on the other side and he didn't go out into the garden. If he had, he might have put himself in real danger of a murder charge."

"I recall he left with Lisa Hunt and reappeared again," Howard said, as though a great mystery had finally been explained to him.

"Lisa was in the car waiting for him, and that bothered me. There was no sign she had gone out back or had any run-in with your sister, but there was something going on. It took me a while to get that one sorted out, but she was completely tied up with worrying about Lee Handel," Silva said.

"Lee?" Howard repeated.

"Lisa was afraid Lee would run into Beth and come out of the encounter even more damaged than he already was. So she was following him around all evening and overheard the last argument between Bob and Beth, who said some pretty harsh things about Lee. It hurt Lisa. And it hurt Lee for her to hear those things," Silva said.

"Yes, it would," Howard said. "The Handels are very fond of Lisa."

"For a while there, they were also the prime suspects simply because of what had happened to them and because they made no secret of their feelings for Beth," Silva said. "But the closer I looked at the family, the more I saw I had to eliminate the Handels."

Howard was shocked to realize that he too had been a suspect. "The family?" he said. "Did you really think we—" He stopped, unable to go on.

"Yes, I'm afraid so, sir," Silva said. "Everyone is a suspect in a case like this."

"I suppose you're right," Howard said.

"It was pretty easy to eliminate three of you," Silva said. "Medge was always with another caterer or a guest, watching for people's reactions to her cooking; she never disappeared for a minute. Your wife was at the door saying good-bye to the guests from ten-thirty until eleven. And during that time she had Hannah Handel in view for almost the entire half hour."

"Does that matter?" Howard asked.

"Yes, sir, it does," the chief said. "Mrs. Handel was the one woman who wore pants and had a motive and was strong enough to actually carry out the murder. She could have been the person the two boys saw following Beth to the cottage."

"Hannah," Howard said to himself as though he were trying to imagine her as the chief had.

"But Hannah was caught by Mr. Steinwell, and when she did finally get away, it was only for a few minutes to hide in the powder room. When she came out, it was all over," Silva said.

"All over?" Howard echoed and Silva began to think Howard would never again be able to have a normal conversation.

"Everyone remembered talking to the host. Your movements were easy to track. Only once did you leave the house between ten-thirty and eleven—to show Lee Handel the new bird feeder. You went out through the door in the side hall, and Frank held the door open for you."

"Ah yes," Howard said. "Frank has excellent manners."

"He was holding it open," Silva said, "because he had just come back from the cottage. He was seconds away from shutting the door and returning to the living room as though he had never left."

"Oh," said Howard as his eyes opened wide.

14

A WEEK LATER

AT THREE O'CLOCK on Saturday afternoon, the Agawam Inn was transformed into the setting for an elegant Victorian-era garden party. The dozen or so tables spread out on the back lawn were covered with white linen tablecloths and set for afternoon tea; the fragrance of the surrounding azaleas mingled with the perfume from the clusters of daffodils bunched in vases on tables set along the veranda. The sunlight glittered on the cutlery, spread in waves along the white cloths, splashed across the thick, spring grass, and slipped into the wall of shrubbery. A light breeze ruffled a single loose curl of a young woman setting out the last of the menu cards. Men and women attired in the starched costumes of Victorian servants were stationed around the garden, ready for the arrival of guests when the doors—figuratively speaking—were opened.

In less than half an hour most of the tables were filled with women in pairs or groups and a few families from Mellingham and the surrounding towns eager to sample the newest local diversion. Trays of sandwiches and cakes rose and fell and rose again like waves on a pond as the caterers worked their way between the tables and through the crowd. Mr. Campbell stood nearby, on the edge of the activity, marveling once more at what enticed the average Mellite from the daily round.

Equal to the owner's sense of wonder was his determination to keep anything and anyone from interfering with his plans, and so when he had absorbed the full measure of the crisis that confronted him, he ran straight for the telephone. The police were willing to come right away, but they were not willing to come in street clothes or in any mode of dress that would enable them to blend in with the crowd. Mr. Campbell tried not to think of how the guests might react to having a policeman suddenly appear at their shoulders, notebook opened and pencil poised as questions fell among the tea cakes.

Chief Silva was not unmindful of Mr. Campbell's concerns as he crossed the veranda in his best summer uniform, but he liked to think that the residents of the town thought of him as just another neighbor who happened to wear blue to work. He stepped onto the lawn, recalling the owner's frantic call earlier in the day that above all else the success of the afternoon tea was paramount. The rest was up to the chief. The chief promised to do his best.

"Would you like a table, Chief Silva?" a pleasant voice asked him.

Silva looked down on a head of golden hair and a polite smile. "Thank you, Mrs. Vinton," he said. She led him to a table and drew a small menu card toward him.

"Are you working here now?" the chief asked, thinking of their last encounter more than a week ago and hoping her composure was not a facade that might crack at any moment.

"Yes. I just quit my job," Medge said. "I sent in my letter of resignation, and now I'm working with Jim full time in the Kitchen Cast."

"Congratulations," Silva said. "I didn't know you were so involved in Jim's business before."

"I wasn't really," she replied, "but things sort of got out of hand." Silva gave her a quizzical look and she explained, "I really had no choice. I was just going to help out part time but

I somehow managed to talk Mr. Campbell into using the roof deck for teas and suppers on the weekends. I don't quite know how I did it, but I did."

"You're probably a very good saleswoman."

"I wasn't supposed to be," she said. "The whole thing seemed to get away from me."

"So now you have to manage serving up there too, is that it?" Silva asked.

"No," she replied. "Jim pointed out how hard it would be on all of us to work up there," she explained. "There's only a broken dumbwaiter and an old elevator."

"Doesn't sound very good," Silva commented.

"It isn't," she agreed, "so Mr. Campbell said he'd fix them and modernize them and whatever else we wanted."

"And did that solve the problems?"

"Not really," Medge admitted. She looked around, then said in a softer voice, "It seems that Jim is terrified of heights. And I mean terrified."

"Really?" said Silva. "How did you find that out?"

"Someone told me, I guess," she said vaguely. "Apparently Jim panics and then blacks out if he gets within ten feet of a balcony."

"I can see why he wouldn't want to work on a roof deck."

"He tried to explain that to Mr. Campbell," Medge said, straightening the single place setting on the table, "but he just wouldn't listen. Mr. Campbell said it had to be the roof no matter what. And of course Jim said it could never be the roof. They almost came to blows."

"Sounds like a difficult business partnership ahead," Silva said.

"It's difficult now. All of us in the Cast tried to talk to Mr. Campbell, but he wouldn't listen. Once that man gets an idea there's no stopping him."

"And so here you are," Silva said, looking around him, "in the garden, right at sea level."

"Yes," Medge said with a laugh. "And it's just as nice as the roof would have been. Two little birds have done what Jim and all of the Kitchen Cast couldn't."

"Have you seen the birds?" Silva asked.

"Yes, have you?"

"No, I haven't been up there yet. Are they all right?"

"I think so. I went up just to take a peek," she admitted. "They're nesting happily in one of those hanging geranium pots, enjoying the view, I suppose."

"Hello, Chief," Jim Kellogg said as he stopped by the table. He was carrying a full tray of tea sandwiches and a teapot. "Nice of you to come for our opening. You're lucky you got a seat," he said as he looked around at the now-filled tables. "A really good crowd, isn't it?" Jim said with obvious pleasure.

"Probably more than you could get on the roof deck," Silva said.

"Oh yes, definitely more down here," Jim said. Medge turned to assist a guest at the next table while Jim went on speaking with the chief. "We could never get this many people up there all at one time," Jim said. "That's a point I should make with Mr. Campbell. Thanks, Chief."

"Don't mention it," Silva said, amused at Jim's enthusiasm. "I suppose the roof deck might be better for a private party?"

"Not really," Jim said, eyeing the chief suspiciously.

"Is that what you told Miss O'Donnell?" Silva asked.

"Well, I pointed it out." Jim ran his tongue over his lips. "I said it was small and awkward and sort of like that."

"I see," said Silva.

"Would you like to order now?" Medge asked when she had returned from helping at the next table.

"No, thanks," Silva said. "I'm really here on business."

Both Jim and Medge paled, but Medge asked, "What business is that, Chief?"

"Possible theft," the chief replied. "Mr. Campbell thinks

the hanging geranium with the birds in it isn't one of the plants he originally put up there."

"You mean the one the cardinals are nesting in?" Medge said.

"That's right," Silva said. "Mr. Campbell thinks someone stole his plant and put the other one up there."

"That's ridiculous," Jim said in a strained voice. "Why would anyone want to do that?"

"Why?" Silva repeated looking at him. "I can't say why, not yet anyway. But Mr. Campbell's suspicions aren't entirely without reason."

"The plants looked the same to me," Jim said.

"That doesn't mean anything," Medge said. "You can't tell a geranium from a lily."

"Well, I don't know if Mr. Campbell can either," Silva said, "but he's suspicious because Mrs. Hight showed up here this morning asking about the birds before Mr. Campbell even knew they were up there. You both know Mrs. Hight, don't you?"

"Oh sure. Steve Badger bought the Harbor Light restaurant from her husband. Nice woman. How did she know about the birds?" Medge asked.

"Lee Handel called her," Silva said, watching Jim while he spoke. "Apparently he got an anonymous phone call very early this morning telling him there were cardinals nesting in the geraniums and the pot was hanging right next to where there was going to be a lot of traffic on the roof deck. You know, guests coming and going and making a racket. The caller seemed to think Mr. Campbell would just go up there and move the plant along with the nest rather than let the birds stay there. The caller hinted that leaving them there during the opening would be bad for the birds and therefore there should be no opening. The caller suggested that Mr. Campbell would never agree to that. He would insist on moving the birds."

"Oh, he would have, he would have," Jim said. "He's

not a bird lover. Definitely not. No, no, definitely not, not a bird lover." So convinced of both propositions was he that he tried to nod and shake his head at the same time and instead ended by waving his head around and around in a circle.

"Mr. Handel must have thought so too," Silva said, "because he called Mrs. Hight."

"Why Mrs. Hight?" Medge asked.

"Because Mr. Handel thought she had the best chance of preventing Mr. Campbell from moving the nest." Silva glanced around at Jim, who was now sidling away from them.

"Gee," said Jim as he noticed Silva watching him.

"When Mrs. Hight got here," Silva continued, "she insisted that it would be too disruptive for the birds to be moved and too stressful for them to have a restaurant around them, even a small one."

"Gee," Jim said again.

"She's very conscientious, Chief," Medge said after taking a long look at Jim.

"Well, we won't make any money standing here," Jim said, and he was gone in an instant.

"I think you should have some tea," Medge said and went on to dictate the rest of his light meal.

For the next two hours, teacups rattled, birds chirped, women laughed, men nodded quietly, and everyone fell easily into the ambience of the garden tea party. Mrs. Hight appeared every half hour to check on the noise level and peer up at the roof, perhaps contemplating the party from the cardinals' position. There had been talk of a picket line, which had degenerated into a debate on whether or not Mr. Campbell should be allowed to assuage his conscience by serving the picketers tea on the front veranda. The seven elderly women and four grandchildren had decided this would be the generous course to follow and had promptly settled themselves for a long afternoon.

After his own tea, Chief Silva had dutifully walked

around the hotel, interviewed a few employees (mainly those who appeared to have little to do in the late afternoon), and pulled one bicycle from the bushes, where its rider landed it after discovering that rubber tires slide at high speeds on gravel driveways. Silva considered the afternoon well spent. When he saw the owner approaching him in the garden, he hoped Mr. Campbell would feel the same way.

"I appreciate your staying, Chief," Mr. Campbell said, casting pained glances over his shoulder at the hotel. "They're still out there," he said in a stage whisper. "Mrs. Hight and her crowd. And still eating. Mr. Handel is coming later to look at the nest. Otherwise business is pretty good, actually pretty good," he said, his mood improving as he surveyed the crowd and contemplated his new income.

"Did you learn anything, Chief? Anything that will help me get the culprit?" he said as he accompanied the chief around the hotel to the front.

"It's too soon to say," Silva replied, "but we'll keep at it."

"Good, good," he said. "He followed Chief Silva to the drive, promising to call if the picketers got out of hand or the cardinals nose-dived into the cake trays.

"Thank God it's only for a while," Campbell muttered. "Hello, Lisa," he said. "Did you come with Mr. Handel?" the innkeeper asked, looking around him.

"Yes, he just went inside to find you," Lisa said.

Believing in his heart of hearts that all businessmen were natural and unbreakable allies against the forces that would put them out of business, Mr. Campbell optimistically bounded up the main steps to the hotel in search of Mr. Handel and imminent rescue. Unfortunately, Mr. Campbell had never before spoken to Mr. Handel for longer than the time it took to say hello, and had not heard of the other man's dedication to the well-being of certain creatures, specifically, birds.

"He's wrong, of course," Lisa said to Silva.

"Wrong about what?" the chief asked.

"About it only being for a while. Cardinals are very settled birds. If they find something they like, they stay," she explained.

"Sensible," Silva said, smiling at her. He wondered why he hadn't noticed the way her eyes twinkled mischievously.

"Do you think you'll find the people who stole the geranium and left the one with the birds up there?" she asked.

"I might," Silva said.

"Do you have to?"

"Do you have something to tell me, Lisa?"

"I might," she said with a twinkle in her eye.